Grace After the Storm

Sandy Sinnett
Author of Hope In the Rain

This is a fictional work. The names, characters, incidents, places, and locations are solely the concepts and products of the author's imagination or are used to create a fictitious story and should not be construed as real.

5 PRINCE PUBLISHING AND BOOKS, LLC
PO Box 16507
Denver, CO 80216
www.5PrinceBooks.com

Print ISBN 13: 978-1-63112-146-3 10:1631121464
Grace After the Storm
Sandy Sinnett

Published by 5 Prince Publishing

Front Cover Ermisenda Alvarez

First Edition/First Printing January 2016 Printed U.S.A.

5 PRINCE PUBLISHING AND BOOKS, LLC.

For Jesse, Wyatt,
Emily and Ethan

Acknowledgments

To my four amazing kids… I am so blessed, and proud to be your mom.

I love you with all my heart!

Jesse, my firstborn, and most passionate child of all… never settle for anything less than the life you want – do what makes you happy and fills you up inside, always keeping God at the center.

Wyatt, you make me laugh, and give me joy each and every day with your sense of humor. You have overcome so much, and now stand proud and tall. Never stop writing!

Emily, my sweet girl, you're the delight of my life! You are a gifted artist my dear – not only with make-up, but also in your writing. My life would be so much less without you in it. Thank you for 'Finding Nemo' with me… my favorite.

Ethan, you are my little miracle! Your generous spirit, your kind heart, your bright smile and your belly laugh fills my soul. I thank God for the gift of your life every day.

And to the two that I never met… you are never forgotten. I look forward to seeing you one day.

Monty, thank you for your unending support and encouragement of me during this long, winding road together. You are a wonderful, loving father to our kids, and my friend forever and always. I'm so proud of the man you are today and will always love you.

To my wonderful mom and dad – thank you for loving me through everything, the good and the bad. I love you both so much! Without you, I wouldn't be the woman I am today. I am proud to be your daughter, and will continue to make you proud as I move forward on this new journey.

To my precious grandmother - I will always treasure all the wonderful memories I have of our time together. You've taught me so much over the years – how to flip burgers, and count change without a calculator; how to put on makeup, and how to be a strong, independent woman.

I love you!

Lastly, to my readers and faithful fans: THANK YOU for all your support and kind words, and for taking a chance on me and my book. I write for you as much as myself.

Grace After the Storm

Prologue

Thud-clank.
Thud-clank.
Thud.

Hannah watched from her porch as the 'suit' pounded the foreclosure sign into the cold, hard ground next to the edge of the road. Every blow of the mallet rang in her ears and the reality of her situation could no longer be ignored. It signified the end of her family's legacy. Of course it was nothing for the man in the suit, as he drove the sign farther and farther into the ground, but for Hannah it meant losing her family's estate. The final nail being driven into her virtual coffin.

She'd lost so much in the last ten years – everything worth living for had managed to slip through her fingers one by one. The love of her life had walked away from her eight years ago and although she hated to admit it, her soul still cried out for him even today. Then the boating accident took her parents away just six short years ago, leaving her to care for the family winery and bed and breakfast – Foxhead Estates. Her choice to move back to Washington and run her family's estate sent her then husband on his merry way. His investment in their marriage had been minimal to say the least. It was hard to admit that she was now a divorcée, but she now realized that she'd only married him to make herself feel safe and secure.

Hannah's 89 year-old ailing grandmother was the only family she had left now and lived with her at the estate. It was only a matter of time before she would lose her too. She watched as the 'suit' climbed back into his fancy car and went hopefully on his way back in to whatever hole he had crawled out of, then she collapsed onto the porch floor. Her insides ached and it was hard to breathe, so she wrapped her arms around her stomach and forced one deep breath at a time, each one like a needle piercing her lung all the way through to her spine. She sobbed uncontrollably, heaving and gasping for air, and soaking the knees of her jeans. Her world was crashing down, and there was nothing anyone could do about it. Except… well, maybe God. In a last ditch effort to find some semblance of comfort, she calmed herself and lifted her tear-stained cheeks to the sky, silently waiting for the courage to make her petition known to the Almighty. She whispered.

"Hey God? It's… it's me – Hannah. I know it's been a while, but hopefully you can hear me. Do you remember me? Please God, please help me! I need your grace now more than ever. Is that still a thing – grace? I know I don't deserve any, but if only for my grandmother's sake, I hope you can send a little our way. We can use all the help we can get. Oh, and I'm sorry about that tantrum I threw at the church picnic last year. I hope you won't hold that against me. Honestly, Ms. Rumple had it coming! She's so snooty and….*ugh*! Sorry, Lord. So… thanks for listening and well… just thanks."

Hannah stood up and wiped her tears. The 'suit' had finally left and it began to rain. "Ugh… t*his* is how you answer me? You know how I *hate* the rain!"

1 - A Season of Drought

Even as a young girl, rain was a source of hope for Laci Kramer, and she believed that good things would always follow it. So what happens when those rains keep falling and falling and don't stop? It becomes a flood; potentially damaging anything in its path. There are times though, when people simply need a flood. Not a literal one, but a personal one. A flood that completely washes away the things in our lives that have been there far too long – a sort of cleansing that brings healing and renewal. Rain is healing, but it's not until after it stops and the land is dry that we see an opportunity to start over and rebuild things better and stronger than they were before.

For Laci, being without the rain for even a time helped her appreciate its value and purpose in the world. Too long without it though, every living thing begins to suffer and dry up… including herself. When she can't see or feel the rain, her heart becomes lifeless, longing for a healing that only rain can bring.

One year ago, she experienced her own personal flood of sorts when she was diagnosed with breast cancer. That diagnosis was definitely a 'washing' – stripping her of a will to live, her dignity and self-worth. Thankfully, she had Mitch, the second love of her life. It was his stubborn love that lifted her up out of the ashes… with a little help from the rain. She's cancer-free now, and the prognosis has remained positive so far, but she was a little nervous about being pregnant so soon after treatment, especially now that she was over 40 years old. The doctor said everything looked good and she shouldn't worry. She did anyway.

It had been three months since she shocked Mitch with the news about their baby, and tomorrow they would have their first sonogram appointment – the first glimpse of baby Young. Tonight though, she would have to endure the weekly family dinner over at Maggie's house, Mitch's mother. Her joyful anticipation overflowed!

I have NO desire to go to Maggie's tonight… but I don't have the heart to tell Mitch, Laci thought to herself. Things didn't start off too well between her and Mitch's mother. After the wedding though, things improved. There were still a few tense moments between them off and on, but overall Laci tried very hard to get along with her. For some reason, Maggie had trouble accepting her and she didn't know why. She hoped the arrival of their new baby would make things better.

Adding even more fun to the occasion, Maggie had asked her to come over early so she could teach her the Young family's secret recipe for cinnamon raisin bread pudding. Apparently, Maggie refused to write the recipe down, not for anyone.

"Laci, Darlin', can you get me some sugar from the pantry?" Maggie asked in her sweet southern accent.

Laci turned and rolled her eyes as she opened the pantry door. *I suppose I should feel honored that she wants to share the recipe with me, but I get the feeling she has ulterior motives. Why is it that I feel like a rooster at a hen party in her kitchen…not welcome until invited in? Yeah for me… I was invited in! Lord help me!* "Sure, Maggie. Here you go." Laci set the sugar next to her on the counter.

"Normally I would ask you to memorize this recipe so it doesn't leave the family, but I know how busy you are with work and all, so I decided to make an exception this one time."

Laci wasn't sure whether to be flattered, or feel guilty by her comment. *How secret can a recipe for bread pudding be anyway? Tiramisu maybe… but definitely not bread pudding.* "Did you teach

Karin how to make this recipe too?" Laci asked, knowing full well she had opened a big old can of thick, southern molasses.

"Yes. Karin loved to cook. She was a natural. But, being a stay-at-home mother gave her time to practice." Maggie's southern tongue had struck, and left a stinging sensation that was hard to ignore.

"Well, I'll do my best to practice in between breast feeding your new grandchild, hosting events at the winery, and raising my other three kids. I'm sure there will be plenty of time in there somewhere." Laci's tone was curt, to say the least.

Maggie turned toward Laci with a puzzled look on her face, then touched her arm gently.

"I'm afraid you mistook my words, Laci. I wasn't trying to insult you because you work. I was merely stating a fact that if you were home, you would have more time, that's all. Please don't be upset dear, it will only upset the baby. Now, where were we?"

A little smirk appeared on Laci's face. *I know where I'd like to send you. Ugh! Sorry, Lord. Not nice… I know,* she thought to herself. The two carried on with the pudding-making class, but very little conversation took place after that. Once Mitch and the kids arrived, he sensed that Laci wasn't herself and pulled her into the living room before dinner.

"Let me guess… my mom pushed your buttons again?" he asked.

"Oh, you could say that. Apparently my less-than-favorable career choice is impeding my ability to cook. It's my own fault though."

"Why is it your fault?"

"Because I asked about Karin and if she had learned the recipe – it took a nose dive from there. Plus I didn't have the heart to tell her I don't even like raisins."

Mitch laughed out loud, "Yeah… I can see how that might not have played well. But cut her some slack, Lace. This is still new for her too. She does love you, trust me." He smiled and pulled her into his strong arms for a warm hug.

"I'm sure you're right," she whispered.

That next morning, Laci woke up still feeling a little miffed at Mitch's mom, but she tried not to let it ruin her excitement.

"Laci, it's time to go! We don't want to be late for the sonogram," Mitch called out from downstairs.

"I'm almost ready – down in a sec!" she shouted in return. *So impatient that man… but so handsome! It's no wonder I let him get away with everything.* Laci smiled.

Laci was so happy to finally see her little baby bump – the small pillow-sized tummy bulge that held an even smaller bundle of joy inside. There were moments when she couldn't take her eyes from it. Even after having had four children, she was still fascinated by the miracle of it all. She finished brushing her hair and gave it a good coat of hairspray. *I'm a North Carolina girl now, so it's my duty to start every day with a heavy coat of hairspray – humidity is the enemy!*

As she looked herself over in the large full-length mirror, turning sideways to see the bump, she couldn't help but notice that it looked a little different today. She was only twelve weeks along, but somehow it seemed… deflated. She shrugged the thought away and gave her little bump a pat, then whispered, "Mommy and daddy are anxious to see you today, little one." She snatched up her purse and walked downstairs to meet Mitch.

"Do I look smaller to you?" she asked.

"Smaller? Um, is this a trick question or are you fishing for a compliment?"

"My stomach, you weenie… you know, the baby bump. Is it smaller?" She pointed to her stomach, as if he couldn't figure out where it was. Mitch walked over behind her and wrapped his arms snuggly around her tummy, resting his chin atop her shoulder.

"You are stunningly beautiful, and your belly doesn't look any smaller – it's huge actually! I was going to mention that you might want to cut back on all those Krispy Kreme donuts you've been inhaling lately," he said, a quirky grin on his face, then laughed.

"Oh you!" she huffed, then playfully slapped him on the arm. "Let's get out of here – I want to see what's on the inside of this bump and hear his little heartbeat again."

"*His* heartbeat? Why did you say *his*?"

"It just came out – seems more natural I guess. No premonitions on the sex, don't worry. There is just as much chance that it's a 'her', *Darlin'*."

"I've got a premonition of my own about the sex, but it doesn't pertain to the baby…" he laughed and kissed her softly. She pushed him away.

"You are a handful, Mitch Young! It's no wonder I'm in this condition." They laughed and walked to the car.

After she checked in at the front desk of the OB office, they took a seat in the waiting area and listened for them to call her name. *I am so excited to see him! At least, I think it's a 'him', but I'd love to have a 'her' too.* She honestly didn't care as long as he was healthy. As she sat waiting, going back and forth on the subject with herself, she realized that her pregnancy seemed to have made her even more scatter-brained than before. She kept rubbing her little baby bump, still feeling that it looked a bit different. She also felt bloated, which wasn't normal for her either. The nurse called Laci's name and she and Mitch followed her back to a small, quiet room – a little TV monitor stationed at the end of the table which held the sonogram equipment. She climbed up on the table and rolled the top of her pants down to expose her belly for the occasion. A few minutes later, the sonographer came in to greet them.

"Good morning, Laci. I'm Amber. How are things going? Are you excited to see your baby?" she asked.

"More than excited! But I admit I do feel a little out of sorts this morning. Nothing big though," Laci replied.

"Well, your body is going through a lot of changes – you'll have days like that. You know that of course, after having four kids." She smiled and prepared the machine.

"That's for sure."

"Okay, I think we're all set here. I'm going to put some warm jelly on your tummy and we'll listen for the heartbeat first."

The nurse pulled Laci's blouse up a little and tucked it under her bra, applied the jelly, then gently moved it across her belly in slow, smooth motions – looking for just the right spot to pick up the heartbeat. She moved it from one side to the other, holding still in several places, but there was nothing there except static.

"Why can't you find it? Is everything okay?" Mitch asked, his voice disquiet.

"I'm sure everything is fine. Babies are notorious for scooting in behind mom's organs or turning in a position where the heart faces the inside, which makes it impossible to hear sometimes. They are very squirmy at this stage," she assured them with a smile. "Let's go ahead and take a look on the screen – once we find him it will help me position the wand." She changed over to the ultrasound wand, and turned the TV monitor toward Laci and Mitch so they could see. It only took a second before she spotted their baby – his little body clearly visible on the screen, nestled in a tiny ball at the bottom of the screen.

"Look, Mitch! There he is! I can see his head and arms!" Laci exclaimed softly, a huge smile spread over her face.

"I see him, Darlin'! Holy cow – it's really real!" He almost sounded surprised to actually find a baby inside.

"See… it's not all donuts in there after all," she laughed, overjoyed to finally see their beautiful baby. He was real. He was theirs.

Amber kept quiet, gliding the wand to different positions around Laci's stomach, taking pictures and measuring baby parts visible on the screen. Her face was void of any emotion though, and the smile that was there just moments ago, was gone. After a few minutes of watching the screen, Laci noticed that their little bump wasn't very active. Actually, he wasn't moving at all.

"Why isn't he squirming around in there – is he sleeping?" Laci's brow creased as a building sense of worry crept over her.

Amber hesitated to reply, knowing full-well she wasn't to discuss anything she saw on the screen, however this was one of those rare exceptions. "Laci," she said softly, "I need to step out and get the doctor. I'm not getting any life activity on the monitor and there isn't a heartbeat. Normally there should be movement by now," a look of remorse apparent on her face.

"What do you mean… no life activity or heartbeat? You're probably just in the wrong spot. I see him!" Laci's voice cracked and she could feel her heart pounding so hard she could barely breathe. Laci looked up at Mitch – his gaze fixed on the screen.

"I'm so sorry, Laci. I'll go get your doctor at once," Amber said in her sweet voice. Without another word, she laid the ultrasound wand aside and quietly stepped out the door, returning minutes later with the doctor.

"Hi Laci, Mitch. Why don't I take a look at what's going on, okay?" The doctor went directly to the ultrasound monitor and placed the wand on Laci's tummy, doing her own review to confirm the results. She looked at Laci, the answer clearly displayed on her face. "I'm sorry, Laci. It appears that you've experienced a miscarriage."

"A what? What do you mean – a miscarriage? How can that be, Dr. Greene?" Laci's hands began to shake and her voice grew louder as the fear and anxiety built up inside. "I can see him – his whole body – right there on the screen! What happened? Why isn't he moving?" Laci yelled, demanding an answer, expecting the doctor to do something to make their baby's heart start beating.

Mitch squeezed Laci's hand and with his other hand, he turned her face, forcing her gaze away from the monitor to look him in the eye. She fought him. *If I look at the screen long enough, he will surely move or wake up! Maybe we just missed it!*

"Laci, Darlin'... look at me. He didn't make it. He's gone. There's nothing we can..." Mitch's voice trailed off as Laci began to cry uncontrollably. He lifted her head, cradling her in his arms, then buried his face on top of her chest. Together, they mourned.

From the deepest part of her soul, she cried out in agony – unable to wrap her mind around what had just happened. It was the kind of cry that rendered one limp and exhausted. Twenty minutes ago they were talking about what color to paint the baby's nursery and who he would look like most... now it was over. Their baby boy, or girl... gone in the blink of an eye. Laci knew that the Lord could give and take away, but nothing about this seemed right or fair. She felt her heart break in that instant, and it caused her physical pain as it throbbed with an empty, hollow ache.

Mitch stood up slowly, still holding Laci's hand as she lay on the table.

"I'm so sorry for your loss. I'm afraid there is nothing more we can do now. Sadly, miscarriages happen more often than people realize, although I know that doesn't ease your pain. Most of the time it's almost impossible to know what went wrong. Trust me when I say it was nothing you did, Laci. The pregnancy just wasn't viable. You're healthy, you take care of yourself, you eat right and you were doing all the right things to take care of your child, so please don't blame yourself for this. There was no way to know. At this point, I would recommend you schedule a D&C procedure for tomorrow. It's the safest and healthiest way to remove the baby."

The doctor explained everything as best she could, but there was nothing she could say to comfort them or take away their pain. Laci wiped the gel from her stomach, and Mitch helped her sit up. Before they left the room, Amber handed her a strip of black and white pictures she had taken during the ultrasound – the words 'Baby Young' printed along the top. *This is all we have – a single image of our baby that is no longer alive! No first birthday photos, no graduation photos, no wedding day photos, just fuzzy black and white images of his tiny body floating inside of me. It isn't fair!* After the D&C was scheduled, a nurse escorted them out the back exit so they could avoid seeing other pregnant women and newborns in the waiting room. Mitch pulled the car around, helped Laci inside, and they drove home in silence – his hand holding tight to hers.

Numb and heavy-hearted, they walked to their room in silence, and Mitch called his mom and his brother to tell them the news. His mother was heartbroken for them. She even picked up the kids from school and kept them through dinner, giving them more time to grieve. Laci decided to take a shower, thinking it would help somehow. She stepped inside, pulled the curtain closed and stood there motionless, letting the hot water pour over her. She still looked pregnant – her stomach unchanged in size and still holding their baby inside. Her tears flowed down with the water and she suddenly felt sick, realizing that the tiny child still within would never feel her warm hug. She would never hold him when he needed comfort. She would never read to him or tuck him in bed at night. She would never see his face or know the color of his eyes. What would he have become? A doctor, an author, a singer? She doubled over, sobbing, then lowered herself onto the floor of the shower so as not to fall. Her breathing was labored as she cried out and mourned for her unborn child. Mitch heard her cries and walked in the bathroom to check on her. Pulling back the shower curtain, he found Laci crumpled in a ball on the floor. He shut off the water and helped her out, gently wrapping a towel around her and pulling her into his arms, dripping wet – never saying a word. Shared between them was only unspoken heartache as they tried to comfort each other.

Later that evening, Maggie brought the kids home and they shared the news about the baby. Emma took it very hard – she had already picked a name. She got up and ran crying to her room. The boys didn't say much. Laci and Mitch tried to answer their questions, but mostly they were quiet and soon retreated to their rooms. Mitch and Laci followed behind. After they retired to their room, Laci reached into a dresser drawer and pulled out a tiny blue onesie, still in the sack. She'd bought it a few days ago, hoping to show Mitch after the sonogram. Clutched to her chest, she looked at him, unable to speak. In her gaze, she was calling out to him to fix everything, to make all the pain go away.

A few minutes passed, then she placed the outfit back inside the drawer and wiped her tears. "It hasn't rained in weeks, Mitch," she said softly, frustrated by how much she missed it. She sat down on the bed, expecting him to offer a profound explanation of why the rain hadn't come.

"I know you miss it, but it's early November, Lace… not exactly our rainy season remember?"

"I need the rain," her voice cracked.

"I know Darlin'. I know." His head hung low, powerless to console her.

The next morning, the kids left for school and Mitch and Laci went on to the hospital. The D&C procedure was quick and virtually painless, but she kept hoping she would wake up – that it was all some horrible dream and her tummy was still growing, and she would see her baby in a few short months. That was not the case. He was gone and it was time to accept that and move forward. All that remained was a sharp, painful ache that emanated from the hole in her heart, and a hole that size would take time to heal.

Laci's healing didn't come though, and neither did the rain. It was an unseasonably dry winter, and the absence of rain was starting to take its toll on her. Her happiness simply left, and she shut down. She stopped smiling, stopped working, and stopped being a mother to the kids she did have. Mostly, she kept to her room, closed off from the outside world. She even stopped going to church. Mitch tried to comfort her, but she pushed him away every time. She would allow him brief access to the surface, but nothing beyond. *This isn't how I want to be at all!* On the inside, Laci screamed out for Mitch to hold her, touch her, love her… but her physical reaction was just the opposite. Losing their baby had hurt him deeply too, but it was different for Laci. She'd carried him. *I am the one who literally had him ripped from my body!* That severed connection was both emotional and physical for her – something that, by no fault of his own, Mitch would never understand or comprehend.

Mitch and his mother took over all the events at the winery to relieve some of Laci's stress, but the guilt from not being able to help consumed her. Thanksgiving and Christmas came and went, but there was still no change. For Laci, and her intense love for Christmas; that was always the one time of year she could normally overcome anything negative. Not that year. It was all a blur since the miscarriage and she was sinking deeper and deeper. Not only that, but she began to relive the pain of the past – losing her first husband, worrying that her cancer would return. She worried about everything.

Now mid-January, there was still no sign of rain, or snow for that matter. Without it, Laci felt as frozen as the hard winter ground, unable to move, consumed with fear and sadness. The sadness kept her stuck inside a black hole, unable to see any light or feel the hope to which she'd always clung. She couldn't eat or sleep, and was at an unhealthy weight. Unable to see it for herself, she had stopped moving forward, and once again began to question God's plan for her. Instead of talking to Him, she became bitter, with no intention of praying or asking God for help. Her selfish pride led her to believe that she could make it on her own, but it was just a matter of time before she would self-destruct. Lucky for Laci, she had forgotten how *big* God really was and how much He cared about every detail of her life.

She lay in bed and tried to sleep, but her mind continued to race. Instead of tossing yet another time, she got up to take a walk and clear her head. Mitch woke as she climbed out of bed.

"What's wrong, Lace?" he asked in a groggy voice, now worried.

"Nothing," she whispered. "I can't sleep – just going down to get some water. I'll be right back, don't worry."

She pulled on her robe, then walked out and headed to the kitchen. About half way down the hall, she stopped at the entrance to the spare room and stared inside. The moonlight poured through the window, casting a soft white glow on the desk directly below, compelling her to go in and sit down. She stared out the window for a few minutes, taking in the view outside and watching as the moon's light danced in the night sky, bouncing off every star within reach – a beautiful night. The small radio alarm clock on the night stand glowed '3:03 AM' in big red numbers. For some reason, she walked over and flipped on the radio. Music was the one thing that could always soothe her soul, but she'd had no desire to listen lately. One song ended, then another began without any commercials or talk between. She listened quietly to a woman's sweet, beautiful voice, singing about how God is with us in all seasons of life, then she slowly slid down to the floor and closed her eyes. Instantly, she felt joy fill her heart, and sensed that God was with her at that very moment. All she could do was cry and let go of the anger and sorrow that had consumed her, and as she visualized her baby in her arms one last time, she said goodbye. *I'll see you again my sweet baby.* She whispered to herself.

After a few minutes, she stood up and walked over to sit in the chair, then took a deep breath. She fiddled with the handles on the desk drawer – still amazed at how perfect a song it was, and exactly what she needed to hear. Remembering that the top drawer was usually filled with paper, she opened it and took out a yellow writing tablet and pen. She turned on the desk lamp and began to write, and write… and kept writing – unable to stop. Words poured from her like the rain she longed to see. As she wrote, she released her pain, and guilt, and the world that had once stopped moving, began to turn again. It wasn't until Mitch came looking for her that she realized the time – a new day was dawning.

"Laci. What are you doing? Have you been in here all night?" he asked.

"I… I guess so. I was writing." She looked up at him and smiled—she hadn't smiled at him spontaneously in months.

Mitch was speechless, and instead of responding with words, he pulled her out of the chair and drew her into his arms. His warm tears fell on her shoulder as he buried his face in the crook of her neck. They cried together, knowing something had changed.

Laci began to write every day after that night, always going to her 'writing room' for inspiration. At times, she would stop writing and simply look out the window above her desk –lost in the view of beautiful trees, colorful blossoms, and the sun peeking from behind their leaves. She watched and waited for the rain, but it kept its distance. A light mist would pass through now and then, but it wasn't enough. She longed for a rain that she could see and touch – a hard rain, and that longing translated into words. On paper, she could express her innermost thoughts – using words to yell and scream – being honest with herself in a way that she couldn't share with others face to face. Mitch tried his best to understand and support her new process, but she saw how hard it was for him. Instead of talking to him though, she wrote, and through her writing, she was changing… even though he couldn't see it yet.

Each day Laci felt a little better, but she wasn't back to her old self yet. She needed more.

I need the rain, she thought.

2 – Visiting the Rain

After the Valentine events had ended, Mitch noticed a long break ahead in the winery's calendar. On some level, he felt like that was God's way of telling him it was time to go. He needed his Laci back. The doctors and psychiatrists weren't helping anymore, and although she was better since she'd started writing, he knew there was only one option left – she needed to visit the rain. Luckily, it was the rainy season in Washington. He talked it over with his mother and Brad, made arrangements for the kids, and booked their flights without ever saying a word to Laci.

Hopefully this surprise trip will jolt Laci back to reality once and for all, he thought.

With tickets in hand, Mitch walked upstairs and found Laci in her usual spot – writing at her desk. "Hey Darlin', are you hungry?" he asked as he entered the den.

"Oh, hi Sweetheart. Actually, I think I could eat." Laci was surprised, not only by the fact that she was hungry for the first time in months, but that she actually verbalized it. Most of the time Mitch would bring her food and stay to watch her eat, making sure she was getting some type of nourishment. Laci wasn't sure what had changed, but she believed that God had grieved with her all those months, and maybe her time of mourning was finally at an end.

Mitch was even a little taken back by her response. "Wow… okay. Well, I'll go down to the kitchen and make you a plate."

"Wait. I – I think I might like to go out for dinner. I guess I'm ready for a change in atmosphere," she laughed at herself quietly. "Would that be okay?"

"Darlin'," he walked over to her chair and knelt down. "That is more than okay with me. It's music to my ears." He smiled and took her hand, gently kissing the top of it – still her favorite display of affection from him since the day they met. For the first time in months, she even had goosebumps from his touch. "You get ready and I'll let the others know that we'll be going out."

"Do you think the kids will mind if it's just us? I don't think I'm ready for a family outing just yet." Guilt from her words took hold, but she pushed it away.

"No, Lace. They won't mind. They will be so happy to see you getting out of the house that it won't matter to them, trust me."

She made herself presentable to go out in public, fussing over her hair and makeup, then walked downstairs to meet Mitch – her palms all sweaty. The last time she was this nervous was before their first date, but this time her nerves were on edge for a much different reason. Fear. Fear of leaving the house, leaving the safety of her writing room, and fear of going out into a world where she could possibly see other moms with their newborn babies, hear their tiny cries, and see little tots walking around holding their mothers hands. At that moment, she doubted her decision to leave and stopped in the middle of the staircase. Then, that familiar itty-bitty-committee in her head surfaced and presented their views. She only heard two this time. Her own voice said, *Don't go Laci. You're not ready and you know it! You're not strong enough!* Then a gentle voice whispered, *Trust in me, Laci. I will never give you more than you can handle. Lean on me – I am your strength.* God's voice was clear and kind, and she wanted to listen to Him, but she wasn't ready. *I have to stay here.*

Her decision made, she slowly turned around and walked back upstairs until she heard Mitch. He called out to her, and with the sound of his voice alone, he pulled her back. *God is right. He will give me strength, but he also gave me Mitch.*

"Hey Darlin', the car is out front. Where are you going?" he asked.

Mitch's voice was loving and kind, and compelled Laci to stop and turn around. Laci's face was flushed with embarrassment, but she took one look at Mitch and all the feelings she'd had when she first saw him came rushing back. He was so handsome, wearing his black button-down shirt and jeans. Somehow, she was able to put aside her desire to chicken out, and made her way downstairs… one step at a time.

"Um, nowhere. I thought I had forgotten my purse, but it was hanging on my arm the whole time. I'm ready." Her reply wasn't confident by any means. Mitch probably knew she wanted to turn around and run back upstairs, but since she didn't, hopefully it earned her some points for not giving in to her fear. Laci realized that's probably what God had been trying to tell her for months now… to push through the fear and keep her eyes on Him – to follow Him despite her fear. *Hmmm… I should write that in my book when I get back,* she thought with a smile.

When Laci entered the living room, the kids' faces lit up with smiles, telling her how pretty she looked. Travis jumped up and ran to her side, throwing his arms around her waist.

"Hi mom! Are you feeling better?" he asked, his voice full of joy. She stroked the soft blonde hair on his little head, realizing how much she had missed his hugs. She bent down and looked into his sweet face.

"Hi Sweetie. I am much better today." They hugged one another tight and Laci swallowed, pushing back the urge to cry. She was tired of being buried under the weight of her sadness.

"Hey Trav, let your mom go, buddy, so we can go get some dinner, okay?" Mitch asked politely.

"Are you sure we can't go? I promise we'll be good Mitch!" Travis asked, slightly begging. Maggie stepped out of the kitchen just in time to save the day.

"What? And miss my special dinner that I cooked for you? I made your favorite – homemade chicken nuggets with sweet potato fries. Besides, I need your help icing the cake!" she said, diverting his attention from their departure.

Travis looked at his mom with his sadness in his eyes.

"It's okay buddy. I think it might be better if Mitch and I go alone this time, but I promise we'll all go out as a family soon. Go help Maggie and be good while we're gone, okay?" Laci replied.

"Okay, mom. I love you."

"I love you too, Trav."

"Okay, Gramma. I'll come help you ice the cake!" he yelled as he ran off toward the kitchen. Travis loved Mitch's mom and Laci was grateful for the way she had supported their new blended family, but her recent departure from 'the living' probably didn't help their relationship much. She wasn't sure it would ever improve, honestly.

They drove to a small restaurant in town and luckily it wasn't busy. Laci was grateful. The few people she saw were older and so far, no small kids were around. The last time she went outside the house was for her doctor's appointment. She had kept her head covered with a hood, staring at the ground as she walked toward the office. She wasn't proud of how she'd handled the miscarriage. One doesn't set out to be diagnosed with post-partum depression, it just happens. Between the sadness, no appetite, having no desire to be with her husband, *which is a crime in and of itself,* and enduring episodes of crying that would last for hours at a time, she lost all semblance of who she was. It's a new day now though, and she felt something big was about to happen.

It was hard to make conversation over dinner, which wasn't like them normally. Mitch updated her on the winery, going over things that she had missed, and then mentioned his concern for Brad, his brother – that he seemed 'out-of-sorts' lately.

A romantic dinner and you're going to talk about your brother? She thought. Brad was Laci's least favorite topic, and she almost lost her appetite at the mere mention of his name, but there was something else going on with Mitch and she couldn't figure it out.

"Okay, now that you've given me the rundown on all things wine and family, how about you tell me what you really want to say. You're hiding something from me, I can feel it," she said.

Mitch took in a long, deep breath and stared at her for a second without saying a word, then pulled an envelope from his jacket pocket.

"I'm not really hiding anything… but you're right. I am holding something back. You always know, don't you?"

"I can see through to your soul – didn't you know?" Laci smiled.

"Okay… hear me out before you say anything, promise?"

"Yes, yes. I promise. Now what is it?" She clicked her nails on the table impatiently.

"There is a nice long break coming up at the winery – no events and nothing big going on. Our stock is good and we don't have any big orders to fill. The kids' school schedule is good too."

"And this means what exactly? Where are you going with this, Mitch?"

"I swear Darlin'… you are the most impatient woman I have ever known! I'm getting to it. Now will you just let me finish?" Mitch laughed through his frustration. Laci rolled her eyes and smiled. "I'm sorry… I'll be quiet." She bit her lip.

"I think it's time to give you a *real* change of atmosphere… and barometric pressure. You and I both need a break from things here." He slid the envelope across the table and her eyes caught the airline symbol showing on the outside.

Her hands shook as she opened the envelope, pulling out two tickets to Seattle.

Mitch reached across the table and set his hand on hers. "We still have a couple of weeks before we leave, so that should give you plenty of time to check in with your doctors. Plus, I've already talked to Mama and Brad, and they are happy to handle the winery and take care of the kids. Everything is taken care of – leaving you nothing to worry about. Caleb is even taking on more duties at the winery, and he can keep Brad in check while we're gone. We need to do this together, Darlin'. It's time we made a fresh start, don't you agree?" he asked.

Staring at the tickets in her hand, she was overcome with joy and the tears came without warning. She stood up and walked around to Mitch, pulling him out of his chair and hugging him right there in the restaurant, in front of everyone. Mitch added a soft kiss, lingering on her lips for some time. So long in fact, that a few couples seated around them began to clap, thinking they were newly engaged or that something 'big' had transpired. They were right. Something big *had* happened.

"Let's go visit the rain," he whispered in her ear, then smiled and kissed her again.

******

Two weeks later, it was time to leave. They said goodbye to the kids, and although Emma had a rough time with the goodbye, she knew it was for the best.

"Take care of your brother for me, okay Sweetie?" Laci asked.

"I will mom, don't worry." Emma smiled and the tears streamed down her cheeks, staining her recent makeup job. Laci hugged her tight, passed out hugs to Todd and Travis, and walked over to Mitch's mom to say goodbye.

"Maggie, I can't thank you enough for helping us with the kids. It means the world to me."

"Laci, I know we've had a rough start, but no matter what you believe… I do care about you. I love you, Sweetheart, and I want you to get better. My son is madly in love with you and you make him happy, so take this time and find your way back to where you belong. Don't worry about anything here, okay?" Maggie replied in a kind voice, on the verge of tears herself.

Laci wondered if those words were difficult for her to voice, but nonetheless, was glad to be leaving on a positive note between them. Hopefully a new beginning lay ahead – for all of them.

Out of Laci's window, familiar mountain tops peeked through a thin layer of clouds hovering below and she knew they were getting close. Mt. Rainier grew bigger and bigger – a full, white moon shining bright above. It was beautiful. The sun had almost set, but she could still see a few faint lines of color spread across the horizon in the softest shades of pink and orange, reminding her of a tropical margarita. *That sounds pretty good come to think of it…* As the plane began its descent into Seattle, Laci smiled and took in the view of the Sound. Mitch took her hand and leaned over to share it with her.

The minute Laci stepped outside, she could smell the familiar scent of a recent rain still lingering in the air. She was home.

"I saw that," Mitch said, smiling.

"What?"

"You know what – you can already feel the rain can't you?"

"Yes… I think we just missed a shower."

They drove into Olympia, and since it was Sunday evening, traffic was light. Even though the skies were filled with gray clouds hovering above, the evergreen trees were vibrant and full of color and there were already a few signs of spring, which was only a short month away. It was the one thing Laci loved about the Northwest– green all year around. After they checked into their hotel, they took a walk and stopped for dinner at a great little restaurant downtown. From across the table, Mitch's gaze locked onto hers and the flicker of the candle between them reflected in his eyes. Laci's heart raced when she looked at him and she couldn't help but smile. He reached across the table and took her hand.

"Are you excited to see the girls tomorrow?" he asked.

"More than I ever realized. I can't believe you arranged all this for me."

"Well, Lena set up most of it, I just made the call."

"Does Sandy know we're coming too?"

"I don't think so – Lena was going to try and surprise her, so we'll see how well that worked out."

They finished their dinner, talking about their plans to see Laci's former co-workers and some other sights around town, then made their way back to the hotel for the night.

Monday morning arrived and Laci woke early – anxious and full of anticipation for the day ahead. She got up and walked over to the window, pulling back the curtains, and saw rain falling from the sky. She closed her eyes and thanked God. *He's so faithful to give me exactly what I need at the time I need it most.* As she watched it pour down, a huge weight lifted from her heart. She could feel the pain drifting farther and farther away and her desire to greet the day with a smile was stronger than ever.

She walked back over to the bed and slid under the covers, snuggling up to Mitch and watching him sleep. She couldn't just watch though… he really needed a wake-up call so he could see the rain! She proceeded to mess with his hair, tickle him under his chin, and anything else she could think of to make him stir… except the *one* thing he truly wanted, which was the one thing she still couldn't give him – herself. It was too soon yet. A smile spread across his face and he swiftly pulled her up on top of him.

"Mornin', Darlin'," he said. "I take it you are ready to go?"

"It's raining, Mitch!"

"That definitely explains your mood," he laughed.

"Get up – we need to go get coffee and start our day."

"Yes, ma'am! How could we ever dream of starting a day without coffee?" he smiled and pulled her closer into his warm embrace, adding a tender kiss for good measure.

They headed out, grabbed a quick mocha from the local coffee shop and walked over to the bank. Lena had sent Mitch a text to come by around ten and they were right on time. Laci knew that seeing everyone again would be bittersweet under the circumstances, but she also knew it would be the first step to healing her heart. *Well, second step,* she thought, *the first one was seeing the rain.*

They walked inside the front doors and Laci's friends gathered within a few minutes. It didn't take long before the tears began, but as they did, she felt the hole inside her heart begin to fill up a tiny bit.

"Laci J – you're here!" Lena screamed from across the lobby, then ran over and threw her arms around Laci in a huge, Lena-like hug, squeezing her so tight she could hardly breathe.

"It's good to see you, Lena!" Laci said laughing, her cheeks still wet.

Mitch couldn't escape her either – before he knew it, she had swallowed him up in a hug too.

"I've missed you, Laci. You look great! Let's go up and surprise the gang, then we can get all caught up!" She escorted them upstairs. Laci felt a little strange being back in the bank, but it felt good. She had such good memories from working there. They snuck past the doors of Laci's old office and peeked in to see if her former boss, Sandy, was in. Sandy caught sight of them, then jumped up and screamed.

"Oh my, gosh! Laci Kram– I mean Laci *Young*! What are you doing here, girl?" Sandy threw her arms around Laci and began to cry, not realizing how much she had missed her.

"Hi, Sandy," Laci replied, and hugged her tight. She heard Sandy sniff and realized she was crying too. As it turned out, Lena had already shared the news about the miscarriage with everyone, and Laci was glad. It saved her from telling the story again and stirring up all those emotions. They visited for a long time then had lunch together.

After they left the bank, the rest of the day was filled with lots of laughter as they visited with other friends around town. It was exhausting though, and Mitch could tell it was time to call it a day, for both of their sakes. For fun, they picked up a pizza from Old School Pizzeria and a bottle of wine, then had a floor picnic back at their hotel room. As they sat there and ate, Mitch looked deep in thought.

"Alright my handsome, 'Creepy-Stalker-Crawdad-Fan', what's going on? I know there is something on your mind, so spill," Laci asked.

Without hesitation, he voiced his thought, "Let's take a road trip, Laci. Go visit a winery or two, see the Columbia Gorge, relax and just have some fun – what do you say?"

"Really? Are you sure?"

"Of course I'm sure – I think we need some time to ourselves and to enjoy a little of God's beauty around us, don't you?"

"I think that's exactly what the doctor ordered! Besides, I have never been to the Gorge."

"Well then, you are definitely overdue for a little southern Washington scenery. I think it will be... therapeutic."

"I'm sold!" and they toasted to each other and their journey of healing ahead.

By nine the next morning, they were driving south on I-5. The drive was beautiful. There were so many quaint little towns along the way too. They stopped to visit a few of them, rested a little, and shopped a lot. As they got closer to Oregon, the skyline began to explode with breathtaking views of hills and mountains – glimpses of spring colors were popping up everywhere. Laci wanted to stop and take some pictures, but she was also hungry and tired of being in the car, so they stopped in a town called Camas to eat lunch. A small family diner came into sight, and they pulled in and made their way inside. There were only a few people inside, which was nice. Laci still didn't like being around big crowds.

After they were seated and placed their order, Mitch reached across the table and took her hands in his, "I am so proud of you for taking this trip. And I have to say, you seem happier today, more like your old self."

"I am happier. I can feel myself getting better and better every day, and this trip was exactly what I needed. I'm still sad and heartbroken, but I can feel God telling me that everything is going to be okay. And this may sound crazy, but I get the feeling that we are on this trip for a special reason – I just don't know what it is yet."

"Well, the main reason for this trip is for us to have some quality time to ourselves and that's the only one I care about right now. I'm glad you are enjoying yourself. Your strength never ceases to amaze me, Laci Young."

Hearing Mitch say her name with his last name still gave her chills – in a good way. "It's not my strength… I'm just borrowing a little from the big man upstairs," she replied.

"A reliable source indeed," he smiled.

They relaxed and ate their lunch. Laci was glad to have Mitch all to herself. After they had returned from their honeymoon, they hadn't gotten much alone time with kids around, a new winery to run, volunteering at the cancer center, and the normal family activities. Their recent loss and her disengaged state of mind only magnified the distance between them. It pushed them so far apart that there were moments Laci could barely breathe not being able to hold him or talk to him like she truly wanted. After thinking about the kids, she decided to give them a call and check in.

"I'm going to go outside and call the kids before we take off."

"Great idea. I'll pay for lunch and meet you at the car. Tell them hi for me," he said.

Laci walked outside and sat on an old bench outside the café, then dialed her mother-in-law's number.

"Hello," Maggie answered.

"Hi, Maggie. It's Laci. I was just calling to check in and see how the kids were doing. Are things going okay so far?" she asked.

"Oh yes, we are having a very nice time Sweetie, don't you worry!"

"Well, I can't help but worry after everything that's happened, but I'm glad to hear everything is going well."

"Those kids are stronger than you realize, my dear. But the real question is how are you doing? Has the trip helped you and Mitch take your mind off… things?" Maggie asked, a genuine concern in her voice.

"It has, more than I ever thought it would. It was a good decision, and I appreciate you taking care of the kids for us. I hope they don't wear you out."

"They're fine and so am I – it's my pleasure to do this, Sweetheart. You just focus on each other and come back refreshed, you hear?"

"We will. Call me if you need anything. And thanks again, Maggie."

Maggie put Emma on the phone first, and then Travis. They both seemed to be in good spirits. Todd was at a friend's house and Laci was glad to hear he was getting out. Maggie was so good to care for them on such short notice, and even though it sounded like she was enjoying it, Laci was concerned about her health. She didn't sound like herself.

Mitch walked outside and sat down next to Laci. He scooted close and put his arm around her. "How is everyone in Crystal Creek? Kids okay?" he asked.

"They are being spoiled rotten. Your mom, however, sounded a little worn out. I hope this isn't too much for her, Mitch."

"She might be a sweet southern belle, but she's tougher than she looks." He gave her a tight squeeze and kissed her on the cheek. "Quit worrying. Let's get back on the road."

Laci could tell he was excited to be on this little adventure, and although he hid it well, their loss and the months of worrying about her had been just as devastating for him. It made her happy to see him smile. They drove another hour or so until they approached a large sign that read, 'Bridge of the Gods Next Right.'

"Stop the car – pull over!" Laci exclaimed.

"What? What's wrong?"

"That's the bridge!"

"What bridge?" he asked, thoroughly confused.

"THE bridge… the one that Charlie and Bella drove across on their way into Forks in the first movie!" Laci's excitement was a bit much for him; she could tell by the glazed look on his face. Laci, on the other hand, was having a minor panic attack.

"Who in the blue blazes are Charlie and Bella?" he asked.

"I'll explain later… will you please just stop so I can get a quick photo of the bridge?"

"Okay, okay… we're stopping at the bridge that fake people drove across," he mocked sarcastically.

Laci's love affair with the recent vampire book series and their movies was no secret to her closest friends, but that was pre-Airplane Man. It was such a small thing, but a fun and healing part of her past – a source of mindless fun and entertainment after losing Andrew. Seeing that bridge brought back fun memories. She and a few of her close co-workers used to attend all the midnight premieres of the movies, waiting in line for hours. It was an annual event – they bought new t-shirts to go with each movie, then swooned over their favorite characters throughout the night. They referred to Laci as the 'vampire mom' since she was over 40 and had kids, but she didn't care. She and those ladies formed a special friendship because of those books, and back then, it eased her pain… even if only for a short while.

She snapped a few photos from a distance, then they continued on their way.

"Happy now?" Mitch asked.

"More than you know… thank you," she said softly.

"Anything for you, Darlin'" He took her hand, and gently kissed the top. Her insides did a little flip and she smiled. *Oh how I've missed that feeling!*

Moments later, Laci caught a glimpse of the river between the trees.

"Keep watching out your window, you don't want to miss what's coming up," Mitch said.

They came upon a wide bridge where several cars had pulled over to the side, and that's when Laci saw the spectacular view of the Columbia River Gorge for the first time. Her body turned sideways as she gazed out the window – mesmerized by the beautiful scene. Mitch pulled the car over to join the others, and once outside, they walked over to the guard rail that lined the road. A thin layer of mist covered the water below, making it even harder to take her eyes from the river's charm.

"I know you want a picture," he smiled.

She looked at him and smiled, then grabbed the camera from the car. The wind whipped briskly, but it was refreshing. They looked over the edge of the railing, staring into the distance. Laci felt Mitch's arms wrap around her to keep her warm as she snapped a few pictures.

"It's cold. We should get going," he said.

"Wait! One more picture," she shouted, not wanting to leave. "Okay, I'm done." They hopped back in the car, and drove off.

"Where are we stopping for the night?" Laci asked.

"Well, let's see what the next town looks like. That sign back there said we're pretty close to Stevenson."

Seconds after Mitch mentioned the town's name, Laci caught a fleeting glimpse of a sign on the edge of the road that read, 'Foreclosure Property'. At least she thought that's what it said, but couldn't make out the rest. It made her a little sad all the same. She used to be a Realtor years ago and she remembered how hard it was when someone was faced with losing their home.

"Hmm…," She mumbled softly. Mitch overheard her.

"Hmm, what? Please tell me it's not another vampire movie monument!"

Laci giggled. "No, no. It's nothing like that – just reading road signs." The beautiful scenery quickly distracted her however, and the thought was gone.

Stevenson was a little town that might have been missed if one blinked, but had a charm all its own. They drove slowly as they entered the town, watching for signs that would point them toward a hotel for the night, but there was nothing around.

"Hey… there's a grocery store up ahead on your right – pull in there. I need to get a few things anyway, and we can ask one of their employees for directions to the closest hotel," Laci said.

"Great idea. I knew I kept you around for a reason," he chuckled softly.

They pulled into the parking lot and got out of the car. Laci looked around and stretched for a minute, then noticed a small women's clothing boutique across the street with the cutest window display!

"Oh! Let's walk over there first, Mitch. I love that blouse in the window! And it looks like there is a café inside – maybe we can finally get a good cup of coffee."

Mitch rolled his eyes and smiled, then took her by the hand. "Happy wife, happy life…" he mumbled out loud.

"You are such a smart man, Mitch Young." She leaned up and kissed him on the cheek for indulging her.

They walked through the front door and a little bell chimed to announce their presence.

"Hello there. I'll be right with you," said the cheerful lady behind the register. Her voice was chipper and she had a smile that lit up the room – it even made Laci smile. She looked around the store, but instead found herself watching the store clerk glide around the room assisting other customers and chatting with them like they were part of her family. She was simply lovely with her short, red hair shaped perfectly for her face, and an exquisite complement to her porcelain skin. She reminded Laci of a young Audrey Hepburn – stylish, graceful and charming. A few minutes later, she walked up to greet them.

"Hello again! I'm Andréa, the owner. Is there anything I can help you find?"

"Hi Andréa, I'm Laci and this is my husband Mitch. We saw the café sign out front – do you serve coffee?" Laci asked.

"Oh Sweetie, you haven't lived until you've had a cup of my coffee. You come right over here and I'll make one for both of you. It's so nice to meet you! Are you just passing through?" She extended her hand to greet them.

"Yes, ma'am," Mitch said as he shook her hand. "We're looking for a place to stay for the night."

"Whoa! You're definitely not from around here are you?" she giggled. "That's quite a southern accent you have there – must drive *all* the girls wild!"

A tad embarrassed, Mitch smiled – his cheeks a pale shade of pink. "Well, it drives her wild and that's all I care about. We're actually from North Carolina, here on vacation. Laci is originally from Olympia though."

"Oh I love Olympia! Sit down and enjoy your coffee so we can chat." Andréa was delightful and Laci found it hard to leave, but it was getting late and they needed to find a place to stay.

"Andréa, is there a hotel nearby?" Laci asked.

"If it's a hotel you want, you'll have another hour ahead of you. But there is an old bed and breakfast up the highway just a little bit farther – it's called Foxhead Estates. I'm sure she has a room available. My sweet friend Hannah owns it and lives there with her grandmother, but it's in foreclosure… the poor thing. They're letting her stay there and keep it open until it sells."

"That was the sign we passed!" Laci squealed.

"What?" Mitch asked, confused.

Laci turned to Mitch and whispered, "Never mind… I'll tell you later," then turned back to Andréa. "That's too bad she's losing her business. Are you sure she even wants guests?"

"Trust me, she can use all the help she can get."

"Well, what do you say, love?" Laci gave Mitch her 'please-say-yes' look.

He laughed. "I think we're going to Foxhead Estates, Andréa. Can you give us directions?"

Goosebumps popped out all over Laci's arms as she sensed there was something much more to this temporary stop – unable to explain it away.

Andréa wrote down the address and phone number to the B&B, and they said their goodbyes. "Ooh! I have such a good feeling about your visit," she said, giving them both a big hug as if they had all been friends for years. "You're going to absolutely love Hannah's place! And don't forget to stop back here on your way out of town and tell me all about it. Besides, I think we're destined to be great friends!"

Andréa beamed her bright smile as she waved goodbye from the store window, and they were on their way.

3 - Promising Opportunities

Signs for the bed and breakfast appeared a few miles down the road. Laci read one to herself. *'Foxhead Bed and Breakfast – Award Winning Winery'. Huh? It seems that Andréa left that little detail out. A winery too? Very interesting.*

Mitch pulled the car into a long driveway that led up to a big, beautiful old log cabin-style house which Laci assumed was the bed and breakfast. The knotty-cedar exterior, most likely a rich red in its earlier days, was now faded and worn. It had two-stories with gables and eaves along the front, and a big bay window still adorned with Christmas lights from the recent holiday season. The two-tiered front porch was the length of the house, complete with a porch swing – swaying slightly as if someone had recently jumped off. They parked, then got out to look around. To her right, Laci saw a large building that looked like the winery, also disheveled and in need of some major TLC, but it had an old-world charm about it. As she looked around, her tell-tale goosebumps came back and she couldn't help but feel like she and Mitch were there for a reason.

Within minutes, a petite, little red-headed gal walked out of the house and on to the front porch to greet them. She looked to be in her mid-forties, give or take a few years. Her long curly hair blew in the breeze and Laci found herself somewhat envious of the muscular arms peeking from under her t-shirt. She was obviously a woman who took care of herself. She looked over at Mitch, realizing he had also noticed her attractive features, and seemed to be enjoying the view. She bumped his shoulder to divert his attention.

"Hey, Romeo. Remember me… your Juliet? You're taken, my love." Laci pinched his side and he laughed.

"Don't worry, Darlin'. I was just admiring God's handiwork, that's all. My heart belongs to you."

Laci smiled, and once again he had sweet talked himself out of trouble. They walked toward the porch and the redhead waved and smiled cheerfully.

"Hi, I'm Hannah Blake. I'm the owner. Please, call me Hannah. I'm afraid I don't have any rooms ready, but if you're here for a wine tasting, I'm happy to assist. If you're nosing around about the foreclosure however, then I'll kindly ask you to get back in your car and leave – I'll be taking that sign down any day now," Hannah said.

Right away, Laci took note of her defensive reaction. Although she was polite, she conveyed a stern, matter-of-fact tone that delivered a clear message.

Laci smiled. "Well, Hannah, it's nice to meet you. I'm Laci Young and this is my husband, Mitch." Mitch waved casually and smiled. "We were actually interested in getting a room for tonight. Andréa sent us – we met her earlier when we stopped by her shop for coffee."

Hannah laughed softly, "I should have known. She's my biggest fan and dearest friend, outside of my grandma. Always looking out for me, that one."

"So, if you're taking the sign down soon, does that mean you've sold the property?"

"No, it's not sold, but it's not for sale either… not exactly. I'm still hoping to raise the money we owe the bank. I have every intention of keeping this place in my family where it belongs," Hannah replied.

Mitch took a step toward the porch. "It's a beautiful place. I don't blame you for wanting to keep it. I don't really know much about the Bed & Breakfast business, but I do own a winery in North Carolina and it's very special to me," he said.

Hannah's eyes widened, "North Carolina, huh? That's… that's where we used to vacation years ago. It's a beautiful part of the country," she replied, somewhat distracted now. Based on her comment, Laci got the distinct feeling that there was more to that story.

"We sure love it there," Mitch said, and paused for a moment of awkward silence. "Well, we should be on our way. The wine tasting did sound good, but we need to find a place to stay tonight. It was nice to meet you," Mitch said.

Laci immediately shot Mitch 'the look' to convey her intense disapproval of his statement. *We are definitely not leaving! I needed to learn a little more about little miss Hannah and this property.* Lucky for her though, Hannah offered up a new option.

"Wait… please don't go. I'm sorry if I've been rude, that's not like me normally. We are fellow wine connoisseurs after all, so the least I can do is offer you a room for the night. Besides, Andréa would never speak to me again if she found out that I turned you away," Hannah said.

Laci looked at Mitch with her 'please-say-yes' look, then smiled.

"Well thank you, Hannah. I'm pretty sure that look from my wife means 'we're staying', as long as you're sure, that is."

"Of course! It's a little run down but I make up for it with my mad cooking skills."

"Great! It's settled then," Laci said, more than a tad excited. Mitch rolled his eyes at her. *I'm a passionate girl, what can I say?*

Hannah escorted us inside.

"Give me a few minutes to get your room ready and let my grandmother know we have guests in the house. We haven't entertained in some time and I would hate for her to suddenly take a stroll down the hall wearing nothing but her skivvies," Hannah smiled and walked away.

While Hannah was gone, Mitch and Laci walked outside to get their bags from the car. Laci was lost in thought. This wasn't a mere coincidence, us meeting Andréa and learning about this place. No, there was much more to this and I already have a few thoughts on what direction this could take. Mitch popped the trunk and Laci stared at him, waiting for him to look at her. Finally he did.

"What? You look like you're up to something," Mitch said, his eyebrow raised in curiosity.

"You know!"

"Uh, well… actually I don't know. You'll have to enlighten me with your wisdom there Darlin'."

"*Ugh!* The winery, Mitch! The foreclosure? She's going to lose her family's business!" Laci said emphatically, hoping to convey her meaning, but it didn't seem to turn on any lights for him. Nope… no one was home.

"Yeah, that's what usually happens in a foreclosure, but I'm still not following. What are you getting at?"

She rolled her eyes and huffed with an audible, exasperated sigh. Hannah stepped out onto the porch before she could continue.

"Do you need help bringing in your bags?" Hannah asked.

"No, no. We've got it – thank you though," Mitch replied.

They walked back inside and Hannah showed them to their room. *It was probably best we were interrupted anyway. This way I can formulate a rock-solid plan that he won't be able to refuse.*

"So, I was just about to fix dinner for my grandma and me. Would you like to join us?"

Laci answered for both of them, "We would love to, thank you. I'm starving!" obviously thrilled for the opportunity to gather more 'intel' on Hannah's situation.

"Great! Give me about thirty minutes and I'll have it ready. Until then, relax or feel free to walk around the grounds if you want. It's a nice night for an evening stroll," Hannah smiled and went on her way.

Instead of unpacking, they took Hannah's advice and decided to go for a walk. Despite the clouds, it was a beautiful evening and the temperature was warmer than expected for mid-March. Mitch wove his fingers through Laci's and they walked over to the small garden nestled between the house and the winery. The sky grew darker, but a small section still glowed from the sun setting below the horizon.

"I'm so glad we're here Mitch."

"Me too, Darlin'. I can see a big difference in you just since we arrived. You look happy."

"It's more than happy… it's a sense of peace that I haven't felt in months. I'm so sorry for everything I put you through."

Mitch stopped and turned to Laci. He cupped his hands around her face and looked in her eyes, "Don't ever apologize again. We lost our baby, and I know it was much harder on you. I'm here for the long haul, Laci Young. For better or worse, remember?"

"Yeah… I remember," she smiled, then he leaned in and gently kissed her, wrapping his arms around her and holding tight. Laci's body tingled and she began to shiver, and for the first time in months, she found herself wanting a whole lot more than a kiss. At that realization, her eyes popped open like she'd been poked with a stick pin, and in her utter joy, she pulled away from Mitch's kiss and spontaneously laughed out loud.

"Wow. Was it that bad?" he asked – a confused look on his face.

"Oh, heaven's no!" Laci slowly calmed down and quieted her laugh, "On the contrary my love, it was a little *too* good." He smiled, knowing exactly what she meant. They walked back to the house, hand in hand, excited for the evening ahead.

They immediately smelled the wonderful aroma coming from the kitchen and made their way to the dining room. Hannah was setting food on the table – pecan crusted tilapia filets, asparagus, and wild rice. Laci almost dove in headfirst she was so hungry. From the other side of the room, a frail little lady walked in and joined them, aided by her cane. She wore a pair of large dark sunglasses and looked over in their general direction, but seemed to be searching for something.

"You're just in time! Laci, Mitch… this is my grandmother, Lois," Hannah said.

"It's nice to meet you, Lois." Laci walked over to introduce herself, but Lois turned slightly past her. Laci realized then that Lois was mostly likely blind.

"It's so nice to meet you both! I'm sorry but I can't see you, Sweetheart. I'm legally blind and can only see shapes and light anymore. It's a real pain in the 'patootie' if you know what I mean," Lois said with a giggle.

"That's okay – I'm right here." Laci guided Lois' hand into hers and patted it gently.

"Jules said we would be having guests tonight – it's so nice to have a table full of people again." Lois quickly turned her head and coughed with what seemed like great difficulty, then cleared her voice. "I hope I didn't hold up dinner. I move much slower these days."

Lois' voice echoed a tired soul within, but you couldn't tell from her appearance. Her hair was mostly white with some reddish roots, and it looked like it had just been washed and set by a hairdresser. The makeup around her cheekbones was a little bright, but nice otherwise. And her outfit spoke volumes; black polyester pants, a long-sleeved white sweatshirt that read 'Steady and Slow Wins the Race', bearing an image of a small turtle with grey hair crossing a finish line. She wore a shimmery pink pearl necklace and tiny gold earrings, complemented by a glittery bracelet on her wrist. Absolutely nothing matched, but she was precious and Laci already adored her.

"Hello, Lois. I'm Mitch. May I help you to your chair?" Mitch walked around and held out her chair so she could sit down.

"Oh mercy, aren't you charming. That's the kind of man my husband was – always the gentleman. Thank you, dear."

"Grandma, don't embarrass him," Hannah said quietly.

"I'll take that as a compliment, Lois. Thank you. I was raised that way I guess – ladies should always come first where I'm from," Mitch replied.

"Did I hear your grandmother call you *Jewels*, Hannah? Is that a nick name?" Laci asked.

"Sort of. My middle name is Jule, spelled J-U-L-E. When I was born, I guess my dad called me his little 'jewel' – like the ruby. Ever since then, my family and some of my closer friends have always called me Jules – I prefer Hannah though. It's just one of those names that mean more to people who love me, or used to love me, you know?"

"Oh, I totally get it! My cousins used to have pet names for me when I was a little girl – Pumpkin, Super Kid and Angel. Not as fancy as 'jewel', but I loved it when they used them. It always made me feel a little extra special in some way," Laci replied.

They enjoyed a lovely dinner and visited about this and that. Laci wanted to dig in deeper and ask more questions about the B&B and the winery, but it didn't seem like the right time. After dinner, she helped clean up the dishes and they said goodnight to Lois before she went to bed.

"So, I know it's getting late, but would you still be interested in a wine tasting?" Hannah asked.

"Are you kidding? It's never too late for a little vino!" Mitch was like a kid when it came to his passion for wine.

Hannah walked them out to the winery and once inside, guided them to a small bar located just past the entry. Laci wasn't sure the bar would hold up one bottle of wine, let alone two or three. It was in pretty bad shape – most likely the original. As they kept walking, a glass trophy case caught her eye, filled with trophies, certificates and several bottles of wine with blue ribbons draped around the necks. *Look at these awards! This is unbelievable, and there is no way this winery can close. We have to do something about this.* Laci thought.

The main room was filled with tables and chairs, obviously a place that Hannah had once used to entertain, but it was covered in dust from being untouched. The far back wall featured a gorgeous stone hearth fireplace and on either side of that were glass French doors that opened to a patio out back. Barrels lined the inside walls of the tasting area and to their right was a door marked 'Employees Only' – leading to the wine making area. It was a spectacular room and Laci imagined it filled with music, glowing lights and people as they enjoyed an evening with friends and good wine.

As Hannah prepared the tasting, she shared details about each wine, about the history of the winery, and bragged on her business, but suddenly grew quiet.

"I… I'm sorry again for my behavior today. I simply can't stand the thought of losing this place! You see, my parents died six years ago in a boating accident and left me the estate in their will. I wasn't living here at the time, but I moved back to run it. My grandmother wasn't doing well, so eventually she moved in with me so I could care for her. I had to let my winemaker go last week – he was one of the best on the west coast. The rest of the staff will be gone at the end of the week because I can't afford to pay them either. My Grandma's health is declining every day and her eyesight is nearly gone, as I'm sure you could tell. It's all I can do to take care of her and run the business. She helps as much as she can though, her and my little sister. I've put so much into this place – I even lost my husband over it when I decided to move back up here. He said he wasn't a *wine kind of guy* and couldn't see himself living in Washington. Actually, that ended up being a blessing in disguise now that I look back on it," she chuckled. "Once the economy tanked, guests stopped coming up as often and I struggled to keep up on the mortgage. The bank finally gave me notice of foreclosure last month and the sign went up the next day." Hannah's voice was both sad and angry, but mostly it was the cry of a broken heart.

"I'm so sorry you and your grandmother are having to endure this, Hannah. I can't imagine how hard it's been on both of you, but I'm glad you have your sister to lean on," Laci said.

Hannah laughed, "Oh, she's not my real sister. She's my 'little' – I'm a 'big sister' with the Big Brothers Big Sisters program here in town. Her name is Clare and she stops by every other day or so to hang out and help me around the winery. After a few months of running this place, I realized I needed something else to throw myself into outside of this business, so I decided to become a Big Sister. That's how we met. She's almost 18 already – it's hard to believe. She's never really had many reliable people in her life. Her mom was an alcoholic and walked out on her when she was just six years old and now she lives with foster parents. They are good people, but they also have several smaller kids and Clare seems to go unnoticed much too often. She's such a great kid, and man does she love to read! I'm always finding her hiding somewhere on the grounds with her nose stuck in a book."

"Wow, you are a busy woman. I admire you for what you're doing, Hannah," Laci said, "And you shouldn't apologize for anything. I know what a big undertaking it is to run a winery, let alone a Bed & Breakfast, and caring for a family member on top of that. It's a competitive business and I'm sure you've done the best you could, given the circumstances. I know it's none of my business, but if you don't mind me asking, how close are you to raising the money to pay off your debt?" Mitch asked.

"Not close enough. I only told you that earlier so you wouldn't ask any more questions."

"I'm sure I would have reacted the same way, don't worry."

"Your wine is outstanding, Hannah – you and your staff obviously know your stuff and it shows. I'm sure you'll have several offers by the looks of your operation here. It's impressive," Laci said, fishing to find out if there were any offers yet.

Hannah sighed. "So far we've received one bid, but the offer was too far below the market value, so they are holding out until there is an offer high enough to pay off the debt and buy the current wine stock at a reasonable price." Hannah walked them out the door, her head hanging low.

It became clear to Laci why they were there – to help Hannah save her family's business. *We are supposed to buy her estate! This is good… but I'll have to wait for the right time to share my idea with Mitch. I'm not sure he'll be quite as enthusiastic as I am.*

"If you can't raise the money, where will you go after the foreclosure?" Mitch asked.

"I haven't given it much thought honestly – it's too hard. I don't want to think about it either because then it means I've given up, and I can't give up yet no matter what. I know that am supposed to be here. I feel it in my bones – it's where I belong. I'm sorry. I don't mean to go on and on. I've only just met you two and here I am spilling my entire life story. Enough about me. Besides, I should get back inside and prep for breakfast. We're having brioche french toast with pear cranberry compote. It's my specialty."

"That sounds mouth-watering, Hannah! What time should we be down?" Laci asked.

"I usually serve around nine – but there's no one here but you, so if you'd like it later, let me know."

"Oh, no. Nine is perfect – we need to get on our way shortly after that anyway," Mitch said.

They walked back into the house and Mitch started upstairs to their room, but Laci had other plans. Mitch looked at her, wondering why she was lingering behind.

"Laci, are you coming?" he asked.

"Actually, I have a quick question for Hannah – you go on up."

"Okay, but don't be too long."

"I won't – I promise."

Laci followed Hannah into the kitchen. "Would you mind if I fixed myself a cup of coffee?" Laci asked.

"Of course not – help yourself. All the supplies are in the cabinet right above your head." Laci pulled down a cup and fixed her coffee while Hannah unloaded the dishwasher. Laci wasn't sure that it was the best time to approach the subject, but she had to know before she went to bed.

"Hannah, what if someone were to buy the winery and let you stay on and manage it? A merger of sorts…" Laci asked.

"I never thought about that. I guess if it meant saving the business and getting out of debt, I would definitely consider it. Although, I'm not sure I'd be the ideal employee after running this place by myself for so long. I can be a bit hard headed at times," she laughed.

"Well, don't worry about that. Let me do some digging and I'll talk to you more tomorrow. I have an idea that just might work if I can get a certain *someone* on board," Laci smiled and pointed her thumb upward in the direction of her room.

Hannah raised her left eyebrow curiously, "I'm not sure what you're up to Laci, but I think I like where it's headed. And for whatever you're about to do… good luck."

A smug smile on her face, and a warm cup of joe in her hand, Laci walked upstairs, but stopped suddenly when she heard a crack of thunder outside – so loud it rattled the walls. She smiled, turned around and walked right out the front door onto the porch. *It's almost here! My rain!* Gusts of wind pushed through and wrapped her in their fierce strength as she waited for the drops to fall. In the distance, lightning flashed to illuminate a silhouette of the hills that surrounded the estate, and she couldn't remove her eyes from the soft white halo that it left behind. *One, two, three, fou-* Another crack of thunder boomed around her. *Less than four miles away now.*

The air was heavy, filled with the rich smell of rain looming nearby. Laci waited patiently. Finally, it was in front of her – a rain that she could see, hear, smell, and touch with her hands. She set her coffee down on the table next to the swing, walked to the edge of the porch, and stretched her arm out to let the warm drops fall on her skin – pricking it like tiny little needles. That wasn't enough though. She inched her head out and beheld the night sky. *This is too good to watch from the sidelines!* It beckoned for her and she replied by walking down the steps and onto the drive – hands outstretched to her sides. Thunder clapped again and she spun around in the rain, laughing like a little girl. She thought back to last year when she stood in the rain – cancer-stricken and heartbroken. It was a source of joy then and still was today.

"Laci!" Mitch's voice echoed, and she turned to find him watching her from inside the front door.

"I couldn't help it, Mitch! Isn't it beautiful?" she yelled, beaming a smile that wouldn't go away.

He lowered his head and shook it from side to side laughing at her antics. "Come inside before you get sick, Lace."

"No! Not yet. Just a little longer, okay? Come join me!"

"Oh no… you have fun and I'll stay right here."

Laci wasn't about to take no for an answer. She ran up the steps, grabbed him by the hands and despite his attempt to pull her inside, she pulled him down the stairs to join her in the pouring rain. White sheets of rain fell on every side of them and light glowed from inside the windows. Laci looked into his eyes and, most unexpectedly, felt a deep longing for him rise up within her – she once worried it would never return. She desired him in every way, and her hope was again restored. Mitch wrapped his arms around her and pulled her in close. Words weren't appropriate, nor needed – his warm, soft kiss was enough.

Drenched from head to toe, they finally decided to go back to their room and dry off. Laci's teeth were chattering as she shivered in her wet clothes. When they walked inside, Mitch grabbed some towels and wrapped them around her. The fireplace was burning bright and Laci stood in front of it to let the heat soak through her clothes. That's when she noticed the candles glowing all around the room and a thick layer of steam rolling off the top of the Jacuzzi tub filled with hot water. *Oh my. This is his invitation. Okay, I can do this – just relax. He's your husband for crying out loud! An incredibly gorgeous, sweet, southern comfort husband!* She was officially a bundle of nerves. She remembered his touch of course, how it felt, how gentle he was and how much fun they had in bed, and she longed for that touch once again. *What if I'm not ready? What if I break down in the middle of it? What if I can't make him happy anymore? How long would he put up with not being able to have a normal relationship with his wife? Get a grip, Laci!* She took a quick glance at herself in the mirror and assessed her current sexiness factor. *Great… five out of ten if I'm lucky! Ugh!* She wanted her fairy godmother to appear, but alas, she was a no-show once again.

Mitch took her by the hand and led her over to the Jacuzzi. He slowly removed her towel, then lifted her wet shirt over her head and threw it to the floor. He took off his shirt, revealing his firm, sun-kissed torso, glistening in the dim light. As she took in the view, she noticed a few flecks of silver at the edge of his hairline that she hadn't seen before. *Very nice!* She thought. She was nervous and still a little scared, but for the first time in months she wanted to give herself to him in every way, without guilt or fear. God had used this trip, and the rain, to open her heart, freeing her from the pain that had kept her from being the wife he needed.

One side at a time, he slid the straps of her bra off her shoulders, then reached around behind her back to unhook the strap. With a gentle tug, he pulled it away, and she closed her eyes as he finished undressing her. It had been months since she'd let him see her naked, let alone make love. As his wife, she knew it wasn't right for her to withhold herself from him, but until now, she wasn't able to get past her grief and sorrow to desire his touch. That time had ended – now she wanted him more than ever.

They stepped into the steaming hot water and sat down, relaxing together for a time. Then Mitch sat up and pulled her onto his lap, facing him. He gently caressed and kissed every part of her. The heat from his touch penetrated her skin, warming her through to her bones. She melted into his lips, running her fingers through his wet hair and drinking him in, enjoying every moment and wanting it to last forever.

The raging fire was building between them, passionate and powerful. Mitch lifted her out of the water, wrapped her in a towel, and then carried her to the living room and laid her down on a blanket near the fireplace. His hands and lips moved all over her body, bringing her intense pleasure and joy, as if he were a musician bringing her back to life. She was his instrument… he was her music. They loved each other as if there were no tomorrow, and it felt like hours had passed as they laid together, resting in each other's arms.

He leaned up on his elbow and looked into her eyes, brushing the hair from her face. "I love you, Laci Young."

"And I love you, Mitch Young," she smiled, feeling the warmth in her cheeks.

"So, what did you ask Hannah about earlier tonight before your frolic in the rain?"

He's asking me this now? After we just… oh well. Maybe it was the perfect time to bring it up. He was quite happy after all.

"I… um, I just wanted to know how old the winery was – I forgot to ask earlier."

Mitch just rolled his eyes at me and smiled. "I know you better than that."

"Well, I might have asked her a few questions about the foreclosure." Laci sat up and pulled the blanket around her. *If you're going to ask, then I'm going to answer,* she thought. "And I've been thinking…"

"Oh no you don't… stop right there, Darlin'. When you start a sentence with 'I've been thinking', it's either going to cost me money or create work for me… which will eventually cost me money," Mitch smiled, knowing full well she wouldn't be able to stop.

"You'll like this idea, I promise! Besides, it's going to help Hannah and grow our business at the same time."

"You want to talk about this now? At two a.m.?"

"Yes I do! And you asked, remember?"

"Okay, okay. I know I'll regret this later, but let's hear it. What's your idea?"

"I think you should buy Hannah's winery and keep her on to manage it. Eventually, she might be able to buy it back or become a partner when it starts to turn a profit again." Mitch's chin dropped a little, unsure of how to respond at first, so she didn't give him a chance. "But wait, that's not all. I think we should send Brad up here to go over everything and run the business with Hannah to protect our investment – at least for a while. She's going to need help for several months to get things up and running, and I think they would work well together."

Mitch tilted his head to the side and suddenly looked as if he'd solved a great mystery. "You are out of your ever-rain-lovin' mind, Laci Jean!"

"Why? Why is this a bad idea? You know we can do it and…"

"This isn't really about saving her winery is it? You are trying to get rid of Brad! I thought you two had moved past your petty differences and were getting along better?"

"What? Oh good grief… no, no, no! I'm just trying to save Hannah's winery – I really like her, is that so bad? And it's good business. We'd be on both coasts – a sister winery of sorts. All of her suppliers are already established and she has an impressive operation here Mitch – you said it yourself. We could even push her label down in Crystal Creek and sell it from both locations. It's a win, win!"

"Well, I agree with you on that. The wine was excellent and there would be little cost on that side. But re-vitalizing a brand takes capital, Laci – and a lot of it. And if you think Brad and that spicy little red-head will work well together, you're crazy! That is a case of dynamite just itching to be lit." Mitch laughed at the thought.

Laci's voice softened, "You don't know that. It could be good for him to branch out. A change of pace is sometimes good for the soul you know. And besides, you even said he's seemed a little 'out of sorts' lately."

"That's true. I'm not sure what he's been going through lately. He won't tell me anything, which is nothing new."

Laci's plan was much bigger than simply helping Hannah keep her estate though, it was about saving Brad too. She knew in her gut that he was lonely, and unless he got out of Crystal Creek, he would never find anyone – and Hannah was perfect for him! But, she knew better than to share that part with Mitch. Once he agreed to send Brad up to look at the business, the rest would happen naturally… in God's time, just like it did when Mitch sat next to her on the plane. Brad just needs a little push in the right direction that's all. She gave Mitch her sad, pouty face, then smiled.

"What am I going to do with you?" He shook his head and returned a smile.

"Hmmm… I can think of a couple of things." She gave him a quick, soft kiss on the lips.

"Laci Young, are you flirting with me?"

"How did you ever guess, Mr. Young?"

"I see," Mitch laughed. "Bribing me with your feminine wiles," he paused and smiled. "Well, it's working, but I need to sleep on it first. If it's something I think we should consider, I'll call Brad after breakfast to get his input and have him run some numbers. I'm warning you though, don't get your hopes up. He may not go for this. He's not only stubborn, but isn't a fan of spending our money."

She leaned over and threw her arms around him, squeezing him tight, then whispered in his ear, "Thank you, Mitch. I love you."

"You're welcome, Darlin'. And thanks for the view."

"What? Oh…" She blushed, realizing that the blanket was no longer wrapped around her. Still warm from the fire, she couldn't waste a perfect opportunity to sweeten the offer with a few butterfly kisses.

"You are a very shrewd business woman, you know that?" he said.

"I know. It took you long enough to figure it out," she smiled.

The next morning brought sunshine, and with it, Laci was filled with hope after last night's rain and the 'reunion' between herself and Mitch. He'd slept on their little discussion and now it was time for his answer.

They walked downstairs to the dining room and Laci darted straight toward the coffee bar. Hannah had pulled out all the stops with a vast array of creamers and sugars to meet anyone's taste choices. *I think she picked up on my coffee fetish right away. I love this woman!*

"Good morning you two! How did you sleep?" Hannah asked as they walked in.

Laci smiled and dropped her head, feeling the temperature in her cheeks rise as she recalled their night together.

Hannah laughed. "Never mind – no answer needed."

"We slept well, Hannah. Thank you for asking," Mitch smiled and kissed the top of Laci's head.

"Good! I hope you're both hungry because I made extra today."

A sweet maple aroma swirled around the room making Laci even more anxious to eat than before. Although she was definitely hungry, the butterflies in her stomach made it hard to focus on food, anxious about Mitch's call to Brad. *He's going to say 'yes'... he has to!* Her motivational self-talk normally helped, but even that had lost its edge today.

"Please help yourself to breakfast behind you on the bar, and I'll be around to check on you shortly," Hannah said.

They filled their plates with the delectable quiche and French toast, then sat down at a table. After a few minutes of staring at her food, Laci burst. She couldn't wait any longer.

"Okay – the suspense is killing me! What's your answer? I can't wait until you finish eating. What do you think?"

Mitch took a sip of his coffee. "Wow. I'm actually impressed that I got a few bites in before you demanded an answer. You should eat first," he smiled.

"Please tell me? I can't eat unless you tell me," she begged.

"Fine, fine! Yes... yes, I like your idea. So, if it's okay with you, I'd like to finish eating now, then I'll call Brad," he smiled and winked at her.

Laci popped up out of her chair and ran over to his side, sitting in his lap and nearly toppling his chair over just to give him a hug.

"Thank you, Mitch. I know this is the right thing to do. This is why we are here!"

"Laci, Darlin'... God brought us here to help you remember what comes before, during, and after the rain... grace."

His reply warmed her heart, and despite the fact that they were sitting at the breakfast table, she couldn't let him go.

4 - The Past Revisited

Brad yawned and stumbled his way into the winery, starting his day exceptionally early, compared to other days, having been rudely awakened by a startling dream. It wasn't just any dream – it was a reflection of his past and a picture of what could have been with a very special woman. Typically, he made every effort *not* to think about her, but today was the day – the day he would write the letter.

He looked at the orders on the desk and began working on them the best he could, but by eleven he couldn't stomach any more. He took a piece of cold pizza from the fridge and walked outside to enjoy it on the front porch, taking in the sunshine. Although he did his best to think about other mindless things, like the pile of dirty laundry at home, and last night's episode of 'Castle', it didn't work. The image of her face was now burning in his mind, and for a brief moment, he allowed himself to stay in the dream, and paid a visit to that sweet familiar place.

*****

Growing up, Mitch and Brad were as opposite as oil and water. Mitch was 'book smart', polite, athletic, and always had a taste for the finer things, as well as a head for business. Brad on the other hand, though smart in his own way, preferred to work with his hands. He hated wearing fancy clothes, didn't like to socialize much, and rarely cared about what others thought of him. One afternoon after school, Brad was tinkering around with the tools and wood inside his uncle's barn, and that's when he realized that he wanted to build things – create something. Brad's uncle taught him everything he knew about woodworking, and eventually,

Brad went on to college to pursue an architectural degree. Not long after that, he got his contractor's license and began to take on projects from Crystal Creek all the way to Charlotte. He was a talented carpenter, and a natural when it came to creating new building designs. After a few years of successful ventures under his belt, he finally received an offer to bid on a new museum project in Highpoint, and got the job.

That's where he met Jules – his first day on a new contracting job. He walked into the site office, took one look at her sitting behind the desk, and everything around him stopped moving. He remembered feeling like there wasn't enough air in the room. The name block on the desk read 'Jules McRae - Project Manager' and she had long, beautiful, curly, red hair that hung down to the middle of her back – stark in contrast as it lay against her black sweater. She stood up and walked over to introduce herself. Her first words to him were, *'You're late, but I like your boots, so I'll forgive you this once'*. Brad was a goner from that moment on, and he recalled that her tight jeans and black knee-high boots were simply icing on the cake.

After a few flirtatious conversations, a couple of morning coffee chats and lunches together, it wasn't too long before they were dating. He didn't need much time to know that she was the one – he knew it from the moment they met. A proposal was imminent, and six months later, he finally popped the question, giving her a handmade wooden box with her ring tucked inside. Of course she promptly said yes and they set a date just six months later. Not long after though, Brad became consumed with doubt and fear, worried that he had moved their relationship along too fast. The museum project was nearing completion and he was already getting that antsy feeling, itching to move on to the next big job. It wasn't long before the call came. It was the best offer of his entire career – a high-rise office building in Raleigh. When he broke the news to Jules, she had begged him to stay and even offered to go with him, in hopes that he would change his mind, but he was scared. Brad agonized for days over his decision, but in the end, the money and prestige that came with the job was more than he could resist, and he accepted the job. He was too ashamed to admit that he was afraid of failing her as a husband. It was easier to leave and he figured it was the best decision for both of them. Besides, it wasn't the right time. His career was finally taking off, and he was better off without her – or so he thought.

The night before he left, he wrote her a letter and tried to explain, hoping that one day she would forgive him. Instead of giving it to her in person and saying goodbye, he stopped by the office and slipped the letter under the door, knowing she was always the first to arrive and would find it before anyone else. That was the first of many letters he wrote to her, but the only one she ever received.

If he'd only known then that his decision to leave would plague his heart for years to come, he would have stayed. He was too stupid to realize back then that Jules was and would always be his forever love. He closed his eyes and kept her face pictured in his mind's eye, longing to reach out and hold her. In the deepest part of his soul, he knew she was still the one. The one woman who managed to steal his heart – the only one with whom he'd ever fallen in love.

About a year after he left, Brad received word that Jules had become engaged to a high school science teacher, and as a man who was still in love with her, the news broke him. Not just his heart, but his spirit. That's when he started writing to her. Every year, on what would have been their wedding anniversary, he wrote Jules a letter as if she were his wife, declaring his love for her and how much he adored their life together. Each letter a work of fiction. Each one sealed inside an envelope, and then tucked in a box… never to be opened again.

Eventually, his work suffered to the point where he could no longer effectively lead projects or his team. They even lost job offers due to his negligence. Everything he'd ever worked for up to that moment was gone, and there was nowhere to go except back home to Crystal Creek, broke and ashamed. A few months passed, and after he stopped feeling sorry for himself, he found a few odd jobs around town. Still, no one wanted to take a chance and hire him for bigger projects.

Mitch's first wife was diagnosed with cancer not long after, and Brad found a new purpose for living; taking care of Mitch and his nephew Caleb. During that time, he even managed to land a good job with a local construction company and worked his way up, eventually able to buy the company. It was a difficult year – helping Mitch cope with his loss, but Brad did what he had to do. His personal life was a non-event.

About two years after Karin passed, Mitch found the winery and talked Brad into running it with him, and he had been by Mitch's side ever since. He kept the construction company for a while, but later sold it and gave his full attention to the winery. Until recently, that had been enough. Not anymore. Something was missing. Someone.

Brad enjoyed working with his brother at the winery, but after Mitch met Laci, everything changed. He didn't approve of Laci at first, but he could see how much they loved each other from the very first moment he saw them together – it was almost sickening at times. Even worse, it became a constant reminder of Brad's choice to walk away from the love of his life, and left him wondering what his life might have been like had he stayed and married Jules.

Brad sat there with his lunch in hand and thought to himself, *I want that.* He finally admitted that he wanted the kind of love that Laci and Mitch had– to find that one person in life that would make him whole – who would fill the void inside – someone he couldn't bear to be apart from, even for a short while. He once had that in Jules. When they were together, it was like breathing. Natural. Effortless. Easy. Unfortunately, a love like that rarely comes along once in a lifetime, let alone twice.

Brad's phone rang, startling him out of his reflective state. Knowing it was Mitch, he smiled and answered. "You know, you have an uncanny knack for either interrupting my sleep, or my lunch," Brad said in fun.

"Sorry big brother… did I interrupt your morning nap time?" Mitch laughed.

"Very funny… you know I don't nap. So what's up? Has Laci seen 'her rain' yet?" Brad's sarcasm didn't go unnoticed.

"Don't start, Brad. You know as well as I do that we both needed this trip, and the rain."

"Yeah… I know. Sorry. How are you doing, seriously?"

"We're good. It's been nice to get away and, interestingly enough, we've uncovered a potential opportunity on our little road trip. Do you have a minute?"

"Sure, I'm just taking in some sunshine – shoot."

"Are you and your cold pizza sitting down?" Mitch asked.

"Very funny… and yes, as a matter of fact, we are. But now I'm worried. What's going on?"

"Well, Laci and I ran across a foreclosure property up here– it's a bed and breakfast, and an award winning winery. It's nice, Brad."

"And… why does this concern me?" Brad had one eye closed and tilted his head, awaiting the rest of the story as if it were a large blast about to hit.

"Laci thinks we should buy it to help the owner keep her family's estate, and we could expand our label up here," he paused to take a short breath, "and I think she's right."

"Wow… since when did Airplane Girl become such a budding entrepreneur?"

"Come on, Brad. I agree with her. It's one of those opportunities that only come along once in a great while and I think we should take advantage of it."

"This is the craziest idea she's had yet, Mitch! Let me guess… it rained while you were at the winery and she took it as a sign. Am I right?"

Mitch hesitated to answer. "Okay, technically you're right. It did rain, but she had this idea just shortly after we arrived which was long *before* it rained."

Brad laughed, knowing full well that Laci's 'thing' with the rain had spurred the idea. "Do you know how much work this will take? How do you propose running two wineries and adding a bed and breakfast on top of that? Last I checked, we don't have any hotel and restaurant experience on our résumé. And why would she want to help the owner save it anyway? Is she a friend of hers?"

"Calm down! One question at a time Sherlock! It's actually not that crazy. We've been talking about expanding anyway, and her business is fully functional. She could stay on and manage the place – she just needs the capital to back the operation, and a new set of eyes to help her market the property. And, no, she isn't a friend of Laci's. We just met her on this trip, but we both took a liking to her. You should also know that she is down a winemaker, so I admit that this will be more work for you than me at first."

"Yep… there it is. I was wondering when you'd finally get around to the part where my life is interrupted by this little venture. Not that I'm surprised."

"Look… you know as well as I do that you are the better winemaker out of the two of us."

Brad thought about it, and surprisingly, was quite intrigued by the potential opportunity, although he hated to admit it. "Okay fine, it's not a horrible idea, but I won't commit to anything until I see the place, Mitch. It could be too risky."

"I know. We won't sign anything until you have looked over everything and given it your full approval. I'll look at her financials while I'm here and make a call to the real estate broker. How soon can you get here?"

"Well, that depends on you, Romeo. How soon will you two love birds be home?"

"We *fly* back this weekend… pun intended," he laughed at himself. "I'll call you in a few days with an update in case something changes, but I would plan on being here within the next couple of weeks if you can. I don't want to waste too much time." Mitch was relieved by his response and anxious to tell Laci the news.

"You know me. I'll be waiting on pins and needles for your call. But wait… where are you anyway? And you said the owner was a 'her'. Does this 'her' have a name?"

"We are in a little town called Carson, Washington. And *her* name is Hannah Blake – she's the owner of Foxhead Estates."

Brad laughed. "Foxhead? That's a ridiculous name. We'll have to change that first."

"No we won't. She's done a lot of work to market her name and the brand. We'd be foolish to change the name and you know it. Stop being a jerk. Besides, her parents named it after Hannah and her 'foxlike' red hair. It's a family thing and we're going to keep it, okay?"

Brad perked up a little when Mitch mentioned the red hair and shook his head. *Great… another red head,* he thought to himself. "Maybe her parents should have reconsidered the name – that's probably why it went under," he replied in a heartless tone.

Mitch lowered his head in response to Brad's callous comment and began to wonder if this plan was such a good idea after all.

"Listen. Her parents died about six years ago in a boating accident. Will you have some respect for crying out loud?"

"Sorry, sorry! You could have led with that you know!" He paused and let out a sigh of surrender. "Fine. I'll come up there and check it out. Is she at least good looking?"

"Is that all you can think about? You are a piece of work! If you must know, then yes. She is very attractive, but I'm warning you… she's a feisty one."

"Like I'm worried about that." Brad's over-confident tone made Mitch worry all the more.

Brad hung up the phone and finished his cold pizza, then went inside and pulled out pen and paper and began to write. This letter would be different though – a culmination of his desires for her expressed in a simple list of wishes. He added the last word, then folded it gently and slid it in the envelope. Another one sealed forever. For the rest of the day, the memory of Jules remained in his mind, as did the curious opportunity that now lay ahead.

*****

Mitch was still outside on the porch talking to Brad, so Laci decided to go out and join him and listen in on their conversation. When she opened the door, all she heard was 'goodbye'. *Dang it! I have the worst timing sometimes.* Naturally, she couldn't wait and immediately grilled him about the call.

"Well? Come on… spill! What did he say?" Laci's overly anxious tone caused him to shake his head, no doubt in frustration. *I know I drive him crazy. I have a tendency to get a little worked up at times… it's what I do.* His face was serious, but it wasn't one that gave her that 'bad feeling' in her gut, so she held out hope.

"I think you should sit down – this could be painful." Mitch's voice was solemn.

Laci immediately prepared herself to go on the defensive, as was her normal stance when she knew she was right about something. She decided against his suggestion to sit and instead, began to pace back and forth. "No, I won't sit down. Ugh! I *knew* it! I knew he'd hate the idea – all because it came from me. If it were his idea, he would have signed the papers sight unseen! But nooooo, 'rain-lovin'-Laci' is '*cuckoo for cocoa puffs'*, so naturally it's a bad idea." Her voice raised a notch with each syllable.

Mitch walked in front of her, then gently grabbed her shoulders in hopes to stop her incessant ranting. It worked… *a little.* "Slow down, Darlin'. If you'll give me a minute, I'll finish. Besides… I was just joking about it being painful. He's going to fly up here to see the estate as soon as we get home. He's not fully on board per se, but he's intrigued, and that's saying a lot for Brad." Mitch's voice was steady and calm, making an immediate impact on her frantic state.

Laci's eyes burst open. "Really? He liked the idea?"

"I'd say 'like' is a bit of a stretch… but I think he'll get there. I'm not totally convinced either, you know. We have to consider every factor here before we sign anything and I need Brad's approval. I won't go forward without it, Lace. For now, let's just say we're both giving it careful consideration," he smiled, and she leapt into his arms hugging him tight. "Are you sure you heard me right? That *doesn't* mean yes," Mitch laughed.

"What I heard, my love, was opportunity."

"Now that is the Laci that I remember… always the optimist. What would I do without you?"

"You'd be miserable, of course."

"That I would, Darlin'. That I would. Now what do you say we go inside and share this little plan with Hannah? She still has to buy into it."

"Something tells me she will," Laci smiled.

5 – Clouds of Hope

Mitch and Laci walked back inside and found Hannah in the kitchen washing dishes, a mild scent of lavender stirring in the air. She lifted up her head from the basin of soapy bubbles.

"What's up you two? Heading out already?"

"Not yet. Actually, we were hoping to talk to you before we leave. Do you have a minute?" Laci asked, giving her a wink.

Hannah smiled, "Of course. Let me dry my hands and we can sit over there at that little bistro table."

They walked over to the other side of the kitchen and sat down at the table. The table was perfectly positioned by a big window that overlooked what Laci guessed to be Hannah's vegetable garden; remnants of last year's crop now brown and lying dead on the ground. Hannah pulled up a chair and sat down.

"Now, what's going on?" Hannah asked.

Mitch looked at Laci and smiled, knowing that she would want to share the news.

"Hannah, Mitch and I talked last night and we have an idea, but you have to promise to keep an open mind."

"Okay, I'll bite. What's your idea?" Hannah's curiosity was definitely piqued.

"What would you think about selling the estate to Mitch and me, and Mitch's brother? It would become a subsidiary company of Crystal Creek Winery. We wouldn't change the name, and although we would own the rights to both the bed and breakfast and the winery, you would still be involved with managing the property until you are in a position to buy it back. If you want."

Hannah didn't reply for what seemed like an eternity. She lowered her head and her eyes remained fixed on the table – lost in thought.

Laci began to worry. *Surely she knows this is the best option for her. She needs this… Brad needs it too. It has to work out, Lord. Please let her say yes!*

Finally, Hannah lifted her head. "So, let me get this straight… you want to buy the estate, and keep me on as an employee; a manager. Then what? Are you going to stay up here and help me?"

Mitch scooted his chair up and the little metal feet screeched as they slid across the old wood floor. "Look Hannah, we're not promising to buy it yet, although Laci likes to think it's a 'done deal'," he looked at Laci and shook his head, smiling. "And no, we can't stay here to run it with our family in North Carolina, but my brother can. He wants to fly up in the next week or two and check out your entire operation, your inventory, and make an assessment on whether he thinks the property would be a good investment for us."

"So your brother makes the final decision?" Hannah asked.

"No, it's both of us, and I think it's a good idea, but I won't do it without his approval. I'll review your numbers, and he can review the operations to tell me if this is a viable business," Mitch added.

"It's viable – but I know you can't take my word for it. Unfortunately, running this business has become the one thing I never wanted it to become… a job. I had no idea what it would take to keep this place running. I am simply lost." Defeat reflected in Hannah's eyes.

Laci took Hannah by the hand. "We want to help you save your family's estate – for you and your grandmother. It will work, I know it."

"I guess the logical thing would be to take some time and think this through – make sure it feels right – but the truth is, I don't have the luxury of time. I'd like to try it. Tell your brother to book his flight," she said in a firm voice.

"Are you sure? You might be wise to take the time and talk it over with your grandmother, make sure she is comfortable with this," Mitch asked.

Hannah's head slowly shook from side to side, "I am losing this place regardless of who buys it. I have no other recourse. With your offer I can still be a part of it, and I don't feel like I'm losing it to a complete stranger. It may sound odd, but I feel like I've known you both for ages. You seem more like… like family." Hannah's voice was sad, but also hopeful in a way.

"Well then, it looks like we may have a promising future ahead. Laci and I need to run into town and visit the realtor, then grab a few things before we pack. You should go tell your grandmother. At the very least, that will give you a few minutes to make sure you're at peace with your decision." Mitch stood up and looked down at the floor. A fresh scratch was now visible, obviously made from the leg of his chair. "I think I scratched your floor, Hannah. I'm so sorry. I'm happy to fix it if you want."

She laughed. "That little scar is the last thing I'm worried about, trust me. Besides, it adds character right? And, if this little plan of yours works out, it will become your problem soon," Hannah smiled and walked out of the room.

Mitch and Laci remained in the kitchen for a minute longer after Hannah left.

"Do you think she's making the right decision?" Laci asked.

"Hard to tell. Right now she believes it's the only decision she has left, and she's probably right. Not easy to read that one – none of you women ever are though," Mitch laughed.

"Hey, I take offense to that statement, mister. I am *not* hard to read, you just have to learn the language, my love." They walked toward the door to leave.

"Oh… is that all? Well, if you'd settle on one language that would be fine. You may not know this Darlin', but you tend to be multi-lingual," he said in fun.

"Yep… it's all part of my master plan to keep the excitement and mystery in our marriage, don't you know?"

"Emphasis on *mystery…*," he added, sarcastically.

"Hey now!" Laci laughed and slapped his arm playfully.

Mitch pulled her into his arms, and after brushing a curl from her face, leaned down and kissed her gently.

Later, their shopping and packing done, it was time to say goodbye to their new friend and potential business partner, and get back on the road.

"I'm going downstairs to pull the car around, Lace. Don't carry anything down, do you hear me? I'll be back up to get the suitcases." Mitch was always protective of Laci, but even more so now since losing the baby.

"I know, I know," she replied. Laci took a quick look around the room to make sure they didn't miss anything, then headed downstairs. When she got to the foyer, she looked through the front screen door to find Hannah and her grandmother sitting outside on the front porch and walked out to join them.

"Hi ladies. It's almost time for us to go and I wanted to say goodbye," Laci said.

"Scoot your chair over here, Laci. I can't see you, Sweetheart," Lois replied.

Laci moved her chair near Lois, immediately taking in the strong aroma of her perfume. She was dressed to the 'nines' again, in Lois fashion anyway. Lois placed her hand on Laci's knee and patted it gently.

"My Jules told me what you are trying to do for her and I think it's a wonderful idea. I agree with her – you and Mitch are special. She's hard-headed though, and it might take her awhile to come around. Giving up her reign on this place won't be easy."

Laci smiled, then looked over at Hannah and raised her eyebrow.

"Grandma, I'm right here. You don't have to speak for me," Hannah said in an extra-loud voice.

"I know you're right there. Don't patronize me. She needs to know how grateful we are and you need to be more appreciative."

"Alright, Grandma… I will be more appreciative." Hannah rolled her eyes, then smiled, nodding her head up and down.

Laci had already grown so fond of Lois – she was a breath of fresh air and made her laugh. She realized then how much she was going to miss both of them, even though they'd only known each other a couple of days.

"I'm glad we could help, Lois. It's been so nice meeting you both and getting to know you. I'll be anxious to come back and visit again soon. Next time we'll bring the kids."

"Oh that would be lovely, dear." Lois took in a big breath and coughed hard, wiping her mouth with a handkerchief – a fancy letter 'L' embroidered on one corner. When she pulled the cloth away from her mouth, Laci noticed a small smear of blood left behind and looked at Hannah with concern.

"You okay, Grandma? Do you need some water?"

Lois coughed again, but this time not as hard. "I'm fine, dear. Water might be nice though."

Hannah bounced her head in the direction of the house, "Laci, would you want to help me bring out a few glasses of ice water?"

"Umm… oh, sure." Laci picked up Hannah's subtle clue and followed her inside.

They walked inside and gathered some glasses, filling them with ice water. Hannah was quiet at first, then pulled a tray down from the cabinet, and placed the glasses on top.

"She's dying, Laci. She falls more often being blind; the last one broke her back in two places. Now her digestive system is out of control and she can barely go to the bathroom by herself. The cough is new though, and getting worse. I don't know what to do." Hannah broke down and Laci pulled her into her arms to provide some comfort the best she could.

"Hannah, your grandmother is a strong lady even though she may not always seem like it. I'm sure she'll bounce back from this and have many years left. Get her to the doctor and try not to worry, okay?"

"Laci? I hate to bring this up, but I don't have any other place to live once you all buy the estate. If we have to leave, I don't know if she'll survive it."

"Why on earth would you leave the estate? If we buy your business, you do *NOT* have to move out. Do you hear me? We would never do that to you."

"Are you sure we can stay? What if Mitch's brother doesn't agree? What then?"

"Hannah, Sweetie. Don't worry. Brad is a lot of things, but he has a heart. At least… I'm pretty sure he does." Laci had a rough start with Brad, and she once questioned that fact herself, but she was sure it was there. *Somewhere…*

"Wait… you said his brother's name is Brad? Brad Young? And they've always lived in… North Carolina?" Hannah stuttered, connecting the lines in her head.

"Yes, Brad Young, same as Mitch. Both from Crystal Creek, North Carolina. Why?"

Hannah's face turned ashen and she seemed a little disoriented for a minute, as if she'd just seen a ghost. She thought to herself, s*urely he's not the same one… the same Brad Young I knew in North Carolina. That's not possible… it's been eight years! It can't be the same Brad that broke my heart. God don't let it be him, please!*

Laci waved her hand in front of Hannah's face. "Hannah, what's wrong? Are you okay?"

"I… umm… I'm fine. It's nothing. I'm just worried about my grandmother, that's all. I wanted to make sure I got Brad's name right for the paperwork."

Hannah wasn't making any sense, and Laci was pretty sure she wasn't being truthful in her reply, but she did have a lot going on right now. They walked back out to the porch and gave Lois a glass of water.

Mitch finished loading the car and came up on the porch to say goodbye. "Are you ready, Laci? It's about that time," he said.

"I know. I'm ready." Laci walked over to Lois and gave her a hug. "Take care of yourself, Lois. It's been an honor meeting you. You have a beautiful granddaughter."

"Thank you, dear. Yes, she's a real 'jewel', as I like to say." Lois smiled but her face was tired and Laci could tell she was drained.

Laci turned to Hannah. "I will call you soon, okay? We'll keep in touch, I promise. Try not to worry about anything. Once Brad gets here and sees how wonderful you are and how beautiful this place is, he will want to buy it as much as we do. I know it."

"Thanks. I hope you're right," Hannah replied, uncertainty heavy in her voice.

Mitch walked over to join them. "Hannah, it was a pleasure meeting you. I'll have our lawyer contact the broker's office to start drawing up papers for our bid. Laci was right – I think we were meant to cross paths."

Laci winked. "I usually am, he just hasn't figured it out yet."

Hannah laughed at her comment and hugged them goodbye. "Thank you, Laci – for everything. I'm so grateful to you both." Tear tracks stained her cheeks.

"It was meant to be, that's all. God's perfect timing. Good luck, and call me if you need me, okay?" Laci hugged her again and whispered, "Give Brad a chance, okay? I've got a good feeling that it will all work out." They climbed in the car and Laci rolled down the window.

"I will. Be careful driving. Those clouds are getting pretty dark and I heard that there were some heavy storms brewing up north," Hannah replied.

"Oh good! That's what I like to hear!"

"Huh?" Hannah asked, a look of confusion on her face.

Laci smiled. "Those clouds are full of liquid hope, my dear. Rain brings good things, didn't you know? It brought us to you! It's something that I've believed since I was a little girl. Probably sounds silly, huh?"

"Well, I never really cared for rain much, but you have fun with that," Hannah laughed.

They waved goodbye and slowly pulled away. Hannah watched them from the porch until they were out of sight.

Laci sighed. "I'm going to miss her. Do you think she'll be okay?"

"I'm sure she'll be fine. Once Brad gives me his review, and if things look good, we'll make an offer. After it's accepted, I think she'll feel much better. I have a good feeling about this, surprisingly enough," Mitch replied.

"It's about time you came around to my idea. I've thought that since the day we arrived."

"I know, I know. I'm not sure why I ever doubt you," he laughed. "So, let's head to the beach for a couple of days, then we'll be nice and rested for our flight back on Saturday."

"Can we make one pit-stop first?" she asked.

"Sure. Where's that?"

"Back to Andréa's for a cup of her coffee!"

Mitch took Laci's hand and laughed. "Anything for you, Darlin'."

*****

A few days later, Mitch and Laci were standing in their designated line, waiting to board their flight home. The scent of Mitch's cologne wafted through the air and made Laci smile. She looked at him and her heart swelled with pride. He looked exceptionally handsome, wearing his blue jeans and white button-down shirt, and his beautiful brown eyes seemed to smile as he looked at her. Then she realized he *was* smiling at her.

"What?" Laci giggled.

"I don't think I'll ever fly again without thinking about the day we met, you standing in your line, staring over at me."

"Wait… you knew I was staring at you?" Laci was shocked. *He never told me that before!*

"Of course I did. I'm pretty sure you smiled at me too. You were kind of hard to miss, Darlin'."

"Wow. I… I had no idea. Why didn't you ever tell me?"

"Once I realized my seat was right next to yours, I didn't see the need. And, the rest is 'history', as they say," he added.

Laci wrapped her arms around his waist and looked in his eyes. "Actually, the rest is still to come. I love you, my Creepy-Stalker-Crawdad-Fan."

He still took her breath away and stirred the deepest part of her soul, and right then, she asked God to never let her lose that feeling again.

"I know. I love you too," he said, and kissed her softly.

Their trip to visit the rain was filled with healing, renewal, and the hope of a new partnership with Hannah. Laci was a bit anxious though – afraid that it would take more than a little rain to show Hannah the way. One thing was certain though, Laci was better and felt like herself again. She smiled and thought to herself, *something good is about to happen here.*

6 – Storms-a-Brewin'

It had been two weeks since Laci and Mitch left, and Brad would arrive later that day – coming to take over her business. Hannah couldn't stay in bed any longer. She got up and went downstairs. The lodge was quiet and cold, so she built a fire knowing her grandmother would be up soon. Set to auto-brew, the coffee pot had kicked on and soon the familiar aroma was coursing through the air. She yawned and watched as the wood caught fire, listening to each pop and crackle. The fireplace in the lodge was made with large, smooth stones and spanned at least eight feet across. The hearth was big enough that she could even sit cross-legged on top of it. On the opposite side of her was an over-sized checkerboard cloth that her dad bought years ago at a Cracker Barrel during one of their vacations down south. They used to sit and play for hours, and the memory of him always letting her win made her both happy and sad at the same time. Now, the guests used it during their stay – building memories of their own.

A high-pitched beeping noise went off, announcing to the whole house that morning was here and the coffee was ready to be poured. Years ago, Hannah had tried to turn the alarm off, but she couldn't figure it out and got mad. After pounding on it a few times with her fist, somehow thinking that would work, she instead activated a permanent alarm in the process, causing it to now go off every morning without fail whether she liked it or not. She chalked it up as a haunting spirit of her mother who always enjoyed waking her before she was ready. It was also Lois' alarm clock, which meant that her door would be creaking open anytime now and she would want her breakfast.

Hannah made her way to the kitchen and started cooking, but there was still no sign of her grandmother. That worried her. After the bacon was done, she turned off the stove and walked down the hall to check on Lois. Standing outside of her grandmother's door, she listened closely. Luckily, Lois snored like a freight train, and after she heard the roar of the engine chugging away inside, Hannah smiled and sighed with relief knowing all was well.

Over the last few months, Lois' health had continued to decline, so Hannah cherished each and every moment with her. Their time together was precious – Lois was the only family she had left – and since losing her mother, Lois had become like a second mother. Even as a kid she spent most of her free time with Lois. She was at her house every summer and even had her own room there – her favorite place to go. Hannah grew up watching her grandmother fuss over things like her outfit, her hair and makeup, the perfect pair of shoes to match her outfit – you name it. Lois was the ultimate 'diva grandma'. Hannah, on the other hand, was mostly tomboy. Still, there was a small part of her that enjoyed putting on makeup and dressing up once in a while – a little Lois managed to rub off after all.

Breakfast was ready and as if on cue, Lois' door finally opened and her footsteps echoed down the hall. When she walked into the kitchen, Hannah could tell something was wrong.

"Good morning, my sweet girl," Lois said, her soft voice was cracked and shaky. She smiled and Hannah noticed her mouth was lined with dried blood.

"Grandma, are you alright? Sit down."

"I'm okay. Don't you worry about me, I want to know about you? Are you ready for your visitor today?"

"Oh Grams, did you have to bring that up now? Can't we eat first?"

"I'm not stopping you from eating. You can still talk and eat, right?"

"Ugh," Hannah let out a big sigh. "No. I'm not ready. I'm scared to death and I have no desire to sell this place – not to that man anyway."

"Aw, honey… this is all part of a much bigger plan. You-," Lois' voice trailed off and she grabbed her chest, then let out a hard cough. "Jules… I'm not feeling so good." She brought the tissue up to her mouth. More blood.

"We're going to the doctor right now, Grandma. I'm going to go get dressed. Drink some water, and I know you probably don't feel like it, but try and eat something."

"I'll eat my eggs, but don't hurry. I'm sure it's nothing." Lois was whispering by that point, hunched over the table and white as a sheet.

Hannah knelt down on the floor next to Lois. "You'll be alright Grandma… don't worry. We'll get you some help and you'll be just fine. Don't give up on me yet, okay? I can't lose you."

"Oh Sweetie. I love you. You'll never lose me," Lois said.

Hannah ran upstairs, threw on some makeup and clothes, and then hurried back downstairs. She took out her cell and called Clare.

"Hello?" Clare answered.

"Hi Clare, this is Hannah. I need you to come over and watch the B&B. I'm taking Grams to the doctor – she's getting worse."

Clare could hear the panic in Hannah's voice. "Of course, I'll be right over! You can leave – don't wait on me. I'm getting in the car as we speak."

"Thank you, Clare. I… I'm expecting a guest today. His name is Brad Young and he's Mitch's brother. He'll be staying a little while to look over the property. I'll explain the details later."

"Yeah… no worries. I'll get him checked in. Go and take care of Grams. Tell her I love her?"

"I will."

Hannah knew that Clare loved Lois almost as if she were her own grandmother. Clare had been a bright spot in Hannah's life for the past several years, and even though they were complete strangers when they first met, they were family now.

Hannah walked into the dining room to get her grandmother. She had eaten some of her eggs, but her face was now paler than before.

"Let's go, Grandma. We're going to get you some help, okay?"

Hannah sat in the hospital room with Lois, waiting on test results. Finally the doctor came back inside.

"Hello, Mrs. McCrae. I'm Dr. Westmore." He reached out and patted Lois on the hand. Not a customary meeting ritual, but it was kind. He was an older man in his mid-sixties, perfectly combed silver hair, and a musky, Old Spice smell to him.

"Hello, doctor. You can call me Lois."

"Well, Lois… it looks like you've had a bad respiratory condition for some time now, and it's now much worse. You've developed what we call 'walking pneumonia', and it will become more severe if we don't get you treated with antibiotics."

"I'm not staying in this hospital – you can just forget it." Lois turned her head away from the doctor, ignoring him like a teenage girl would ignore a bossy parent. She had hated hospitals ever since her brother broke his hip years ago. He'd gone in for surgery and rehab, but due to an infection, he never came out.

The doctor smiled politely. "I understand Lois. Walking pneumonia isn't something to take lightly. It can be treated at home, as long as you promise to take your medicine for me, okay? Can you do that?" His brow was furrowed as he talked.

"Doctor, can I talk with you out in the hall?" Hannah got the distinct impression that there was something he wasn't telling them. They walked out of Lois' room to speak privately.

Hannah dropped her shoulders. "Doc, I need to know everything here. Your words say one thing, but your facial expression shows something much different. Is it worse than you're letting her believe?"

"Ms. McCrae –,"

"It's Ms. Blake."

"Ms. Blake. Your grandmother's condition *can* be treated at home with antibiotics, however at her age and in her frail state, she may worsen quickly if she's not watched. I can hospitalize her now and give her IV antibiotics, but knowing her distaste for hospitals, I fear that would actually make her condition worse. She has pneumonia and she'll need constant supervision and care. She'll have the most trouble breathing at night, so you may want to consider sleeping very close to her. Can you do that?"

"Yes, no question. She lives with me and I'm around her all day. I'll make sure she is well cared for. Is there anything else?"

"Keep her well hydrated and watch her food intake. Has she been eating regularly – good meals?"

"Her appetite has definitely diminished, but some days are better than others. I'll make sure she eats."

"Alright then. Call me if you need anything. Here is my card. If she gets worse, call an ambulance or get her to the hospital. I'm afraid it will escalate to that eventually, so be prepared."

"Thanks. I appreciate you allowing her to go home."

"My pleasure." He walked away and Hannah paused for a few minutes before going back into Lois' room. *Don't take her away from me, God. Not yet. I don't want to be alone.*

Hannah walked back inside and helped Lois gather her things, then they headed home.

*****

Brad's flight to Portland was long and loud, filled with crying babies and whiny toddlers. He was exhausted and looked forward to checking into his room and crashing. After renting a car, he made his way to Carson, still a solid hour's drive from the airport. That hour was a gateway for his mind to wander – going from place to place, thinking about the estate, what it would look like, and what the owner might look like. He smiled mischievously. *I just hope she's good looking – that will make this whole process a lot easier to deal with,* he thought. The enthusiasm to buy the property was lacking on his part, but he promised Mitch and Laci that he would keep an open mind. *Alright God, I'm not sure why you've orchestrated all of this, but this lady had better appreciate what we're doing for her, that's all I can say.*

Brad didn't mention God often and rarely talked to him out loud or in silent prayer; and although church was a big part of his childhood, he'd long since given up his faith after his Dad died. Watching Mitch lose his first wife didn't help either. Mitch gave up on faith too, for a time, but once Laci came into his life he managed to find his way back. Brad continued to push God farther away though, became cynical. Once again, on the outside of everything – love, faith, and even family. He was everyone else's 'go-to' guy, the babysitter, the big brother, the cool uncle, but he longed to be something special to just one… *his one.*

Before he realized it, he had made it to the estate and saw the sign up ahead. He pulled in and parked, then got out and took a few minutes to look the place over. *Not bad,* he thought. He walked up the steps of the lodge-like building which he assumed was the Bed & Breakfast, and knocked on the door. No answer. He turned the doorknob. It was unlocked, so he started to walk inside when a young girl came barreling up the porch steps and startled him.

"Hey! What are you doing? Everybody's gone right now. I'm watching the place until they get back," Clare said, out of breath.

Brad turned toward the girl. She looked to be around 16 or 17, wearing faded blue jeans filled with holes and a grungy hooded sweatshirt. She was staring a hole through him. *No wonder they are losing customers.*

"Okay – do you know when the owner will be back? I'm here to check out the property for purchase."

"Are you Mitch's brother?" she asked.

"Yeah – how did…"

"Hannah told me you would be arriving today. I can get you checked in if you want. You look horrible," she giggled.

Brad's eyebrow lurched up, figuring that to be a typical teenage remark, but still a little surprised by her outspokenness. "Gee, thanks. And who are you exactly?"

"I'm Clare."

"Where is Hannah?"

"Not that it's any of your business, but she took her grandmother to the doctor. She called a few minutes ago and they are on their way back – should be home any minute now. Come with me and I'll get your key."

Clare walked inside and left the door ajar for Brad. He followed, and Clare came right back to give him his room key. "You're in the Bay View Suite. First door on the left at the top of the stairs." Clare walked away.

"Thanks," Brad called out.

She turned her head back toward him. "Yep – that's what I do."

"Not much on small talk are you?" he muttered under his breath, but Clare was already in the other room by then.

He went back out to the car to get his bags, and then headed up to his room and decided to lay down and rest for a few minutes. It was short lived, his nerves were a bit on edge, so any efforts to relax were futile. Instead, he got up and went downstairs, thinking he would take a self-guided tour around the property. On his way there though, his stomach let out a rumble loud enough to shake the walls. *Now where did that* **teenage being** *go off to? Surely she could help me find some food around here.* He looked all around the house, but Clare was nowhere to be found. *It's a kitchen… can't be that hard to find.* Finally he stumbled upon the kitchen, and even managed to locate a banana to satisfy his pang.

Walking back into the foyer, Brad heard the door squeak open and watched to see who it was, figuring it was Clare. It wasn't. It was Hannah, walking through the door backwards. She was pulling her grandmother in a wheelchair, struggling to get it up over the door jam. Brad couldn't see her face, but her long, curly red hair swung from side to side. He smiled in anticipation, and waited patiently for them to get inside so he could introduce himself.

Hannah closed the door behind them and turned Lois around. Brad was standing quietly at the back of the foyer and was about to say hello… until he saw her face. It was her. *My Jules.* Shocked at the sight, he couldn't move and took in a sharp, quick breath. His jaw dropped first, his banana second, landing on the floor with a dull thud. They were both frozen in place, stunned as they beheld each other.

For Brad, time stood still. She was even more beautiful now than the day they'd first met nearly nine years ago. Her long red hair flowed into the sassy look on her face, and she was wearing what he remembered to be his favorite outfit – blue jeans, boots, and a tight long-sleeved t-shirt, untucked.

"Jules? Is… is that you?" Brad stuttered.

Hannah didn't say a word. No 'hello'. No, 'how are you'. No reply – not one syllable left her lips. She stood motionless, staring into the face of the man who left her eight years ago. Her fiancé. The love of her life. Slowly and methodically, she walked toward him, her boot heels clicking against the wood floor. Now directly in front of him, she reached up with her right hand and slapped him across his cheek as hard as she could. So hard in fact, that her hand burned from making contact. She turned around and slowly walked toward her grandmother.

"Son of a biscuit-eater…," she quietly mumbled under her breath, shaking her hand to ease the sting. Brad overheard her and smiled, looking down at the floor to hide his face.

"I take it you two know each other?" Lois asked in a soft voice, a little smirk spread across her face.

"I suppose I deserve that. But what are you doing here, Jules? I was supposed to meet someone named Hannah Blake. Where is she?" he asked, clearly confused.

Hannah was reluctant to turn and face him, but when her grandmother patted her on the hand, she figured he deserved some sort of reply. She turned around and looked him in the eye, her face stern and serious. Right about that time, Brad reached up and pushed his dark brown hair backward with his fingers, like a model in a photo shoot.

After seeing that, Hannah's insides boiled – she was a complete basket case! *Why does he have to look so stinking hot? I didn't know jeans could be that tight. Why couldn't he have a chunky middle with forty or so extra pounds, or bad teeth? Good grief just look at him… he looks like a famous country music singer getting ready to take the stage for his adoring fans! He's even more gorgeous now than he was then. How am I going to pull this off? I hate him for what he did to me! I hate that he gave up on us… but if I let myself feel what still lives in my heart, he'll think I'm weak or desperate. Well, not this girl. After that slap, I certainly don't look weak. Now THAT felt good! Here goes nothing…* She thought, encouraging herself internally.

"I *am* Hannah Blake!" Hannah's voice was cold and tense, remembering the pain he had caused her. "Jules is my middle name and McCrae was my maiden name."

"Oh yeah, that's right. I heard you got married. A school teacher, correct? So where is the lucky ball and chain?" Brad couldn't deal with the surprise of seeing her after all this time, so he replied with his ever-so-dry sense of humor and sarcasm – a veritable defense mechanism when things got tough or too emotional.

"Let's just say it didn't work out. I never bothered to change my name back – too much of a hassle I guess."

Brad laughed, almost enjoying the display unfolding between them.

"Well, well, well… Jules McRae. What's it been now – six, seven years? I remember you telling me your parents owned a small business near the Oregon border, but I think you left out a few details, love."

"Don't call me 'Jules'! You lost that privilege a long time ago – right about the time you walked out and gave up on us. It's 'Hannah' to you. And for the record, it's been eight years and I gave you as much information as I could back then. Maybe if you'd stuck around a little longer, you would have learned the full story or maybe even had a chance to meet them." Hannah lowered her head, saddened by the thought of her parents not having the chance to meet the love of her life.

Brad looked down at Hannah's grandmother, still smiling at the two of them as they bickered. Suddenly, he remembered Mitch telling him about Hannah's parents, and a fleeting moment of remorse entered his thoughts.

"I'm… I'm sorry about your parents by the way. Mitch told me you lost them."

"No you're not, so don't pretend like you are. I know you better than that, which is why I'd like you to get out of my house. It'll be a cold day in… well you know where… before I ever sell this place to you!"

Brad chuckled, "You still can't curse can you? No matter how bad you want to."

"Get out, Brad! And pick up your banana!"

Brad smiled, stooped over to pick up his banana as instructed, then walked over to Hannah, his face now inches away from hers. "You need me here, Jules, and you know it. Plus I'm a paying guest and I've already checked into my room. You might as well get used to me being here. We have a deal to finalize and I don't plan on disappointing my brother or his 'rain-lovin' wife. Trust me, Laci is not a person you want to mess with – I've tried and it doesn't work."

His deep southern voice made Hannah's whole body quiver, which she hated and loved all at the same time. Although disgusted by this new turn of events, she was even more afraid of turning him away and losing everything to complete strangers. She lowered her eyes to the floor in defeat and huffed, then looked into Brad's eyes. "Fine. But don't expect this to be like old times, Brad Young. This is business – nothing more. That should be pretty easy for you given your history and all. We'll start tomorrow at nine a.m."

"Yes, ma'am. Nine a.m. it is," he said softly, then smiled and headed up to his room.

Hannah's gaze followed him as he walked, never blinking. *His voice still makes me weak in the knees – so ridiculous! And, he still wears my favorite cologne… figures.*

Lois yanked on Hannah's sleeve. "Psst… Jules, wake up girl," Hannah turned.

"What Grams?" She leaned down to hear her better.

"Ask him to join us for dinner," Lois whispered.

"No."

"Yes, Hannah Jules. Be polite to your guest," Lois replied, using her 'pay attention' voice – or what little of it she had left.

Hannah threw her head back, knowing she couldn't refuse her grandmother's request. She turned around and yelled out his name.

Brad was already on the staircase when she called, but stopped and smiled. He enjoyed hearing her say his name out loud after all these years. He removed his smile, then turned around. "Yes… *Hannah*?" he replied, his tone rich with sarcasm.

Hannah bit her tongue at first, then took a deep breath. "Would you like to join us for dinner tonight? Around six?" Her teeth were grinding together as the words came out.

"I'd like that. Thank you," Brad smiled smugly, like he'd just won the first prize blue ribbon in the county fair, then continued on to his room.

7 – A Sweet Reunion

Back in his room, Brad paced the floors trying to decide whether to be furious or thrilled about the circumstance in which he now found himself. Buying and becoming the new owner of his first love's family estate wasn't really on his bucket list after all. He needed to vent and there was only one person to call, so he pulled out his phone and dialed Mitch's number.

"Hey Brad – how are things? Have you made it out to the estate yet?"

"Mitch… I can't do this. We can't do this!" Brad was worked up and had no idea what to say or tell Mitch. He'd never mentioned his love for Jules to anyone, or how badly it had ended.

"Slow down big brother! Is something wrong?"

"I can't be here. She's… ugh! She's the one, Mitch. It's Jules – Hannah is *Jules*."

"Umm… I'm not much of a psychic translator, Brad so you're going to have to spell it out for me. What in the heck are you talking about? Start at the beginning. And who is Jules?"

"Jules was the woman I fell in love with up in High Point when I was building that museum. She… she would have been my wife if I hadn't left her."

The phone was quiet. Mitch was stunned by Brad's confession, and utterly speechless that he had just used the words 'love' and 'wife' in the same sentence.

"I… wow, Brad. I had no idea you had ever fallen in love like that. Why didn't you tell me when you came back home?"

"Well, I wasn't exactly proud of how it ended – how *I* ended it. I was embarrassed. Then after I came back, Karin got sick and my mission became you and Caleb. Time moved on and I didn't see the need to bring it up. I wanted to forget her and leave it all behind me I guess."

"Brad, I'm so sorry. Man, you should have told me. I'm your brother for crying out loud!"

"Yeah, I know. I never really figured I'd see her again. This was definitely a curve ball I didn't see coming. What do I do, Mitch?" Brad's stress spilled over.

Mitch could sense that his brother was in turmoil over seeing Hannah again, and although he felt somewhat bad for his current situation, he didn't feel a bit sorry for him. Mitch laughed out loud just thinking about how poetic this whole thing had turned out, and now it all made sense.

"Why are you laughing at a time like this, Mitch? I am in dire straits here! I need a solution, brother!" Brad's shoulders dropped and he sat down on the bed, holding his head down between his knees.

"Brad, buddy… I can't help you. This is a situation in which God alone has placed you, and he is the only one that can help you through it. I do believe this was planned long before you and I ever existed though, so you're going to have to come to terms with it and accept the fact that you are exactly where you are for a reason. Maybe the man you are now, is exactly the kind of man she needs in her life to get through this. You never know. I *do* know a thing or two about the man you used to be however, and he probably wasn't ready to be a husband, if you get my drift. Maybe that's why your story was put on hold for a while."

Hearing Mitch's calm, rational voice and listening to his words of assurance brought Brad a much needed sense of peace. That was Mitch's gift – he was always the one who gave everyone else strength during stressful situations. When their dad died, it was all Brad could do to keep going, even being the older sibling. Mitch held it together though, and they got through it one day at a time.

"I hope you're right. I'll give you a call in a few days to let you know how things are going. In the meantime, will you… will you pray for me? And Jules?" Brad asked.

"I'm sorry. Could you speak up a bit? I could swear you just asked me to *pray* for you. Did I hear that correctly, Brad Young? I do believe God has just worked a miracle in my brother's life! *Hal-le-lujah!*" Mitch said jokingly, adding a little 'southern preacher' flair for effect.

"Don't push it, Mitch. That took a lot for me to ask. Just do it, okay? You're always saying how well it works. I figure it's time I give it a try."

"Yeah it does. So why don't you try it yourself? That would help even more, you know," Mitch replied, smiling on the other side of the phone. "By the way, what was it like… seeing her again? I'm going to go out on a limb here and say you still feel the same way about her, right?"

"Yeah, that's a pretty solid limb to say the least. I know it sounds crazy, but I never stopped loving her even after I left. And she looks amazing, Mitch, even more beautiful now than she was before. My heart stopped when I saw her. She's changed, but in all the right ways. She's flat out gorgeous! What am I supposed to do with that? How am I supposed to work under these conditions?"

Mitch chuckled. "Knowing you, I'm sure you'll find a way."

"Well, I'd better go."

"Hey Brad, one last question. Why *did* you leave? What happened?"

"I left because of dad," he replied softly.

"Dad? What did dad have to do with it?"

"I know it sounds crazy, Mitch, but you remember how much trouble I had after we lost him. If it hadn't been for you, I wouldn't have made it. I guess I didn't want to love anyone that much ever again – that way I wouldn't have to feel the pain if they ever… well, if I ever lost her. I know you lost Karin, and then you almost lost Laci, but you're stronger than me. I didn't think I could handle it," Brad's voice cracked.

"It's not crazy, brother. I get it, but you have to remember one thing… you caused yourself more pain by walking away, and robbed yourself of the fullness and happiness her love could have given you. Knowing that kind of love makes all the other 'stuff' that happens in life – good and bad – worth living. It's time to live a little, Brad. Live the life that dad would have wanted you to live."

"Yeah. Easier said than done. Anyway – I've gotta go. I'm supposed to have dinner tonight with Jules and her grandmother. And please don't tell Laci about this yet… she'll never let me live it down."

"I won't tell her, not yet at least. She'll find out eventually, you know."

"I know. I just need some time to process this first."

"So… she asked you to join them for dinner, huh? I'm impressed!"

"Don't be. It was her grandmother's idea – she forced Jules to ask me. It was pretty funny actually." Brad smiled at the thought.

"Well, don't start pushing her buttons right off the bat. You tend to do that, you know? Can you mind your manners for the first meal at least?" Mitch pleaded.

"Too late. I pushed her button merely with my physical presence. She's not happy about me being here, I can tell you that. It's going to be an interesting few weeks around here."

"Few weeks? What do you mean? You're there for at least two months… maybe longer. Didn't you know that?"

"What? Two months – are you kidding me, Mitch?" Brad shouted. "You said to come up, check the place out, sign some papers and make some suggestions to improve the place. You never said anything about taking up residence here!"

"Calm down. I did, but you were so worried about going to see the 'hot chick' that you probably missed all the important details. Get a grip, Brad! I need you there to see this through if it's going to work. You are there to finalize the sale, make changes, put them in place, then make sure she has enough help and support to run the place so she doesn't fall flat on her face again. She needs your help, Brad. Don't you get that?" Mitch was flabbergasted by Brad's lack of focus and neglecting his responsibilities.

"Fine. I'll stay. But I don't have to like it."

"Well, only time will tell on that."

"Mitch… I want to make an offer on the estate."

"What? You haven't even been there a full day yet! Shouldn't you check the place out first? What if it's a lemon?"

"Make the offer, Mitch. Please?"

"Yeah, yeah. I'll make an offer. If you're good with it, I'm good with it," Mitch replied.

"I have an idea about the sale however – doing it a little different. Are you open to that?" Brad asked.

"Well, what do you have in mind?"

Brad shared his idea about how to handle the sale of the estate, then Mitch spent a few minutes talking about things back home and hung up. After their call, Brad collapsed on the bed from exhaustion, longing for sleep. Hard as he tried, he couldn't stop thinking about Jules and how she was back in his life after all these years. *Is this my second chance, God? Is she still the one?* Worried that he would fall asleep and miss dinner, he set the alarm for five thirty, then rolled back over and closed his eyes.

"Well, it looks like I'm cooking dinner for three now, thanks to you," Hannah said, escorting Lois to her room.

"It was the right thing to do Jules, and you know it," Lois replied. Her cough had improved since they'd returned from the doctor, thankfully.

"So you say, but now it's time for you to sleep so I can cook. You've had a long, hard day. I'm giving you orders to stay in bed until I come and get you for dinner, okay?"

"Oh, alright Sweetie. I am pretty tired."

Hannah got Lois settled into bed and took off her shoes, then sat down next to her and stroked her soft, white hair.

"Get some sleep, Grandma. I love you."

"I love you, sweetie ."

Now, to figure out dinner! Hannah thought to herself. *Just what I wanted to do… cook a meal for the man who left me! Ugh!* She fumbled around in the kitchen trying to decide what to make, when finally she settled on liver and onions, baked potatoes, and boiled spinach from the can. This was one of her favorite meals growing up and knew her grandmother loved it, but she also knew that Brad *hated* liver. Suddenly, she felt quite light and giddy as she prepared their meal.

Around five-thirty, she walked down the hall and helped her grandmother get dressed for dinner, then they headed to the dining room. Outside of setting the table, everything was done for the most part, and she'd even managed to cook dessert – cinnamon raisin bread pudding. She didn't really know if Brad liked that or not, but she was hoping he wasn't a fan.

"Dinner is almost ready, Grandma. Do you want some tea?" Hannah asked.

"Nope."

"Well, what *do* you want?"

"I want you to come over and sit down, then tell me about Mr. Banana Brains up there."

Hannah couldn't help but laugh at her grandmother's comment. It was so fitting!

"Oh Grandma, I love you. But there's not much to tell really. I met him when I lived in North Carolina and worked for that construction company."

"That was during your rebel years, wasn't it? Didn't you move down there after you got mad at your father?"

"Yes, but we patched things up not long after I moved. By then, I'd found a job that I really liked, plus, I'd met Brad and… well, I fell for him, okay?"

"Really? I would have never guessed!" Lois was a bit sassy for her age, and even managed to sling a few zingers now and then.

"It wasn't serious. Not for him anyway. He had bigger and better things to do – like go build tall skyscrapers and earn a big fat paycheck." Hannah's bitterness was more than evident.

"It was a choice he had to make for himself. It doesn't mean it was the right one. I could hear it in his voice – he still feels something for you."

"It won't do him any good if he does. I'm about to lose my parent's estate that they worked tirelessly to keep running since the day I was born. I have nothing to offer him or anyone else for that matter."

"Hannah, you did everything in your power to save this place. No one could have done any better with what you had to overcome. Don't be so hard on yourself."

"Maybe you're right, but it sure doesn't make it any easier. I don't see much hope at this point. Can you believe that man is back in my life after all these years? I think God is surely punishing me!"

"It may seem like that now, but sometimes those moments can be blessings in disguise," Lois smiled.

Brad's alarm went off and he freshened up a bit before dinner. As he made his way downstairs, he heard the ladies chatting in the dining room. It sounded a little intense, so instead of going in and making his presence known, he stopped short and stood silently in the lobby – out of sight. He knew it wasn't right, but he inched closer and listened in on their conversation…

Hannah's voice was elevated. "I don't think so, Grams. You weren't there! He crushed every dream I had – he gave up! All I wanted to do was to spend the rest of my life with him, and he walked away for big money!"

"We all make mistakes Jules. Maybe there was more to it than that, and maybe he regrets what he did."

"He doesn't – trust me. He only cares about business. Why else would he be here? He's just in this for the kill – the power that comes from taking on another big project."

"Well, it's been eight years, Sweetheart – everyone deserves a little grace. Besides, it's in your blood," Lois said, her voice a little shaky.

"What do you mean 'it's in my blood'?" Hannah was intrigued by the notion.

"The McRae's are Irish, and the Irish meaning of our name is 'Son of Grace' – or in your case, 'Daughter of Grace'. You see? It's in your blood, my dear. In fact, one of your ancestors settled in North Carolina in the 1800's, so maybe it's not a coincidence that you found your way there all those years ago."

"That was then, and this is now, Grams. Besides, I moved back here – to my real home."

"Home is where the heart is Jules, and I'm not sure your heart ever left North Carolina."

"Grandma – I think you need to take your meds," Hannah smiled.

Brad couldn't bear to listen any longer – afraid of what Hannah would say next. It was too hard. He tip-toed back upstairs a few steps, only to turn around and come back down, making a loud, deliberate entrance. He set his foot down on each step, hard and heavy, then yawned with great emphasis as he got closer to the dining room.

Hannah heard Brad coming down the stairs. "My heart is not –," she whispered, but stopped mid-sentence as Brad entered the room. She looked up and gave him a big, toothy smile.

"Good evening, ladies. I hope I'm not interrupting. The food smells delicious. What are we having?" Brad took a seat next to Lois, figuring it was safer on her side of the table.

Hannah smiled and said, "Liver and onions… your favorite right?"

"Huh? Oh, umm… sometimes I guess. That's really kind of you to remember," Brad replied. His face was contorted at the thought of eating the one food he hated the most, then his gag reflex kicked in and he almost lost it. *Well, I'll give her credit… she at least remembered how to torture me.* He smiled a half-smile, then took two pieces to spite her.

Dinner was mostly a conversation between Lois and Brad. They danced around big topics like politics or religion, and settled on his winery in North Carolina, Brad's brother Mitch and Laci, and Laci's struggle with breast cancer, plus a few other random facts. Hannah kept silent, enjoying every bite of her dinner, then excused herself to the kitchen to clean up. Brad started to get up and help, but Lois set her hand on his to stop him.

"Let her be, son. She's suffered a great deal over these past few years. Losing her dad's estate is the last straw – she's going to need some time to figure things out. Selling to your brother was one thing, but now that you're involved… it makes things very difficult," she said.

"I gathered that with the liver and onions. I hate them. I hate them worse than any other food on the planet – I know she remembered that," Brad laughed.

"Then you should feel flattered."

"Flattered? Why would I be flattered that she made me eat my least favorite meal and almost caused me to throw up?"

"Men… when will you ever learn?" Lois laughed.

"You've got me, Lois. Help a guy out?" Brad smiled.

"She still has feelings for you, and you have them for her as well. I've been around the two of you for all of two hours and comes through loud and clear. I can't see, but I bet it's also written all over your faces. You ate liver and onions for crying out loud! Open your eyes, son. You're both still in love with each other, and you know it," Lois coughed. Brad laughed, anxiously watching for Hannah to come out of the kitchen, but she remained inside.

"I'm afraid love is the furthest thing from her mind, Ms. McRae."

"So you don't deny it then?"

"Deny what?"

"That you still love her… that's what." Lois took a sip of her water.

"I'm here at my brother's request to get this business up and running. That's it." Brad stared down at the table, playing with his spoon.

"Oh pish-posh. You kids need to learn that life is too short to waste on something that happened years ago. It's time to get over it." Lois' words were firm, but gentle and motherly at the same time. He already liked Lois – she had sass… which was obviously passed on to her granddaughter.

Hannah came out of the kitchen juggling three bowls of bread pudding. Rich with attitude, she slid Brad's bowl across the table to him, as if it were a mug of beer being slid across the bar at a local saloon. She walked around the table, and gently set her grandmother's bowl down in front of her, smiling.

"Nice! Bread pudding is my favorite dessert – for real!" Brad said in a lively voice.

Hannah twirled her pointer finger around in a little circle. "Well yippee… score one for the innkeeper."

"You know, I think I'll enjoy this dessert in my room. I'm pretty tired. You ladies have a good night."

"Breakfast is served at nine sharp. We can start after that," Hannah stated.

"Yes, ma'am. Nine a.m. sharp." Brad gave her a little salute, then walked upstairs.

Hannah stared into her bowl, playing with her bread pudding but never taking a bite, then finally she pushed it aside. Lois was quiet and ate her pudding in silence.

"Are you ready for bed, Grams?"

"I guess so."

Hannah walked Lois to her room, helped her into her pajamas, and then tucked her in bed.

Lois took Hannah by the hand. "Jules – you have to do this if we're going to keep the winery. There's no other way. I know this won't be easy for you, but I believe God allowed this to happen for a reason. He brought Laci and Mitch up here, and even Brad, and the sooner you embrace the situation, the better off you'll be." Lois coughed, then took a sip of water from her glass on the bedside table. "I love you, Sweetheart. It's all going to work out."

Hannah squeezed her grandmother's hand. "I love you too, Grams, and I'll do my best, but I can't make any promises. I'm not even sure *God* has enough grace to get us through this storm," Hannah paused, "… but don't worry, I'll be fine. You get a good night's sleep – it's been a long day for both of us."

Hannah returned to the kitchen, cleaned up the rest of the dessert dishes, and then made her way upstairs. As she sat on the edge of her bed, a strong memory of her mom came to mind. She could almost hear her voice – the voice was so loud in fact, that she almost thought her mother was standing right next to her. Her mom always said, 'Don't worry about the problems of tomorrow, for today's problems are sufficient for themselves.' She smiled, remembering that it was a verse from the Bible. It had been so long since Hannah picked one up though, she had no idea where to find it. Tears trickled down her face, unsure of why that particular memory came to her. She was grateful nonetheless. Memories of her mother were rare anymore, and it was getting harder to picture her face. Hannah wiped her face, then crawled into bed – her mother's voice still ringing in her head. She whispered her words over and over, then fell fast asleep.

8 –Rocking the Boat

Hannah woke early, hoping to get downstairs and enjoy her coffee in peace, but apparently Brad had the same idea. He had already made the coffee and was sitting at the table reading over the estate sale paperwork.

Hannah stopped at the table and stared; 'bad attitude' written all over her face. "Do I need to sign my life over before breakfast or will you allow me to eat first?" Hannah's heart broke as she saw the papers under his hand, realizing this was really about to happen.

"For your information, we made an offer on the estate yesterday. I need to educate myself on everything, Jules."

"Stop calling me Jules – I'm tired of telling you. I don't want to hear you say it again."

Hannah stormed through the kitchen door and started cooking breakfast, dreading the day ahead. Once everything was done, she made Brad a plate and suddenly felt her heart rate speed up rapidly – almost beating out of her chest, a subtle reminder that she had forgotten to take her blood pressure pill last night. She sat Brad's plate down on the counter so hard it made a loud clank. She closed her eyes and took a few deep breaths to calm down. *It's hard enough to give up my home, but why do I have to hand it over to the one man that crushed my heart, Lord?* She thought. *That makes it ten times worse!*

Hearing the loud noise, Brad rushed through the kitchen door.

"Hey, are you okay?" he asked. Hannah was so startled by his sudden entrance that she hit Brad's plate with her hand and sent it flying off the counter – egg casserole and bacon hurled through the air. "I'm so sorry, Jules. I didn't mean to scare you."

"I told you to stop calling me Jules!" His insistence to keep calling her by that name – the name he used to say over and over – was like rubbing salt in an open wound. In a furious rage, she began cleaning up the mess.

Brad grabbed some paper towels and knelt down to help her.

"I don't need your help – just leave!" She looked at him, the heat palpable in her cheeks, and realized he wasn't leaving.

"You're too proud, *Hannah*. "It's okay to let people help, you know," he said softly.

Brad's deep voice was sweet. She always loved his voice, and for a second, he almost fooled her into thinking he actually cared. *I can't fall for him! He hasn't changed.* Hannah's heart now raced for a totally different reason. *One thing certainly hasn't changed… he's still stinking gorgeous!* She thought to herself.

She let out an exasperated breath. "Thank you for helping. Now, please let me finish so I can get you a new plate of food. We need to get busy, and then you can do whatever it is you have to do and be on your way."

Brad laughed. "Be on my way? Ha! I'm not going anywhere until this place is up and running at profit level again. That's what I learned yesterday at least. I figured Mitch would have told you."

Hannah stood up slowly, and the anger stirred in the pit of her stomach like liquid fire. She felt sick as his words sunk in – driving home the undeniable truth of what she was about to lose.

"I… no… he didn't tell me that part. He didn't tell me much actually."

"Well, it makes sense if you think about it. We can't just buy your place and leave you to run it without resources or staff."

Hannah paused and stared down at the food. She filled a clean plate with eggs, fruit and bacon, then handed it to Brad. "Yeah. Of course… you're right. You'll be the new owner and I'll be your employee. Forgive me. This whole losing-my-livelihood thing is kind of new for me. You enjoy your breakfast, Mr. Young. I'm going to take some food to my grandmother, then I'll wait for you in the winery when you're ready." Hannah walked out without another word.

She walked to her grandmother's room and looked in to find Lois still sleeping, so she held off on taking her breakfast inside. Hannah was actually grateful to avoid another lecture. She tiptoed away and closed the door behind her. As she made her way out to the winery, her head was spinning – so much hurt and pain. *He is finally back in my life and all I can do is hate him for leaving me!* She thought.

The fresh air was nice so she decided to walk around the estate for a bit before Brad came outside. Her favorite spot was around the back side of the winery – a perfect view of the hills behind the estate. It was no surprise when she found Clare there as well, sitting under the magnolia tree with her nose stuck in a book.

"Hey Squirt. How long have you been here?" Hannah asked.

"Not long. I ran down after breakfast and yes, my foster mom knows I'm here, don't worry," Clare replied.

"I wasn't worried. Besides, I'm glad you're here."

Hannah plopped down next to her, pulled her knees in and wrapped her arms around them for warmth and comfort.

"Uh, oh. What's up? You only sit in that position when you're sad, contemplating life, or trying to resist the urge to dive into a tub of Rocky Road."

Hannah laughed. "Wow. If you know all that, then you are spending way too much time hanging out with me, girl."

"Seriously, Jules. What's up? I know something is wrong."

Fighting back tears, Hannah swallowed and then rested her head against the tree. "I've been better, kid. We need to talk."

"O-k-a-y… now I'm worried."

"You should know that things around here are going to drastically change soon – really soon."

"That guy is buying Foxhead, isn't he?"

"Yes. Him, and Mitch and Laci of course. This will be Brad's newest conquest though, his new pet project… at least until he gets bored and moves on to the –"

"Wait a minute," Clare interrupted. "You sound like you know this guy. Spill, Jules."

Hannah dropped her head down on her knees then plucked a few blades of grass from the ground beneath her. "I do know him," she said solemnly.

"What? No way! He just got here – how could you possibly know him?"

"He's the 'Putz' from North Carolina, the one I told you about from a long time ago."

Clare's mouth fell open so wide that her gum fell out. She quickly picked it up, brushed it off, and then put it back in her mouth.

"That's gross, Clare! You don't put your dirty gum back in your mouth, girl…" Hannah felt more like a mother to Clare than a 'sometimes-big-sister'. Clare was around almost every day, all day, except when she wasn't in school. She had good foster parents, but Clare was one of six other foster kids in the same house, and the oldest. They weren't very attentive at times, and it had been tough on her.

"Don't change the subject Aunt Jules… out with it! How can he be 'Putz'? It's been what, like a hundred years since you've seen him, and he just shows up?"

Hannah laughed, half-heartedly. "Yep. I think God is punishing me for the sins of my past."

Hannah and Clare had spent hours working together in the B&B and the winery over the last few years. One slow afternoon, Clare asked about Hannah's love life, or lack thereof, and why she never remarried. So, Hannah filled her in on the very short but sweet 'affair of the heart' between her and Brad, including the part about Brad leaving her – thus earning him the nickname of 'Putz'. It was easier than saying his name out loud – even that still hurt at times.

Brad stole her heart from the moment she set eyes on him, and Hannah knew deep inside that those feelings were still there – they had never left. The pain he had caused though, still hung on like a dark shroud that she feared would never go away. Seeing him again was something she had always wanted, but never let herself believe it would actually happen, least of all like this.

"So, now what? Will you have to move out?" Clare asked.

"I honestly don't know yet. I don't think so, but it depends on the conditions of the sale. If I want to save this place, I have to do what they ask. Mitch and Laci said I could stay on to manage the place, but I have a feeling that it might get rather sticky with 'Putz' in charge now."

"This is wrong on *so* many levels, Jules! Why is this happening?" Clare was not only sad about Hannah losing her family's estate, she was scared of losing the one person that had become her only family.

"Now you listen to me, Clare Robbins. You have *nothing* to worry about, okay? Whatever happens, it's you and me and Grandma Lois. We are a family and that will never change – are we clear?" Hannah's quiet, assuring voice seemed to calm Clare's fears.

Clare smiled. "Yeah, we're clear. And, since we're family and all… my birthday *is* coming up soon."

Hannah laughed. "Oh good grief – it still three weeks away! You're getting a little anxious aren't you?"

"Duh… it's my birthday. I'm supposed to be excited! Besides, I don't really want a gift. I want the two of us to go horseback riding together instead – like we used to. You haven't been out to ride Storm or Molly in years, Jules. They probably miss you."

"Wow, I haven't thought about mom and dad's horses in a long time. Once I left them at the stables, I had a hard time going back."

"I know, but that's why you need to go see them. It will be good for you and we'll have so much fun! Please?" Clare smiled, then folded her hands folded together in a prayer-like manner and begged.

"How can I say no to that?" Hannah pulled Clare into a playful hug.

"Sweet! We are going to have so much fun, Jules!"

"I hope you're right…"

"It's like riding a bike, or something like that, right?" Clare laughed.

"Yeah, something like that. Now, I have work to do kid, and you need to do your homework. It's time to go *schmooze* the 'Putz'."

"Sounds good! You have fun schmoozing… I'll watch your back."

Hannah laughed out loud, "Deal." They got up and walked back to the winery. Brad was already inside and seemed anxious to get busy – his clipboard in hand.

"Wow, you don't waste any time do you?" Hannah gave him a look that could freeze ice.

"Look, *Hannah*… I have a very short time to turn this place around and get it up to profit level – hoping our offer is accepted and the sale goes through, of course. There's really no time to waste."

"Fine, then let's get to work… *boss*."

"I think that's the best idea you've had all morning," he replied sharply.

That day was the beginning of several long weeks for Hannah as she tried her best to get along with Brad. Between showing him all the day-to-day business operations for the B&B and the winery – what worked, what didn't work – and caring for her grandmother, she was physically and mentally exhausted. The hardest part was sharing all of her parent's wine stories with him – their techniques and how each blend meant something to their family. Hannah was relieved when he decided to spend an afternoon away from the estate to visit a few local wineries and restaurants. She didn't quite understand what he was up to, but was grateful for the time alone to clear her head. Hannah grew more upset every day having to work around Brad – forced to remember how they used to be years ago. Every now and again though, she would catch a glimpse of the man she fell in love with, then dismiss it as quickly as it came.

By the end of the third week, they had established a fairly good routine. Hannah would review a few things about the winery or B&B operations each morning, then they would go their separate ways in the afternoon. Brad would work on the estate, fixing things up, and she would work inside and take care of the few guests that came in and out. It was Friday, and unfortunately no guests were coming in that weekend. By six o'clock, Hannah realized she hadn't even thought about dinner. She hurried downstairs and scanned the cupboards for something to fix. Brad walked in the kitchen and Hannah did a double-take, trying to stare inconspicuously, but lingering the second time. He had cleaned up and changed clothes, and was now wearing khaki shorts and a black polo shirt – her favorite. *He's doing this on purpose – he remembers that I always loved it when he wore black. It's not fair!*

"Do you need any help?" he asked.

I need you to go away so I don't fall in love with you again! She thought. "No, but thanks for offering. I'm trying to decide what to fix for dinner, but so far I'm at a loss. It's just you and me tonight – Grandma didn't feel like eating so she went on to bed. You changed clothes. Are you going out?"

"Well, I thought I might treat you to dinner out tonight. What do you say?"

"That's really nice, but I couldn't."

"Why not? Come on – it will be a nice break and you need it. I know this week hasn't been easy on you," he added.

Hannah was reluctant, but she was tired and the thought of not having to cook was worth the price of putting up with him for a few more hours. "Okay, I guess you're right. It does sound nice. I'd like to change first, if that's ok. I'll be right down."

"Take your time, but wear something warm. We might be outside for a short time."

"Outside?"

"They have outdoor seating. It's a nice place – don't worry."

She came back a few minutes later and Brad couldn't help but stare. She wore black leggings with leather trim on the sides, tucked neatly in her black leather boots. Her gray and black sweater had a few sparkles on the front and was a little snug in places, but he liked that. Realizing his jaw had dropped a little, he closed his mouth.

"You look really good. I hope it's okay if I say that," he said politely.

"It's okay, and thank you," Hannah smiled, very happy with his pleasant reaction.

After a few minutes of driving, passing every restaurant in town – all of two – Hannah wondered where he was headed.

"Where are we going? You'll be in Hood River if you keep driving this way."

"I know. That's the plan."

"Oh… okay then. You do seem like you know where you're going. Have you been there before?"

"I drove over here last week to check out some restaurants."

"What for?" Hannah was curious, hoping he would divulge his reasoning.

"I just like to know what's around. It's nice to be able to share with guests when they ask for recommendations for local places to eat."

"I guess you're right. I never thought about it much." Hannah was embarrassed, realizing how little she offered to her guests. *I really do need help running this place… that makes so much sense! Why did he have to think of it first?*

"Here we are. You ever been here?" he asked.

Hannah looked out the car window and saw the familiar, beautiful restaurant. It was a strong link to her past, unbeknownst to Brad. "Romuls. Of course. I loved coming here with my parents. It's been around for a long time," Hannah smiled, but her heart was sad at the memory of her parents. To some degree though, it brought her comfort and she sensed her parents were there with her.

Brad was embarrassed for causing Hannah to relive what might have been a painful part of her past, not realizing her history there. "Hannah, I'm so sorry. If this place brings back too many memories for you, we can leave. I didn't know."

"It's okay, really. It will be nice to see the place again, and they have an amazing Shrimp Orecchiette. At least they used to," she smiled.

Inside, the smell of fresh bread, oregano and garlic filled the air. It was beautifully decorated – a 'Little Italy' experience in every way. Hannah closed her eyes for a moment, allowing the memories to flood her mind of the many dinners spent there, and they brought joy to her heart. She suddenly felt right at home. Brad put their name on the waiting list for a table, then they walked over to the bar and ordered a glass of wine while they waited.

"Let's go out on the deck – it's a nice evening. If that's okay with you."

"Sure – that sounds nice," she replied.

The sun had almost set, but the skyline was still a faint shade of orange. The deck overlooked the Columbia River Gorge – a beautiful view of the hills in the distance. Brad looked at her, his wine glass in hand, and lifted it up to her.

"A toast," he said.

She laughed. "To what? You leaving me years ago, or you taking over my family's estate and leaving me penniless?" Hannah regretted her words the minute they left her lips. "I'm… I'm so sorry. That was uncalled for. I didn't…"

"Jules… it's okay. I'd feel the same way if I were you. I hope you know that Mitch and Laci simply wanted to help you by offering to buy the estate. Laci has it in her head that they were meant to find you. She believes the rain *led* them here."

"Yeah, I remember her getting all excited when it rained the night they were here. She was like a little kid, even went outside and stood in it. I watched her and Mitch from the window – they were both getting soaked. Those two are crazy about each other. You don't see that very often in couples these days," she replied. *I remember feeling that way about you once.* She thought. He had slipped and called her 'Jules', but she didn't correct him that time. Secretly, she wanted him to say it.

"Yeah, they were definitely meant to find one another. After both of them lost their first spouse, they needed each other more than any two people I know. I didn't think Mitch would ever fall in love again after he lost Karin, but Laci stole his heart in less than four hours – literally."

"What? You're kidding me right?" Hannah was intrigued by the story.

"They met on plane – fell head over heels for each other. That whole 'love-at-first-sight' thing."

"Wow… that's crazy! Let's toast to that – to the rain that led them here, and their second chance at love." Hannah smiled and lifted her glass to his.

Their glasses clinked and they sipped their wine, enjoying the view.

"So what about you? Your marriage. Were you happy? If you don't mind me asking, that is," Brad asked.

"Let's just say he was the safe bet, so I figured 'why not'. He was nice, did his part with the housework, and even cooked now and then. I loved him, but not like I… well, let's just say I would have made it work. When my parents died though, I had no choice but to come back home and take care of the estate and my grandma. He wouldn't budge. His career was going well and he had invested a lot in his school. I sometimes think we were both just settling for one another – together for convenience. I can honestly say it was the longest year of my life. But, it all worked out in the end. The divorce was really mutual, and I kind of think he had his eye on another teacher at the school," she giggled. "I like to think we'll both get a second chance someday, maybe with the person whom our soul was originally meant to find."

"I'm sorry it didn't work out, but I'm glad you're a fan of second chances," Brad smiled.

"Ah… well, second chances are pretty hard to come by in my book. It would take a great deal for me to give a guy a second chance."

Brad's heart deflated a bit at her comment. The hostess called his name before he could reply, and they were escorted to their table. After ordering, the conversation dwindled, and in an effort to avoid even more awkward 'moments-of-silence', he shifted the conversation.

"Tell me about one of your favorite dinners here with your family – if you are up to it."

His compassion for her loss was evident and she was pleasantly surprised that he'd asked her to share. She missed being able to talk with him like this.

"All of them were great, but the nights when my dad would start going on and on about how he met my mother were pretty special. He loved her more than life itself. Then there were nights when he would brag about how the Italians 'do food' so much better than the Irish, just to irritate my mom of course. That debate was always a fun one."

"I wish I could have met them. They sound like very special people."

"They were. It's hard not having them here anymore. But right now, with me losing the winery, I admit I'm glad they're not here to see this. My dad would be so disappointed."

"No he wouldn't, Jules. You did everything you could to make it work and did an amazing job! Not many people can run a winery, a B&B, take care of an ailing grandmother, and help a wayward teen without losing a little of themselves in the process. I can see the toll it's taken on you to keep it up. Everything you've done to that place is an extension of who you are, and I know that any guest who walks inside can feel the love you've put into it."

Brad's passionate words moved Hannah more than she realized, a lump formed in her throat. "Thank you. That was very nice of you to say. And, thank you for dinner tonight. I can't remember the last time I enjoyed a night out."

"I want to help you make your family's estate a success if you'll give me the chance. I want us to work together. And… it may be hard to believe, but I still care about you." Brad reached over and took her hand, hoping he wasn't overstepping his bounds.

Hannah's heart jumped into her throat at his touch, enjoying how nice it felt. Until then, she hadn't given in to her feelings of loneliness and longing, and although hard to admit, they did exist. Now, with Brad back in her life again, she felt her heart caving in little by little, day by day. She tried to ignore it, but the more time they spent together, the harder it was to push him away.

Back at the estate, Hannah went in to check on her grandmother and found her sleeping peacefully, so she walked to the kitchen to fix a cup of coffee. It was late, but it was always the one thing that seemed to relax her, and she needed it tonight – still a tad worked up from dinner.

The coffee aroma wafted through the air, and after smelling it, Brad couldn't help but want a cup for himself. He made his way to the kitchen and walked in quietly. Hannah's back was toward him, so she didn't hear him come in. Her long, curly red hair brought a smile to his face, still one of his favorite things about her. It was more than that though. It was the way she took such care in doing the everyday things – doing the dishes, making meals… even making coffee. The love he had for her long ago surged inside of him, still as strong today, if not stronger, and he was taken aback at that thought. He cleared his throat to announce his presence.

"Hey, I figured you'd be in bed by now," he said.

Startled, she turned toward him and smiled, surprised by how happy she was to see him. "Yeah, I should be, but I'm not tired yet. Coffee helps."

He laughed softly. "Doesn't coffee stimulate the brain?"

"Normally yes. That's why I only drink decaf this late at night. I think it's the warmth that helps me relax more than anything, although caffeine never bothered me much until I developed high blood pressure."

"You have high blood pressure? Do you take something for it?"

"I didn't at first, but with the stress of my grandmother's health and running this place, it got worse. My doctor finally put me on medication. I'm not that good at remembering to take my pill though," she admitted.

"I get it. I've never liked taking medicine much myself."

"Can I fix you a cup of coffee?" she asked, a blush of red peaked on her cheeks. *I'm letting him get to me… I can't do this! He'll just hurt me again. Why won't he just kiss me for crying out loud! Wait… what am I saying? This is the Putz! I can't let him do this.*

"No, no. I can do it – you go on up and relax. It's been a long day."

"Okay then. Well, I'm off to bed. Enjoy your coffee, and thanks again for dinner." She started to walk away.

"Jules…wait," Brad couldn't hold back any longer. He reached out and pulled her into his arms, then leaned in slowly – about to kiss her.

Hannah desired his kiss more than she ever imagined, but her head was getting in the way and the walls around her heart were strong and tall. *He'll hurt me if I let him in… I know it. I'm not ready.* She immediately pulled her head away and looked down, staring at the floor. "Oh, Brad, I can't. If I gave you the impression that I was interested in you, then I'm sorry," she said, then looked into his eyes. "It's been too long and the hole is still there – it still hurts. I think it's best if we stay friends." Small tears trickled down her pink cheeks.

Brad let go of her and backed away. "It's okay, Jules. I understand. I…I'm sorry. You have to know how sorry I am, for before."

"Goodnight, Brad." She walked out of the kitchen.

9 – Winds of Change

Brad decided it was best to keep his feelings in check and simply work on being friends with Hannah, but it proved difficult for him. He longed to share his true feelings, but knowing they wouldn't be returned, he waited. Instead, he worked hard and learned everything he could about her family's business. He wanted the best for Hannah, and making her business successful was his main objective, especially since his plan was to turn the estate back over to her. Hopefully that would help win her heart back for good.

Each day they grew a little closer, talking and finding new things to laugh about. Once in a while they would reminisce about the past, but it wouldn't last long. Hannah tried her best to resist his charm, but much to her surprise, she was beginning to see him in a new light. There were changes going on inside of her too, and even Lois was taking notice despite her worsening condition. Hannah looked forward to what the days would bring, and although she was losing her family's estate to Brad's family, the sting of the loss had begun to fade. A small part of her was almost happy it would be in his hands.

April had finally arrived, and the sun was shining bright through her window. No rain in sight either, which was rare. She woke up and spent a little extra time on her hair, and then carefully selected her outfit for the day. *He always did like my jeans and boots. Oh crap! I'm dressing to please him now… what am I doing?* Hannah still had moments when she felt frustrated, sad, and mad for what he had done to her, realizing that her feelings for Brad were still raw, but slowly… she was coming undone.

After breakfast, they finished washing the dishes together, which was happening more frequently. Standing next to him at the sink, she could smell the fresh soap smell from his morning shower and it made her smile, distracting her from the task at hand.

"The broker will be here later today to go over the paperwork, but before he gets here I thought I would take inventory of our B&B supplies. Care to join me?"

"Oh, wow… that's today?" Hannah had forgotten about the broker coming. It was really happening – she was officially losing her estate.

"Yeah, but I can meet with him alone if you like, and go over things with you later – it's up to you. I know this won't be easy on you."

Hannah didn't reply and Brad could see a shift in her mood – like a switch had flipped and turned off the light inside of her. He quickly changed the subject. "You know… why don't we walk out to the patio behind the winery instead?" he asked, an excited tone in his voice.

Hannah raised her eyebrow and her interest was piqued. "Why the patio? There's nothing to inventory on the patio."

"Just bear with me – if that's not too much to ask."

"Fine… boss," she said sarcastically. They walked outside and Hannah stomped off, walking out ahead of him. *Why I wasted my time trying to look nice for you today, I'll never know. You're taking my life away today… again. Guess I'm not quite as 'fine' with all of this as I thought.*

Brad smiled as he watched her walk, her long red curls flopping in the breeze. He ached to reach out and fiddle with them like he used to. One of his favorite memories of their time together was sitting on the couch after dinner, drinking wine and talking about life. She would lay her head on his lap and her hair would sprawl across his legs. One at a time, he would gently pick up a curl and stretch it out, then let it go and watch it spring back into place. She loved it and not long after he started, she would fall asleep in his lap.

They walked behind the winery and stopped at the patio entrance. Hannah turned around and looked at him. "Okay, we're here. Now what?" Her bad mood was getting worse by the minute.

Brad walked to the other side of the patio and turned around to face her. He needed to see her face while he explained. "Tell me how you normally use this space." Crossing his arms, he walked around the table that separated them, somewhat coy.

"What do you mean, 'how-do-I-use-this-space'?" Her arms were flapping up and down as she spoke. "People sit out here, they drink wine… what else is there?"

"Well, Laci would probably have a heart attack that I'm actually saying this, but you have a great space to entertain and host events back here. Look around you! There's an amazing view of the hillside and a perfect space to build a fire-pit right here," Brad walked over to the 'future' spot for the fire-pit and held out his arms for her to see his vision, "… and it's covered."

"I don't get why you're telling me all this. Why does any of this matter?"

He marched over and stood in front of her, so close he could feel her breath on his face. "Close your eyes," he said.

"Why?"

"Hannah, just close your eyes! For crying out loud, is it that hard to do this one thing? Please?" Brad's patience was starting to wear thin, but he smiled the minute her eyes were closed.

Exasperated, she let out a huge sigh and closed her eyes. His voice was commanding and confident. Although she didn't want to do it, mainly out of spite, part of her couldn't resist following his directions and doing what he asked. "Now what? What is the purpose of all this?" she asked.

Brad quietly moved around behind her and softly whispered in her ear. "Will you just *trust* me? At least with this," he pleaded.

Hannah's heart rate shot up and her palms began to perspire. What on earth is he doing? And why does he have to smell so good?

"Fine," she replied.

"Now, imagine for a minute that it's a cool summer evening and a small group of about twenty people are gathered around drinking wine, laughing, and having a wonderful time. A few others are sitting over there by the warm fire. There are a few banquet tables set with black linens, candles glowing, beautiful centerpieces, and a full place setting for ten at each table. The chef has prepared—"

Hannah burst out laughing, interrupting Brad's elegant account of his 'vision'. "Chef? You actually think we have one?" she asked, still laughing.

"No. I *know* you don't have a chef. That's the point! You need to partner with one to hold dinner events here and bring in more people. That's how I found Romuls. I've already talked to their head chef about this and they're very interested."

Feeling somewhat foolish for jumping to conclusions, she let him finish. "Fine, go on… I'm listening." Her eyes rolled, then closed again.

"Thank you. Now, as I was saying, the chef would make seven small courses, each one paired with a different wine, using both your wines and a few from Crystal Creek."

"People would really come to something like this?" she asked, growing more intrigued.

"I *know* they would, Jules! I've seen it. We can call them Twilight Tasting Dinners. Not only will they come, but they will pay top dollar if the chef is locally well-known and has a good reputation. Tickets would probably sell for over a hundred dollars a head, depending on the menu."

As much as she wanted his idea to work, she couldn't wrap her head around the thought of actually pulling it off. She lowered her head and shook it side to side, doubtful of its success. "I don't know, Brad. It seems a little far-fetched."

"You have to trust me on this. You and I both know that wine changes every taste bud when paired with food! Mitch force-fed me Wine101 over the past two years and I think I've attended every winemaker class, conference and seminar ever offered in the South. I know this can work." He was more excited than a kid with a new toy.

Hannah cracked a smile at his comment, but suddenly it hit her as to what he was trying to do. He was taking over *her* business – taking everything she had ever worked for!

"Wait a minute… what do you think you are doing?"

"What do you mean? I'm trying to give you –"

She didn't let him finish. "You're giving me a migraine! I can't listen to this anymore. They're all just empty promises and you won't be happy until you take over my entire estate and push me out forever. That's what you do best isn't it, Brad? You walk in, take the world by storm, then walk out once you've conquered the job; never allowing yourself to become too emotionally attached!" she shouted, letting it all out. Hannah's emotions had finally gotten the best of her as the painful memories resurfaced, no longer able to keep them bottled up.

"If this is about our past and how I left, then just admit it! You've been wanting to ever since I walked through the door. Tell me off, slap me. Oh wait, you already *did* that. I get it, okay? I'm a jerk, a loser, a no-good, non-committal Neanderthal. I was so scared of not being good enough for you that I left. I'm sorry. Is that what you want to hear? Because I am. I'm sorry I never told you face to face and took off without saying goodbye. I'm sorry I didn't marry you and take you with me, because believe it or not… you were the love of my life! I tried to explain everything in the letter, but obviously that didn't work out too well." Defeated, he dropped his head.

"I… I wouldn't know. I never received any *letter*," she said.

"What? I wrote a letter! I left it under the door of the office the morning I left. I swear!" The look of surprise on his face was priceless. Hannah felt a little guilty for lying to him about the letter, but he deserved it. She wasn't being totally dishonest, though. She did get the letter, but she never opened it. She couldn't bring herself to learn the truth, to learn that she wasn't enough for him or that he didn't love her. Instead, she ripped it in half. *Wait… did he just say I was the love of his life? If that's true, why did he leave? What did I do? Maybe it's time I read that letter.*

He stood in front of her and looked into her eyes. "Don't believe me, I don't care. I wrote the letter and told you exactly how I felt and why I couldn't stay. Apparently it was all for nothing."

Hannah didn't have the words to reply immediately, and by then, she was starting to get a real migraine. "I'm going inside to take a pill and check on Grandma."

"Fine," he said, and walked away.

There was no point in trying to talk to her anymore so Brad took a few minutes to calm down and went back inside the B&B. He'd no sooner walked through the front door when he heard Jules scream at the top of her lungs and immediately ran to find her, his heart in his throat. She was in Lois' room, her grandmother lying face down in Hannah's arms choking and gasping for air. Hannah was pounding on her back to help clear her lungs, but her breathing was so labored that Lois' lips were turning blue.

"Brad! She can't breathe! Call an ambulance, please!" Hannah cried out in agony.

Brad ran to get the phone and call 911, but Clare beat him to it and was already dialing, running down the hall toward him. They waited for what felt like an eternity, but the ambulance finally arrived and took Lois out on a stretcher. She was alive, but unable to breathe without oxygen. The pneumonia had worsened.

Hannah climbed into the back of the ambulance and looked at Clare. "Please don't leave, okay? I need you here to watch the 'Putz'."

"You got it, Aunt Jules," Clare replied.

Brad's eyebrow raised after hearing Hannah's statement. After the ambulance left, he turned to Clare. "Let me guess. I'm the Putz?" he asked.

"How'd you guess?" she answered, then blew a bubble with her bubble gum and popped it. A mischievous smile spread over her face.

"Great… this day just keeps getting better and better. And I suppose you know all about me then?"

"Not everything, but enough. Enough to know that you must be a real scum-sucking leech of a guy to ever leave Jules. Are you really that stupid?" Clare's teenage, abrasive tact was in rare form.

"I refuse to have this conversation with a kid who knows nothing about me or my previous relationship status with Jules. You have no idea what happened."

"I know enough to see right through your little plan you've got going here."

"Oh yeah? And what plan would that be? Please enlighten me *Oh-Wise-One*," his voice continued to rise.

"You're going to kick her and Lois out after the sale is final aren't you?"

"What? Why would you think that? Does Hannah think that too?" Brad ran his hands through his hair in frustration. "How could she think I would do that," he whispered out loud.

Clare heard him muttering. "Oh gross! You still love her don't you?"

"Again… *not* going to have this conversation with you, Squirt."

"Yep… that's a yes. I can tell. You're like a little puppy around her."

"I am not!"

"Yes, you are!" Clare snapped. "It's so obvious a monkey could see it."

"I've got work to do and a meeting in an hour. Don't you have something to keep you busy?" Brad was growing more frustrated with her by the minute. "Why are you here anyway? Who are you to Jul… Hannah?"

"She hasn't told you?"

"Told me what?"

"I'm her 'Little'."

"Her 'little'? You mean little sister? I didn't realize she had a sister."

"She doesn't. I'm not really her blood sister. I'm her 'Little'. She took me under her wing after her parents died. We met through the Big Brothers Big Sisters program here in town. That was five years ago." Clare scuffed the floor with her foot.

"So, she just hangs out with you? And you work here too?"

"Well, I didn't at first. As I got older, I started helping out more and really enjoyed it. Before I knew it, Jules had me working and even paid me. It's fun, and I like having something to call my own. I live with my foster parents, but they're really busy with their younger kids. Jules and I were matched up through the organization and I've kind of become, well, part of her family. She helps me with homework, encourages me, listens to all my crazy stories about school and friends, you know… all that stuff."

"That sounds like something Jules would do," he smiled.

"Now that I'm older, I just walk here after school and help her where I can. It's harder for her to do much now with her grandma so sick. I just want to help her like she helped me."

"That's pretty cool, kid. But why aren't you in school today?"

"Today is parent-teacher conferences, so we got out at eleven. Besides, I don't need your approval," Clare replied in a sharp tone.

"I… *ugh*! What is it with teens these days? Look, Clare, I don't have time to argue right now. Go do whatever it is you do. I'll be fine."

"You *are* my job, remember… Putz? I'm supposed to watch you and make sure you don't get into trouble," she laughed.

"I'll give you twenty bucks to leave me alone." Brad pulled out his wallet and took out a twenty-dollar bill.

"Make it forty and you've got a deal."

Brad laughed, "Forty? Are you –?"

"Otherwise I will sit here and stare at you until she gets back. And I don't blink." Clare sat down at the kitchen table and cast her steady gaze on him.

"Fine. Forty." He pulled out another twenty and handed her the crisp bills. "Now go, please."

"I'm gone, but I'm never far," she giggled and walked off.

"That's comforting," he replied, then went up to his room to rest and review the papers for the sale.

The wood floor creaked as he walked through his room over to the window, staring at the old rug that lay beneath his feet. The edges were frayed, the southwest colors now faded from the years of sitting in the sun. It was shining bright, so he took a few minutes and let its warmth sink into his skin, consumed with worry about Jules and her grandmother. She was the same amazing woman he had fallen in love with long ago, yet better in every way. He greatly admired her taking over her family's estate, caring for Lois, and taking in Clare like family.

Please get better, Lois, he thought. Lois was the only one in his corner right now and he would need her support to help get Jules back. *How can that silly teenage girl tell that I still have feelings for her? It's true though. I've loved her since the day I laid eyes on her, and I only hope she is willing to give me a second chance, once I prove to her that I won't hurt her again. She didn't correct me today when I called her Jules, so I guess that's a good start.* His mind continued to race.

After a few hours, still no word from Jules, Brad made his way back down to the dining room and ate a small snack to calm his nerves. Clare had managed to give him the space he needed thankfully, but the solitude made things worse. The doorbell rang.

"I'll get it!" Clare yelled from the family room and came running toward the door.

"I've got it, Clare. It's the broker," Brad said and opened the door to let him in.

"Are you Mr. Young?" the man asked.

"Yes. And you are?"

"Hello. I'm Alan Reynolds. I'm from the broker's office."

"Please come in, Mr. Reynolds. Can I offer you anything to drink?"

"No, I'm fine thank you. We should get down to business. I have another client meeting in an hour. The bank has accepted your offer to purchase the estate and I think you'll find the contract outlined exactly as your brother and I discussed over the phone. You've made a generous offer, and I must say, your conditions were rather… unique. I've never had someone buy a business in foreclosure and then donate it right back to the original owner. May I ask why?"

"This estate belonged to the owner's parents, and it's all she has left of them. It's her home. We couldn't just run her out. That's not really the southern way, Mr. Reynolds," Brad smiled.

"She's a lucky lady. I hope she knows that."

"Outside of the basic sale contract, I'd like to keep the other conditions confidential if that can be arranged." Brad didn't want Hannah to know their plans, fearing it would make her feel like a charity case. For now, he needed her to believe that he and Mitch were the sole owners until he could explain everything.

"Of course. The conditions regarding the donation will remain undisclosed, and there is no need for her signature on anything for that arrangement. Once the 90-day mark has passed, however, she'll need to re-file the deed of trust for public record. All I need is her signature on the contract and you'll officially be the new owner of Foxhead Estates. Congratulations, Mr. Young."

Clare stepped out of the family room and into the foyer, going unnoticed by Brad and the 'suit' at the table. She could tell they were talking about the sale, and it was her job to protect Jules. She tiptoed around the corner and listened in on their conversation.

"No congratulations necessary, Mr. Reynolds. It's only a short-term formality. In another couple of months, it will be out of my hands," Brad stood up and shook his hand.

"Well, I wish you and the 'next owner' all the best. Good day," Mr. Reynolds said as he shook Brad's hand. He closed his briefcase and walked toward the door.

Clare was shocked by what she heard and quietly hurried out of sight, hoping Brad hadn't heard her leave the room. Once the suit was gone, she walked back into the foyer.

"What do you want now, Scooter? You're supposed to steer clear of me remember? I paid top dollar for that as I recall."

"You are a first-class jerk, you know that?" Clare's accusation took Brad by surprise.

"What did I do now? I paid you forty bucks and *I'm* the jerk? I demand a refund!"

"You're going to need a lot more than forty bucks once I tell Aunt Jules what you are doing with her family's estate."

"What are you talking about, Clare? What did you hear? You can't tell her!"

"I gotta go." She pushed open the front door and ran out.

Brad stood in the foyer, stunned at her reaction and wondered what she *thought* she had heard, but all he could do was worry about Jules and Lois, that bad news was coming. It was nearing five o'clock now and still no sign of them, so he went into the kitchen and searched around for something to cook for dinner – figuring they might be hungry after their ordeal. The gold Amana refrigerator looked like the original 1970's model, complete with wood handles and no automatic ice maker. *That's going for sure.* He dug around to find some fresh romaine lettuce and a few frozen shrimp, then found a box of fettucine pasta and a jar of Alfredo sauce in the pantry.

It was nearly seven when he heard Hannah walk through the front door. Brad went out to greet her and found her standing in the foyer. Alone. She looked exhausted and worn, her eyes fixed on the floor.

"Jules… how is Lois? Is she alright?"

Hannah slowly lifted her head, tears spilling from her eyes. She quickly wiped them away and took a deep breath. "It's pneumonia, and influenza. Both. She's holding her own right now and they've got her on a breathing machine, but her lungs are filling up with fluid faster than they can remove it. She's… she's dying Brad." Hannah folded over at the waist, wrapping her arms tight around her stomach as she let out a loud, broken cry. Brad walked toward her, longing to hold her and console her, but she lifted up her right arm and with the palm of her hand facing him, she motioned him to stop.

"Don't. I don't want your pity," she growled.

"I'm so sorry, Jules. I want to help, Darlin'. Please… just tell me what I can do," he pleaded.

"I think you've helped enough, haven't you? You *being* here just makes everything worse!" she yelled.

"I'm sorry. I'll… I'll leave you alone. Dinner will be ready soon if you're hungry."

"I'm not hungry. I need to go take a nap, shower and get back to the hospital." Hannah ran to her room and slammed the door behind her.

Brad returned to the kitchen and finished making dinner. He was starving, but had no desire to eat. He figured Hannah might come in when he was gone, so he fixed her a plate and covered it with foil. On a small piece of paper, he wrote her name, and underneath it wrote 'I'm here for you'. It was after seven and Jules was still holed up in her room. Rather than go to his own room and pace the floor, Brad felt a strong desire to visit Lois at the hospital before Hannah decided to return. He picked up his keys and quietly slipped out the door.

Hannah cried for the better part of that evening, her eyes stinging. She stared at the closet door, hugging her tear-soaked pillow, stained with streaks of black mascara. *Maybe if I hide in there, this will all go away. I've hidden other things behind that door to make bad memories disappear. It worked too… at least until he showed up.* In a last ditch effort to take her mind off the inevitable, she walked over and opened the door. Buried behind a stack of shoe boxes and a bag of old clothes, she dug out a little wooden box – the words 'My Jules' carved into the lid. She returned to the bed and set the box down in front of her. A thick layer of dust covered the top, and the rusty hinge creaked loudly as she opened it, revealing two items. The first, a faded old envelope, yellowed by time. Her name was written on the front. Brad's letter. The second, a small blue velvet pouch that contained her engagement ring. He'd given her the box and the ring the night he proposed. Unable to look at the ring, she moved it aside.

She lifted the letter out of the box, her hand shaking. It happened just like Brad said it did – she found it laying on the office floor the day he left. Knowing it contained his goodbye, she chose not to open it. Ever. Instead, she took it home and in a fit of red-headed anger and stubbornness, ripped it in half, only to regret it later and tape it back together. That night, she hid everything inside the box… the letter, the ring, and her pain. All of it in that little box… never to open it again. Never to think about him again. Until now.

Even the tape was now brown, the edges curled and peeling away from the surface. Tears welled in her eyes as she stared at the letter – her memory of that day still marred by the agony she had endured. Brad turned out to be the first in a series of bad moments and decisions in her life, all of which she conveniently blamed on him. His leaving caused a permanent stain, but as it turned out, his love had also left an indelible mark on her heart that she could never remove.

Very gently, she opened the envelope and pulled out the still-torn letter, laying the two pieces side-by-side in order to read it.

His words read…

> Hey Jules,
>
> I'm not good with words and I'm even worse at saying goodbye, so I won't say it. I love you more than I ever thought a man could love a woman. My dad died when I was only a sophomore in high school, so I don't remember much about how he treated my mom and I never really learned the right way to treat a woman, let alone love one or marry one. The truth is, I don't think I'd make a very good husband to you. I build things all the time, but building a life with you scares me to death, Jules. I'm afraid I'll disappoint you and I can't bear to do that. You deserve better than me. I need you to know that you hold my heart in the palm of your hand and you always will. I will never forgive myself for leaving you, but it's the only way I know how to make sure you have a good, happy life. I know you'll fall in love with someone else one day, and I want you to have the best that this life has to offer. No matter what, just remember that I love you. You are my forever love – and I knew it the day I laid eyes on you in that office. I'll

never love another like you, Jules. I only hope that someday you can forgive me for not giving us the chance we deserved. It's weird, but I believe there is a plan for us floating out there somewhere, and if God can find it in his heart to lead us back to each other again, I promise I'll never let go.

Still Yours,
Brad

Sadness overwhelmed her at first, wishing she had read his letter years ago. *He was so scared, but he still loved me when he left! Why didn't he just tell me in person?* On some cosmic level, it brought comfort to her as she lay there worrying about her grandmother and their future.

Hannah heard a loud growl emanate from her belly, so she got up and took a shower, then walked downstairs to the kitchen. When she opened the refrigerator, she saw the plates, her name written on a piece of paper affixed to the top one – a note from Brad. She read it, tore it off and crumpled it in her fist, and threw it across the room. *It will be a miracle if this is even edible*, she thought spitefully, knowing very well that he'd always been a better cook than her. She removed the foil from the plate to find a beautiful Caesar salad. The second plate was filled with shrimp fettuccini alfredo. It almost looked too pretty to eat. A smile spread across her face. *Now that is the man I remember… the man I loved. The man I still love.* She warmed her pasta and devoured everything in a matter of minutes. Delicious.

*****

"I'm here to see Lois McRae, please," Brad said politely to the front desk nurse.

"Are you a family member?" the nurse asked politely.

"No ma'am, but I hope to be. You see, I'm in love with her granddaughter and I need to ask her permission to… to marry her before it's too late. Please? I won't be long, I promise."

The nurse could barely hold it together. She simply smiled, nodded her head and whispered, "Room 204."

"Thank you."

He walked inside Lois' room. She was hooked up to hoses and wires, sleeping. Her chest would rise and fall as squeaks and groans echoed from her mouth. It was a sad sight, and Brad nearly walked out without saying a word, but she opened her eyes and looked right at him. Lois lifted her arm and motioned him over to her side.

"Hi Lois. Sorry I woke you. I wanted to check on you. Hannah is home resting. Can I get you anything?" Brad asked.

Lois took her oxygen mask off her mouth. "Come closer."

Brad leaned down closer and took her hand. "What is it, Lois?"

"You need to tell her," she said in a scratchy voice.

"What do you mean? Tell her what?"

"Tell her… how much… you love her," she said, taking deep breaths between words.

"I can't. She hates me right now. How do I get her back, Lois? I don't know what to do."

Lois closed her eyes and Brad continued to hold her hand, waiting. After a few minutes, she continued, "She needs to see you living out your commitment." She paused to take several breaths. "She needs to know you'll never leave her again." Lois smiled and placed the mask back over her nose.

"I want to marry her, Lois. I can't live the rest of my life without her in it. Will you allow me to marry your granddaughter?

Lois coughed, removed the oxygen mask again, and looked at Brad. "You are the answer to my prayers son, and you're the answer to hers. She just doesn't know it yet. Give her time, and don't give up on her. You two are meant to be together." She placed the mask back in place, laid back and closed her eyes.

Brad was overwhelmed with her approval and her words. "I feel like I've known you my whole life, Lois. How can that be when we only just met?"

Lois was overcome by exhaustion, simply smiling in reply, and fell fast asleep. Brad stayed and continued to hold her hand. "I need her more than air, Lois. She's the best part of my unfinished story, my happy ending, and it's time I let her know," he whispered, and gently laid her hand back on the bed and slipped out.

10 – Letting Go

Hannah was exhausted, now spending the majority of her time at the hospital with her grandmother, and still trying to run the estate – doing what she could in the evenings. Per her grandmother's wishes, Hannah decided to be the bigger person and slowly relinquish control of the estate to Brad. He was constantly spewing new ideas to increase traffic and had created a new website, which to Hannah's surprise, was already generating business. They even received their first online reservation for the summer. She hated to admit it, but he was doing everything right and giving her the space she needed at the same time. Among other things, he also built a fire-pit, power washed the patio, and started to remodel the wine tasting area. It was hard *not* to notice all his efforts. His demeanor was different too – more at ease, comfortable… happy even. Part of her was grateful that he was there, but it constantly fought against the part that hated him being there. Even after reading his letter, she still struggled daily with their past, how he'd hurt her, and she worried that he would just hurt her again. It was hard to let it go.

*****

With her grandmother still in the hospital, Hannah was hesitant to take Clare riding, but Lois had insisted upon it, so she picked up the phone, and dialed the stables.

"Hi Sarah, this is Hannah Blake. I'll be out at the stables tomorrow. Could you have Storm and Molly prepped to ride? Yes, I know. It's been far too long. Around eleven would be fine, thank you. See you then."

After she hung up, she smiled, more excited about riding her parents' horses again than she'd realized. For years after their death she avoided riding altogether, and thus avoided the memories associated with it, both good and bad. If she were being honest though, they were mostly wonderful memories. Hannah's dad had taught her to ride when she was barely big enough to walk or talk, against her mother's wishes. Mother had never been a fan of horses – always the prima donna – but she loved spending time with Hannah, and on a few rare occasions they would enjoy a ride together. It was time for Hannah to embrace the good memories, and put the past behind her once and for all – to move forward, starting with tomorrow's ride with Clare. She threw on her red pea coat, and headed out to the winery. There was work to be done before the fun.

Hannah walked inside to find Brad already there, as usual, busy working on the wine bar. He was buried behind it, using some type of hand tool, undisturbed by Hannah's entrance. The construction was finally to the point where she could visualize the end result, and the sight took her by surprise – not at all what she expected. She stopped to take in the view, noticing the sleek contours of the bar, how smooth it was with its clean lines. The best word to describe it, had she the nerve to say it out loud, would have been *sexy*. The frame had a strong character, with large posts positioned underneath, evenly spaced along the length of the bar. As she walked closer, her mouth dropped – realizing that he was carving twisted grapevines into each post from top to bottom. Even unstained in its natural wood finish, it was a work of art. She smiled, then moved closer and squatted down to admire Brad's handiwork up close. That's when she saw it. The figure sculpted at the top of the post…the head of a fox. One on every post. She took in a sharp breath, amazed at the sight, and keenly aware of how much time and love he had invested.

"Mornin' sunshine," he said smiling, looking down over the bar at her.

Hannah shot up like a rocket, startled by his greeting. "Oh, hey! Good morning. Uh, I was just admiring your handiwork here. Looks like you're making progress – I… I like it." Hannah's face was flushed, embarrassed at her clumsy reaction.

He grinned at her – his shiny white teeth gleamed against his tan face. Brad never did lack in the 'external beauty' department. The worst part was that he got better with age and she felt her heart do a little jump. He wore a snug sweatshirt – the sleeves of which were ripped off of course. And against every fashion law, he was wearing cargo shorts! She smiled, noticing the thin layer of sawdust sprinkled on the top of his tousled, dark brown hair. *Okay, Jules… simmer down! You are NOT going to let him get to you again. You're stronger than that!*

"What did you say? I'm not sure I heard you right… did you just say, 'I like it'?" he teased.

"Very funny. You heard me. I really like it. It's more modern than I thought it would be. I figured you would give it a 'log cabin' look, being from the south and all. I'm glad you didn't. You surprised me."

"I guess it's never too late to learn something new is it? Besides, Mitch is more of the 'log cabin' guy. I may be the carpenter in the family, but I've always been drawn to the more modern look," he paused, almost like he was nervous, "Um… if you come around here, you'll see where I'm making room for two wine coolers behind the counter."

She stepped around the back of the counter to see his progress.

"When it's finished, it will have a smooth, black quartz countertop. Then I'll add a foot bar and some lighting under the front for a nice effect. I think you'll like it."

Hannah could feel her face glowing and knew it was time to get out of there. "I remember your apartment back in North Carolina… it was pretty contemporary I guess, but I never figured it was by choice."

"I remember that apartment too. It always looked better when you were in it." Brad's own candor caught him off guard, not realizing what he'd just said until it was too late. "I'm so sorry. I shouldn't have said…"

"It's okay. We can't pretend like we weren't *together*. We were. It's a fact, but it's in the past."

"Yeah right. In the past. So, do you want to help me?"

"Oh, trust me… you don't want me to help. I've never been real handy with power tools – I would probably end up shooting you with a nail gun or blowing something up," Hannah laughed.

"I'm not worried, and it's only a small belt sander. Just hold onto the handle, press down lightly, and push it back and forth. It's easy. Here, you give it a try."

Brad set the sander in front of her, then handed her a pair of safety glasses. She put them on, reluctantly, then grabbed the handle and turned it on. It lunged forward and she pressed down, guiding it back and forth across the counter's surface like he told her. *So far so good… this is kind of fun actually!* After a minute or two though, she noticed some big divots in the wood and freaked out, then turned off the sander in a panic.

"Oh no! See? I've already ruined it! I told you I'm horrible at stuff like this." She looked at Brad in defeat, another addition to her portfolio of recent failures.

"Calm down and let me show you." Brad stepped around behind her and put his arms around hers. He placed her hand on the sander and rested his hand on top, weaving his fingers through hers. He turned it on, then together, they gently guided it back and forth on the bar surface, slowly nudging it and letting it do the work.

Hannah's heart ached as it pounded inside of her chest, feeling his warm body snug behind her, his breath blowing down her neck. *He smells like sawdust and… fresh berries? Odd combo, but wow does is work! He's good at this… too good. I've missed him so much!* Memories of their time together flooded her mind, how they used to laugh and giggle, act silly and just enjoy being with each other. It didn't matter what they were doing. Spending time with Brad was when she felt most like herself. He was her favorite place. That, she realized, had never changed. He was everything to her then, and now. *What am I doing?* Hannah used her other hand and quickly turned off the sander, then wiggled out of his embrace.

"What's wrong? You're not done – we have this entire counter to do yet."

"I… I just remembered that I need to go get a room ready – we've got a guest coming in tonight," she said.

"I see. Of course, duty calls. That reminds me actually. I took a call this morning before you woke up and left you a note in the reservation book. There is another guest coming in tonight. Can you make up two rooms?"

"Wow, that's great! I can't even remember the last time we had two rooms filled. I'll make sure everything is ready," she smiled. "Oh, and afterward, I need to head up to the hospital to check on Grandma, then I can come back and help sand later if you want. Sorry. I don't want you to think I'm trying to get out of doing work or anything. It's not that. I'm just hot… I mean, I'm *not* good at this stuff." Embarrassed at her blunder, she rolled her eyes and turned her face away from him. *Hot? Really, Jules?*

Brad smiled. "It's okay. I know you're working – there's a lot to do around here. Go on, and if you have time and want to come back later, the sander will be here. How is your grandmother anyway? Any news?"

"No. She's stable and holding her own, but there isn't much improvement. I just want her home."

"I know, Jules. I do too… for you, of course."

"Can you greet the guests if I'm not back in time or do you want me to call Clare?"

"Don't worry about it – I've got it covered. You do what you need to do. Don't call Clare – she's not too fond of me anyway."

Hannah laughed. "Clare will do whatever it takes to make sure no harm comes to me or Lois. She's family."

"That girl is a teenage pit-bull – she has more grit than I've seen in most construction workers!" he laughed. "It's great what you are doing for her. You're a strong woman, Hannah Blake. I admire you."

"She's done more for me than I could ever do for her. She saved me and brought me back to life when I needed it most. I don't know what I would have done without her. This week is her birthday. She's so excited! We're going horseback riding tomorrow for her present. Will you be able to watch the place while we're gone?"

"Sure, no problem. I never knew you liked to ride."

"Well, it's never too late to learn something new about someone is it?" she turned and walked out, smiling.

By the time Hannah arrived at the hospital, Lois was eating, which was a big improvement in her condition. The medicine was finally starting to work and her lungs were slowly improving.

"Hi Grandma! You must be feeling better – you're eating."

"Hi, Sweetheart. I'm doing alright I guess. Are you doing okay?"

"Don't worry about me. I'm fine, the estate is fine, Clare is fine – we're all fine. You just concentrate on getting better so we can get you home."

"How is Brad?" she coughed, struggling to catch her breath afterward.

"Oh he's fine, I suppose. He's quite happy taking over my family's estate – almost too happy. He's making repairs, coming up with crazy marketing ideas, and he's being very nice to me. I guess if I were in his shoes, I'd be pretty happy too."

"Jules, honey. When are you going to realize that *you* are the reason he's so happy."

"I think they've given you a few too many doses of that pain killer, Grandma."

Lois scooted up in her bed and pulled on Hannah's arm to draw her closer. "Sweetie, you need to listen to me, because I don't know how much longer I have on this earth, and if you don't remember anything else I've ever told you before, you need to remember this… if you don't let go of the past and the pain it carries, you are going to be alone forever. You have to trust the love you have for him now – it's still right there in your heart, sweet girl! I know it didn't work out before, but it wasn't the right time then…," she coughed, then cleared her throat. "You're both different people today, and you still share the same love my dear. *Now* is the right time. After all, isn't life all about God's perfect timing?"

"I understand what you're saying, I really do, but my timing has always been a little off. I'm the one who is late for everything remember?" she joked. Lois grinned and nodded in agreement. "And please don't talk like that. You're going to be back at home before you know it, silly. I love you."

The nurse walked in and cleared away Lois' dinner tray, then proceeded to check her vital signs. "I'm going to step out for a bit, Grams. I'll be back soon okay?"

"Alright, Sweetie. I love you, Jules. You'll always be the jewel of my heart," Lois said softly.

Hannah kissed her on the cheek, then got up and walked out, replaying her grandmother's words in her head. Maybe she's right, but I don't know if I can forgive him. I won't let him hurt me again! He's definitely changed though – I can see it… and I feel it. I'm lying awake at night thinking about him for crying out loud! My heart still belongs to him, I admit it. I'm so scared though – letting go means tearing down all those walls and forgiving him. I suppose that's part of the risk in loving someone, and I do love him. I guess he's earned his second chance after all. She smiled.

The nurse came out of the Lois' room. "She's already fallen asleep, Ms. Blake. You might want to let her rest for a while. She hasn't slept much today."

"Oh, of course. I'll come back in the morning. Please call me if… "

"We will dear. Don't worry," the nurse replied.

It was late when Hannah returned to the estate and the guests had already checked in. Brad didn't seem to be anywhere around, which relieved her somewhat, so she put on some grubby clothes and went out to the winery to do some work. *I have a date with a belt sander. It might get rough.* "Ha!" she laughed aloud at her own bad joke, then began to sand the bar.

An hour later, it was finished. She turned off the sander, then took a step back to admire her handiwork.

Brad had walked in unbeknownst to Hannah, admiring her tenacity with the sander. "Nice work, Jules!" his deep southern voice boomed behind her.

"Ah!" she screamed, then turned around and scowled at him. "You scared me to death Brad Young! That's twice today. How long have you been standing there?" Her cheeks were the same shade of red as her hair.

"Hold on, Red – don't freak out. I heard the machine after I got out the shower and wanted to see if you were doing okay." He walked over and ran his hands over the surface of the counter, checking the quality of her work.

"Does it meet your standards… *boss*?" she asked sarcastically, a little upset that he'd interrupted her alone time, but also glad he did.

Brad swiftly walked over to her and got right up in her face, gently pulling her safety glasses off her head. "You're absolutely beautiful when you're holding a power tool, did you know that?" Without hesitation, he reached around behind her and pulled her close, sinking his lips into hers for the first time in eight long years.

This time, Hannah surrendered and melted into him. Immediately, she felt their souls connect, two long lost friends and lovers destined to be together. The warmth of his touch brought her back to a place when she was his and he was hers, and it was better than anything she could have ever imagined, but once again, fear set in. She pushed him away and backed up.

"What are you doing?" Hannah was disappointed in herself for allowing it to happen.

"I thought I was kissing you and it sure seemed like you were enjoying it!"

"I… I didn't enjoy it. We can't just pick back up again where we left off Brad – too much has happened between us!"

"Why can't you just forgive me? I never wanted to hurt you – don't you know how much I loved you? I still love you, Jules!" he shouted. "There… I said it."

"It doesn't change anything! You left me. You walked out on everything – on our future. You'll do it again!"

He stepped toward her, inches from her face, and she felt the heat between them.

"Stop pushing me away, Jules! You still love me too and you know it – just let it go!"

"I don't know how, Brad," she said, vulnerable and honest.

"Then let me show you… please?" Brad took her in his arms and leaned in, gently kissing her soft lips. His grip tightened with the intensity of his kiss, filled with passion and warmth. Hannah couldn't fight it any longer, and she gave in to her heart's desire. The love she had kept hidden in a box for so long, along with his letter, was now free. She returned his passion and Brad felt her body relax – finally.

He always knew they were meant to be together – despite the detours in life that had kept them apart. She was his once again – and this time it was forever. Hannah broke his kiss, leaning her forehead against his, catching her breath.

"Does this mean…"

"Yes! I love you, Brad Young! Are you happy now? I never stopped loving you, not *once*. I simply learned to bury it to protect my heart. There's something you should know though…" She hesitated telling him the next part, but knew she had to come clean.

"Okay. What is it?"

"It's just that… well, I kind of lied to you about the letter." She bit her lower lip and squinted, prepared for his unfavorable response.

He laughed. "I knew you were lying, silly."

"What? You did not!" Hannah slapped his arm playfully

"I totally did – you are a horrible liar, Jules. Remember when you used to plan our surprise dates and tried to make me believe we were just going grocery shopping? I always knew you were up to something. Your mouth always curls to one side when you lie."

"How could you possibly remember that?" She was amazed.

"I remember every moment we had together – each one. I never wanted to forget any of them… or you. I was so stupid and couldn't admit I had screwed up."

"It's okay – I forgive you. I guess it was more of a half-truth, really. I did get the letter, but I never opened it. I ripped it in half, then taped it up again and stuffed it in the box. I never read it until this week."

"I get it, Jules. Oh… is it okay if I call you Jules now? It's really all I know."

She laughed, "Yes. I'd like that."

"Good – it was so hard trying to say Hannah all the time."

They walked arm and arm back to the house. Hannah's heart was light and burden free for the first time in years. When they reached the door, Brad stopped and turned to look her in the eyes.

"What's wrong?" she asked.

"I'm curious about something. If you kept the letter, I… I don't suppose you kept…" He stammered, hesitant to finish his question.

Hannah blushed, already knowing his question. "Yes, I kept the ring too. Why? Did you want it back?" *No, no no… please don't ask me to marry you – you'll ruin everything!* she thought.

"Oh no, of course not! I was just curious – that's all. I'm glad," he stammered.

"This is a new journey okay? Let's just take our time and see what happens." She leaned up and kissed him again, then they walked inside. "Are you sure you're okay to watch the place tomorrow?"

"Absolutely. I'll have the place booked solid before you get back."

"Ha ha… very funny. But thanks for thinking positive." Hannah was still leery about the success of the estate, even if it was under new ownership.

"Go and have fun. I've got everything covered. Oh, and I talked to the chef. He is good with hosting our first wine dinner in July. Do you want me to send out the invitations and put it on the website?"

"That's great! Yes, let's send them out. We only have two months to prepare," she giggled. "You know… you being here – back in my life after all these years – it's crazy, and exciting, and scary all at the same time. Do you feel that way or is it just me?"

"Yes, and no," He closed the gap between them and took her face in his hands. "I always hoped for this day, Jules. I kept living my life and going through the motions after I left you behind, but on the inside I never stopped loving you. You're my one. You've always been the one – the reason I could never be happy or settle down with another woman. No one else was good enough compared to you," he laughed softly. "My brother would say that this was all God's perfect timing, and although I haven't been the most willing to believe in God at times, I have to agree with him on this. Only God could have planned for us to find our way back to each other again, and I'm never letting you go," he paused, then whispered "Never."

Hannah was rendered breathless by his sweet words, unable to reply. Slowly, Brad leaned in and his lips met hers, parting them slightly. He pulled her body close, into his warm embrace, then backed her gently against the wood door, sinking deeper into her wet kiss. Brad's soft hands slid under the back of her blouse and she moaned softly, reeling from the sensation of his touch and longing for more, but after a few minutes, she suddenly stopped and pulled her head away – fearing things would get out of hand if they kept going. *I admit I've let go, but I'm not quite ready to let go of everything just yet.*

"Um… wow… that," she smiled, letting out a short breath, "that was… very nice. I'd like to slow down a bit though, if that's okay? My head is still spinning from this whole thing. I think I need some time to adjust," she smiled, hoping she hadn't upset him.

Brad smiled and pulled her to his chest, his chin resting on her head. "Having you back in my life is all that matters. We can crawl, walk or run, whatever speed you need, as long as you're by my side. If I can see a *glimmer* of forever spent with you, then I'm good," he paused for a minute, then chuckled softly, "and to think all of this began with a crazy lady who loves the rain…"

"Do you mean Laci?" Hannah asked, looking up at him.

"Yeah, but that's a story for another day." He opened the door for her and they walked inside.

"Well, sleep tight," Hannah said. "Thanks again for… for helping me let go." She turned and gave him one last hug. "I do love you, you know. And you have no idea how nice it is to say that again after all this time." She smiled up at him, cheeks still aglow.

Brad bent down and kissed her softly. "I couldn't agree more. I love you too. 'Night, Jules."

11 – Forgiving Rain

Clare stormed in the house like a bull in a china shop – yelling at the top of her lungs.

"Let's go Jules! The horses await!" she shouted.

Hannah was still getting ready when she heard Clare's announcement. "Make some coffee – I'm almost ready!" she yelled down the stairs.

Clare started a pot of coffee and Brad walked in – helping himself to the first cup.

"Great – you're still here? I was hoping you had fallen off of a steep cliff by now, or gotten caught in the grape musher thingy," Clare snapped.

"Very funny, Pit-bull, but I'm not going anywhere." Brad's smug face was more than she could take.

Hannah walked in on the two of them, sensing the tension in the air. When Brad turned around, they smiled at each like two high school teenagers with their first crush. "Hey gorgeous," he said, leaning down to kiss her.

"Morning handsome," Hannah replied.

"Oh gag! You two are…? What is this, Jules? What's he done to you? You know he's up to no good right! This is the PUTZ remember? You can't cave in now!" Clare was furious at the obvious display going on in front of her.

"Slow down, Clare. No one is caving in. What are you talking about – why is he up to no good?"

"His little plan to kick you out of here – that's what. Didn't he tell you yet? I overheard him talking it over with the broker the other day."

Brad realized then that Clare overheard only *part* of their conversation that day, skewing it all out of proportion. "Now wait just a minute, Clare – you have no idea what you're talking about," Brad said harshly, his temper flaring.

Hannah turned to Brad. "Well, why don't you enlighten me? What is she talking about?" Hannah's brow furrowed.

"It's nothing – not really. I'll explain it all later. It's just a special stipulation we had put in the contract – it's not a big deal." Brad hated to tell her about giving back the property this soon, fearing she would let her pride get in the way and reject their offer.

Clare crossed her arms in front of her chest. "I heard him say this place would be out of his hands in a couple of months. He's going to sell the estate out from under you, Jules!"

"Is that true? You need to tell me *now*, Brad!" Hannah was furious, realizing what a fool she'd been for allowing him back into her heart.

"No, Jules. She's got it all wrong!"

"I should have never trusted you again! Jeez – I was so stupid to let you get under my skin. You don't care about me! This is what I suspected – I'm just another capital business venture to you aren't I?" She turned to Clare. "Grab the snack bag and coffee thermos. Let's get out of here. I can't stand the stench any longer… I'm done."

"Jules, wait! Let me explain, please?" Brad pleaded, following her out the front door, but she wouldn't turn around. They climbed in Hannah's car without another word.

"Wait, Jules! It's not what you think!" he yelled from the porch, but they were halfway down the drive already.

Brad was beside himself – worried about what Jules thought of him, knowing that Clare had the facts all wrong. *Why didn't I stop her and tell her the truth? She hates me now, and I just got her back.* Over the next few hours, he tried to stay busy to keep his mind off things. He added some finishing touches to the fire pit, then polished the new quartz on the bar, but nothing helped. Disgusted with life in general, he went upstairs and took a shower, then sat down on the bed, took a deep breath, and called Mitch.

*****

Laci paced back and forth in the bathroom, staring down at not one, not two, but three pregnancy test sticks sitting on the counter – each one reading 'positive' in bright pink words. *This can't be right! It's only been a month since… oh good grief. I was late – but I'm also 44 years old… this doesn't happen to a woman my age, does it?* She collected the tests and shoved them in a sack, hiding them under the cabinet in case she needed the evidence later. Mitch was waiting patiently for her downstairs, about to treat her to lunch.

"It's about time – everything okay?" Mitch asked as she walked up to him.

Laci didn't reply. Her mind had drifted – still in shock from the results.

Mitch waved his hand in front of her face. "Woohoo… hey Darlin', come back to me."

"Oh, sorry. I'm ready when you are," she replied, half-heartedly.

"I asked if everything was okay. You were up there a while."

"I don't recall asking about all of your *long* visits to the 'loo'… give me a break! Can't a girl have a moment to herself?" Laci playfully poked him in the gut.

"Fair enough. Let's go – I'm starving."

They were about to sit down at their table when Mitch's phone rang. Laci saw Brad's name on the screen. "Yeah! An update!" she said, her face filled with excitement as Mitch answered. *Thank you God! I needed the diversion. I'm not ready to tell him…*

"Hey brother, what's up? How goes the B&B 'reno' project?" Mitch asked.

"I've got a problem," Brad said in a serious tone.

"Uh, oh. What's wrong, bud?"

Laci's expression changed instantly, worried that something had happened. She leaned in closer in hopes of hearing some of the call.

Brad poured his heart out to Mitch, going over the events of the last few weeks, Lois' worsening condition, the progress he made with softening Hannah's heart, and how things had even taken a turn for the better – with their relationship. Then he shared about Clare's little 'eavesdropping' escapade.

"I think Clare overheard the broker talking to me about the 'new owner' that would be taking over. She thinks I'm selling Hannah's estate to someone else, taking it out from under her or something."

"I see… and she doesn't realize that Hannah will be the new owner?"

"Correct. She's a hot-headed teenager who was in the wrong place at the wrong time. I knew she heard something that day, but honestly wasn't sure what until now." Brad was devastated. He flopped down on the bed and stared up at the ceiling, scared that he'd lost Hannah for good this time.

"Look, I know we were going to wait and tell Hannah after the sixty days were up, but you're obviously going to have to tell her."

"Trust me, I tried, but she stormed off with Clare and drove out of here so fast you'd have thought her hair was on fire – for real."

"Where was she headed?"

"To the stables – she's taking Clare horseback riding for her birthday. She's fuming mad, Mitch. I don't like it."

"Maybe this is better – it will give her some time to cool off. Women need that," Mitch added, smiling at Laci across the table.

Laci heard his comment and kicked Mitch under the table, smiling.

"Ouch!" Mitch yelled.

"Laci punched you, didn't she?" Brad laughed, knowing she had done something.

"Nope – kicked me…"

"Serves you right little brother."

"Yeah, yeah," Mitch said, winking at Laci. "It will all work out Brad – don't worry. Just tell her the truth and let God handle the rest."

"You're right. I'll talk to her as soon as they get back." A crack of thunder sounded in the distance and Brad stood up to look out the window, a dark sky overhead. "Hopefully sooner than later. I don't like the looks of this sky right now," he said, an uneasy feeling churning inside.

"That's crazy – I heard the thunder through the phone."

Laci's eyes got as big as quarters at the mention of thunder and she smiled. Mitch covered the phone and whispered, "Don't smile, Lace. Hannah and Clare are out horseback riding and there is a storm on the way," he said.

Laci shrugged, unaware of the circumstances of course. "Sorry," she mouthed in silence.

"She'll be fine, Brad. You worry too much," Mitch said.

"Yeah – you're one to talk about not worrying," Brad replied sarcastically.

"Touché. Text me after you two talk okay? I'll let you go."

"Sounds good. Oh, and tell Laci she's starting to rub off on me. I'm planning an event… or I *was* planning one at least. Not sure I'll get to finish now."

"Wow. She'll have heart failure – not sure she's ready for that kind of news yet," Mitch laughed, then winked at Laci.

Laci tilted her head, curious. "What's he saying?"

Mitch whispered, "He's planning an event."

"Oh dear Lord, help us," Laci replied, rolling her eyes.

"Hey, if I can straighten things out, it will be the talk of the town – you wait and see," Brad said confidently.

"I have no doubt, brother. No doubt at all. I'll talk to you later," Mitch said, then hung up.

Laci was anxious to hear Brad's news, and more than happy to delay sharing her own. She tapped her fingernails on the table. "Well? I'm freaking out, Mitch! What's going on?"

"Everything is fine – or will be. They had a little misunderstanding that's all," he replied.

Mitch explained the situation to Laci as they ate lunch, trying to put her mind at ease, but something was gnawing at her and she couldn't ignore it.

"I'm worried, Mitch."

"You and Brad both. Will you stop worrying? There is nothing we can do except wait. Brad's got this under control, trust me."

"That's what worries me."

Mitch took Laci's hand and squeezed it. "We have to have faith, Darlin'," he said.

"It's not the winery – it's Hannah and Lois. Something doesn't feel right, Mitch."

"Well, at least it's getting ready to rain there – that's good right?"

"Yeah – I suppose so." Laci wasn't sure this time.

"Now, what is going on with you? Our lunch is almost over and all we've talked about is Brad and Hannah. Are you sure you're okay? I get the feeling you aren't telling me something."

"Oh, it's nothing. It can wait," she said, staring at her plate.

"No – I know that look. Something is up and you need to tell me before you burst. Now what is it?" Mitch pressed.

"I… I'm not sure how to say this, but…" she hesitated, still in shock herself.

"What is it, Lace? What's wrong, Darlin'?"

"I'm… I'm pregnant, Mitch." Laci exhaled after she said the words, her cheeks rosy red.

Mitch's eyes popped open wide, but he remained silent.

"Did you hear what I said?" she asked, unsure what to make of his reaction.

"I heard you, but… it doesn't make sense. You can't be… it's only been a month since we…," he paused to calculate the time in his head. "Oh. Wow. You're *absolutely* sure?"

"I've done this a few times Mitch… I think I'm well aware of the signs at this point, and it's been 5 weeks," she replied, a little miffed at his reaction.

"That's true." He smiled wryly, looking as if he'd just won a 12-month membership to the 'soap-of-the-month' club instead of the lottery.

"You're not happy." Laci's heart was broken by his lack of emotion, and she stood up to leave.

"No, heavens no! Wait, wait… I mean yes. Yes, I'm happy! Don't leave, Lace. I'm so sorry. I love you! Of course I'm happy – I'm thrilled, Darlin'. It's just… it's a lot to take in, that's all." Mitch stood up and walked around to her side, leaned down, and kissed her softly. "I'm sorry I didn't sound more enthusiastic. I'm guess I'm a little nervous after…"

"I get it, don't worry. I'm nervous too. I wasn't sure whether I should even tell you or not. I should have waited."

"Why wouldn't you want to tell me? I'm your husband. That's what I'm here for – we go through this together remember? You and me." He stood up and returned to his seat.

"I didn't want you to get your hopes up and then something happen. I don't want to disappoint you again," she said, her cheeks still moist from her tears.

"Laci, look at me, Darlin'," he took her hands in his, "you are my whole world and nothing else in this life gives me more pleasure than to stand by your side – no matter what life brings us. Good, bad, or otherwise. Do you hear me? You could never disappoint me. I love you." He kissed the top of her hand.

Laci smiled and her heart filled with love, love for her man – her Airplane Man – who took her by surprise each and every day and made her life worth living. "I hear you, Mr. Young. I love you, too."

*****

The stables were only about thirty minutes away, but it was far enough to give Hannah some time to calm down. Once there, she and Clare saddled up, then reviewed their trail with the guides and headed out. Hannah still remembered the trails well, so she felt comfortable taking Clare out on her own.

"Are you sure you're up for this Clare?" Hannah asked.

"I am *so* ready – let's go!" Clare's enthusiasm overflowed and made Hannah laugh. "How do I make him go faster?" she shouted to Hannah.

"Well, first you need to keep your voice down. I'm not 'hard of hearing' – it's just you and me out here. Second, *he* is a *she,* and you don't need to make her go faster. Once we get up past the tree line, there is a nice open pasture and I'll show you how to post and trot. For now, just try and enjoy the ride okay?" Hannah giggled.

"This is boring, Jules."

"Hey – you wanted a true horseback ride experience and this is it girl. Sit back and relax. We have some hills coming up, so keep hold of those reins – you don't want Molly to think she is in charge."

Thirty minutes into the ride, they came up to the pasture and Hannah showed Clare a few tricks – giving her some freedom to run Molly out in the open. Clare was a natural on a horse, and it brought Hannah joy to see her having so much fun and being a kid.

"Hey, let's take a break!" Hannah yelled.

Clare gave Hannah a 'thumbs-up', then brought Molly over and tied her to a tree close by. Hannah had already laid out the picnic blanket, pulling food out of her pack.

"Sweet! I'm starving!" Clare said.

"Good, I brought plenty. I'm glad I had everything packed last night. The morning was a little tense," Hannah sighed, her voice heavy and sad.

"I'm really sorry, Jules. You love him don't you?" Clare asked.

"It's not that simple."

"Why does it have to be hard? You're either in love with him or you're not. What else is there?" Clare popped a grape in her mouth, then laid back on the blanket.

Hannah smiled. "Trust. That's what else."

"So, you love him, but you don't trust him?" Clare asked, trying to understand.

"It's hard to explain. These last several weeks of being forced to work with him, I finally saw the man I fell in love with again, but this time there was more compassion and tenderness – I saw more of his heart. When he first walked into my office all those years ago, my insides lit up. It was like he brought me to life and I instantly felt a strong connection between us. I can't even describe it. Every time we were together, I felt it. Brad made me feel whole and complete. I was crazy about him," she paused, picking at her food, "and then he left and I fell apart. He hurt me, and I changed. I lost hope in true love. And like a crazy woman, I tried loving someone else – the teacher – even married him, thinking it would help. I gave our marriage all I had, but that didn't turn out so great either. The truth is, even though I tried to move forward, my heart stayed in the past. I was still in love with Brad, and trust me, there's a big difference between loving someone because they are good and kind, safe even… and being madly *in-love* with someone."

"So you *were* falling back in love with him again?"

"Yes. I didn't have too far to fall though…" Hannah smiled, then flopped back on the blanket and stared up at the sky. "That's why I have such a hard time believing he would sell my business out from under me! I'm furious for letting him trick me into believing he was doing this for me – for us. I thought he loved me too." Her anger deafened by the cry of her broken heart.

"Oh, he loves you, Jules. Trust me. He's just greedy."

"You could tell he was in love with me?" Hannah asked, a hint of a smile appeared on her face.

"That man is mad about you, girl! Every time he looks at you it's like the stars have all aligned over your head or something," Clare laughed.

"Well, that's too bad. He ruined any chance we had with his big plans to sell my estate. *Ugh!* Whatever… I'm done with him. Let's just eat our snacks and talk about you – any love interests at school?"

Clare laughed. "You're kidding right? I won't fall in love – it's against my religion. I don't think there is anyone in my entire school who would meet my laundry list of requirements anyway. It's a very shallow gene pool there."

"Oh yeah? What's on your list of requirements for a guy? Do tell. Apparently I could use a few new tips," Hannah giggled.

"Let's see… smart, funny, active in something besides himself, likes adventure, reads books, likes music – maybe even sings or plays an instrument, holds his own opinion, likes to help his community, treats a girl with respect… just to name a few."

"Wow – that's quite a list. You don't mess around do you?"

"Since I read so many books, I started to pick out some qualities from my favorite characters. It's kind of fun. Plus, I don't really care about his looks that much. All the other girls get hung up on that, but not me."

"Good for you, Clare. It's refreshing to know a young woman who has a mind of her own and knows what she wants in her future man." Hannah's heart swelled, so proud of the beautiful young woman Clare had become over the last few years.

"I'm not rushing it though. Most of the guys I know would rank right up there with 'Putz'."

Hannah laughed again, but Clare's comment forced her once again to think about how disgusted she was with Brad and his plan. It was short lived however, interrupted by a crack of thunder in the distance. "Uh, oh. Sounds like we have some rain coming our way – we'd better get back."

As they cleaned up their picnic, another clap of thunder sounded in the distance. Clare looked over at the horses stirring around.

"They're starting to freak out. Will they let us ride them back?" Clare asked, worried about their return back.

"Of course. They might be a little skittish, but we'll be fine, don't worry. They're used to this type of thing – they live in it."

Clare looked up at the sky. "Those clouds are black, Jules. That's not good. I learned that much from science class." The thunder rolled again, this time a little louder and a thin streak of lightning split the sky at the horizon.

"Stop looking at the clouds and let's go. This storm is moving in fast." Although she didn't show it, Hannah was nervous, not having ridden in a while herself, and now riding with Clare who was so inexperienced. She knew the horses would sense their fear, and that made the journey back home even more dangerous.

They mounted up and took off. Hannah chose an easier trail going back, which also provided them with more shelter from all the surrounding trees. The lightning and thunder continued, growing in both volume and intensity. Then the rain began to fall, hammering down and forcing its way through the air. It pounded against the fall leaves that still covered the ground – the clatter deafening.

"Jules, I'm scared!" Clare yelled.

Hannah was riding ahead of Clare, but kept the distance tight between them. She slowed down and turned Storm to face Clare. "You're doing great, Clare! We only have about fifteen or twenty minutes to go. Stay close, okay? I don't want Molly to take off too fast."

Hannah rode on, slow and steady, but the next peal of thunder caused a vibration that shook the ground so hard it spooked Storm, and he galloped off. Clare panicked and started screaming – the distance between her and Hannah growing farther and farther. Hannah tried to steady Storm and slow him down, but couldn't get control. Directly ahead, a bolt of lightning came down in front of her and split a large tree, and the pieces plummeted toward the ground below – one half falling directly in Hannah's path. She looked up and saw it, desperately trying to guide Storm out of the way, but he jerked his head and reared back. The reins flew out of her hand and Storm turned into the falling tree.

Clare had almost caught up when she saw the tree fall. "Jules, watch out!" Clare screamed as a huge branch of the tree knocked Hannah off Storm. She flew backwards and landed on the hard wet ground, now pinned underneath the tree.

Clare felt like she was watching a movie in slow motion, unable to stop it from playing. She was terrified, but kept pushing Molly hard until they got to Hannah. She managed to stop, tied Molly to a tree, and then ran to Hannah's side.

"Jules, can you hear me? Please say something!" Clare cried out, scared to death. No response. Hannah lay lifeless under the tree, her red hair blowing wildly, and her head bleeding. Matching blood smears were still somewhat visible on the large rock sitting next to her, but quickly being washed away with the heavy rain. It was merciless, falling so hard that Clare could barely tell if Hannah was even breathing, trying to watch her chest rise and fall.

"Jules – wake up! I don't know what to do!" She tried to lift the tree off Hannah, but it was too big and she didn't have the strength. She took off her jacket and scooted close to Hannah's body, laying it over her face to shelter her from the rain. Clare was shaking, and cried out for help, albeit useless. When she looked up though, she saw Hannah's horse, and remembered the phone in her bag. She stood up and looked around first, figuring the bag had flown off too, but she couldn't find it. Storm stood in the distance, calm and still, almost as if he was watching over them. As Clare walked toward him, she saw the bag hanging on the saddle. She slowly approached Storm from the side, gently stroking his back to announce her presence, then lifted the bag off, careful not to scare him. The cell phone had very little signal, but she dialed the number and prayed he would answer, calling the one person she knew would help.

*****

Brad had already checked in one of two guests that day. The second couple were arriving late, so he left an envelope in the lobby which contained their key and check-in instructions. It was an easy system. His mind raced aimlessly though, unable to focus and pacing back and forth. His phone rang and he breathed a sigh of relief when he saw Hannah's name appear.

"Hey! I was starting to – ,"

Clare cut him off, "Brad – it's Clare! Jules is hurt! I don't know where we are or what to do!" she yelled. The connection was cutting in and out.

Brad could barely hear her over the din of the storm in the background, but definitely heard the words 'Jules' and 'hurt'.

"Clare, is that you? Are you okay? Is Jules hurt? What happened?" he shouted, scared for both of them.

Clare sobbed uncontrollably, but took a breath and tried to reply. "Lightning struck a tree! It fell on top of her – knocked her to the ground. She's trapped underneath, Brad, and her head is bleeding! Please…," the phone cut out. Seconds later her voice came back. "… send help!"

"Okay. You need to listen to me, Clare… I need you to take a deep breath and calm down. Can you can reach her?" he asked.

"Yes, I'm sitting next to her."

"Good! Do you have a t-shirt or cloth that you can wrap around her head to stop the bleeding?"

"Uh, yeah. I can use the table cloth. It's in her bag." Clare reached over and pulled the table cloth from out of the bag.

She ripped a large strip from it and reached through the tree branches to wrap it around Hannah's head like he told her.

"I did it!" she said proudly. "Now what?"

"Great job! Now just stay by her side and don't leave. I'm going to hang up and call the stables so they can send a rescue team. Did you follow the same trail back?"

"No. Hannah said she knew a short cut – an easier trail through the woods. We're at the base of a ravine and there is a creek right next to us. The creek is rising, Brad, fast!" she shouted over the rain.

"Someone will be there soon, Clare – I promise! Hang in there, okay?" Brad tried to reassure her the best he could.

"No! Please don't hang up! I can't do this."

"You're wrong, Clare, you CAN do this. You're a strong young woman and Jules needs your strength right now. I'll call you right back okay?"

"Promise?" she asked, sniffing.

"I promise, Scooter. I promise."

Brad hung up and looked everywhere to find the number for the stables, finally spotting it on the fridge. The stable owner answered, and by the time Brad explained who he was calling about, the owner had already sent out a rescue party to search for them based on Hannah's original trail route. Brad shared Clare's information about them taking an alternate route, being near the creek, and the owner radioed to the search team to give them the update. The stable owner tried to assure Brad that they would find them soon. Brad hung up the phone, got in his car, and called Clare from the road.

"Brad, is that you?" Clare asked.

The rain had let up some and he could finally hear Clare's voice more clearly. "Hi, Clare. Yes, it's me. I'm on my way to the stables. How are you? How is Jules?" he asked, hoping for some improvement in her condition.

Brad's voice was soothing and put Clare at ease. "She was moaning a minute ago, but stopped. She won't wake up or answer me." Clare's teeth chattered as she talked and her whole body was shaking as the temperature began to drop.

"That's great news, Clare! If she's making noise, then she's alive and that's all that matters." His relief was met with tears of joy. "The stable sent a team out to find you – they should be there any minute, okay? You're doing great." He took a deep breath to calm down.

Clare had found a patch of grass near Hannah's head and wiggled in between the branches that covered her body, stroking her wet red hair as she continued to talk to Brad. "Brad, I'm so sorry."

"For what, Sweetie?" he asked, knowing what she meant of course.

"I shouldn't have told Jules about you selling the estate to someone else," Clare cried louder.

"Oh Clare, Darlin', I'm not mad at you, and I'm not selling the estate to anyone. I'm donating it back to Jules – *she* will be the new owner. She's the love of my life... I could never take her business and home away from her, and no one ever will again," Brad said in his sweet southern voice.

"I'm such an idiot! I got it all wrong and I'm sorry. I really screwed up, didn't I?"

"You were protecting her, Clare. That's what any little sister would do – that's what family members do for each other, and Hannah is your family. I'm proud of you for looking out for her."

"You're proud of me? But what about today? It was my idea to go riding! She wouldn't be here if it wasn't for me. I'm scared for her."

"Something else you two have in common – you're both pretty darn stubborn. Jules loves you and this was her gift to you. Don't blame her for loving you. She is a strong woman, and she is going to be fine. You'll see." Brad was scared, and although trying to sound confident and strong for Clare, he knew that Jules being unconscious that long wasn't good.

"Okay," she paused. "She loves you too, you know. She never stopped loving you – even after you left. She told me that today."

Brad took a deep breath of relief. "Thank you for telling me, Clare. I never stopped loving her either," he smiled.

Clare heard a whistle in the distance and looked up to see two riders, both wearing bright yellow rain coats. "Brad, the rescue guys are here! I'd better go."

"Okay. Don't worry, Clare. I'll meet you at the stables with warm clothes. See you soon."

Brad hung up and broke every speed limit between him and the stables. About twenty minutes later, he pulled into the parking lot and the EMT's were already loading Hannah into the ambulance, sirens blaring. He ran to the ambulance as fast as he could, but the doors slammed closed in his face. Pressing his hands against the doors, he peered through the window and saw Jules' body lying lifeless on the stretcher – her blood stained head wrapped in bandages. Impossible to ignore were her grayish-blue lips, and the sight caused his stomach to seize. He slammed his hands against the doors as hard as he could, yelling her name. "Jules! I'm here, baby. It's gonna be okay. I love you, Jules!"

The stable manager walked up to Brad. "Sir, you need to step away from the ambulance – they need to get her to the hospital. You can meet her there," he said calmly, trying to ease Brad's state of unrest.

Brad backed away and the ambulance tore out of the drive. He broke down, unable to hold back his emotions.

"I'm sorry. I'm guessing you're the man who called me?" the stable manager said.

"Yes, sir. Thank you for sending someone to help them. I'm in your debt," Brad replied.

"Thanks to you, we found them much sooner. Your call probably saved her life. It took both men to lift the tree off her body, but I'm afraid they couldn't tell the extent of the damage. Try not to worry – she's in good hands now, and you've got a young lady waiting for you over there," he added.

Brad wiped his face and looked over toward the office. "Clare!" he yelled, then ran to her side.

Clare stepped off the porch, wrapped in a blanket and still drenched from the storm.

"Brad!" she replied, crying.

"Are you okay, Scooter?"

She threw her arms around him, practically cutting off his circulation.

"Wow… she hugs," he said in jest. A rush of relief shot through him, grateful she hadn't been hurt as well.

Clare sniffed, and looked up at him. "Tell anyone and I'll deny it 'til my death," she replied with a little smile.

"Your secret is safe with me, kid," he smiled. Clare had made quite an impression on him in the last few weeks, and within the last hour, their friendship was at a whole new level.

"She never woke up, Brad. Is she going to be okay?" Her voice shook as tears rolled down her dirty cheeks.

"She will. I know it with everything inside me, Clare," he whispered. "Now go change clothes. We need to be there when she wakes up, right?"

"Right," she replied.

While Clare was changing, Brad called Mitch to give him the grim news.

12 – Silent Goodbyes

Laci and Mitch drove home and decided it best not to share the 'baby news' with the family just yet. She walked up to her writing room to relax, but called her mother instead. *I have to tell her. She would never forgive me if I kept this from her. Besides, I can't hold it in any longer.*

"Mom, did you hear me?" Laci asked.

"Oh Sweetie, I'm very happy for you, but are you sure you should be announcing it yet?" her mom asked.

"We decided to hold off telling everyone just yet, but I had to tell you."

"That's probably wise… until you're farther along that is. How do you feel?"

"I feel fine – great actually. It feels worse having told you and you not be happy for us though."

"Oh honey, I couldn't be happier! Are you kidding? You are having a baby with the love of your life and *that* makes me very happy. I'm just a little nervous I guess."

"I know, I get it. Trust me, I'm nervous too. I can't even think about a nursery or a name yet. It's too soon."

"Well, stay positive okay Sweetie? Don't give in to the voices in your head – the worry and doubt. If you do, they will win. You need to focus on yourself and that baby. Take it easy, eat right, and do things that make you happy to keep your mind busy. Are you still writing?" her mom asked.

"Are you kidding me? I can't go a day without it – it's addictive. I even have a blog now," Laci chuckled.

"What's a blog?"

"Oh mother… really? You don't know what a blog is by now?"

"Why would I? You know I never get on that computer unless I'm playing one of my games, and I never go into that internet place."

Laci laughed. "It's not a place Mom. And a blog is like a diary, only I don't write secret things. I just write whatever is on my mind… that's blogging. Sometimes I write about events, life, silly stuff – anything really. A blog is on the internet. Anyone can read it if they want to."

"Why on earth do you put it out there? Do people really read it?"

"I think so. I know I have a few fans out there," Laci replied.

"Well, your dad needs help with his email – can I put him on?"

Laci laughed. "Sure, Mom."

Laci's parents were probably the least techie people on the planet. Most of the time when she called home to talk, there was always some sort of 'tech support' involved, and that day was no exception. Her dad had forgotten his email password and tried to follow the instructions to reset it, but he'd clicked 'reset' so many times, he had ten different reset codes and it finally locked him out. It took her almost twenty minutes to walk him through it over the phone, and once she managed to get him access, he found over 600 emails in his inbox. Laci laughed so hard she almost wet her pants. Turns out it had been over a year since he'd checked his mail. They were a constant source of entertainment, frustration, love and support – which is exactly what she needed that day.

*****

Mitch unloaded the truck and yelled out for Caleb. He figured he was inside the winery.

"Caleb, get out here – I need your help!"

When Caleb didn't answer right away, Mitch walked inside and found him snoring on the couch in his office.

"Wake-up lazy bones," Mitch shouted, nudging Caleb's knee so it would fall over.

"Go away. I'm tired, Dad."

"I need your help unloading the bottles from the truck, Son."

"Right now?" Caleb grumbled.

"Caleb – it's after two o'clock. Get up."

"When is Brad coming back – he does most of this."

"Your uncle has his hands full right now – he could be there a while. That's why I need you to step up and help out a little more around here. What's gotten into you lately?"

Caleb sat up and rubbed his face. "Dad, I don't… *ugh,*" he sighed.

"What is it? Spill it, Son."

"Dad – I love you, and this winery was the best thing that could have ever happened to you. It helped you find a new purpose after mom died. But it's not for me. I want to go to college in the fall."

Mitch sat down on the couch. "I always knew this day would come – when you were ready. I won't lie. I always hoped we could run the winery together as a family, but I knew it wasn't likely you would feel the same way."

"I wanted to at first, but after you and Laci met and got married, then lost the baby… it stopped being fun. I hear Evan talk about how much he loves school and I want to experience that too."

"Son, I've never been more proud of you than I am right now. I would never want to hold you back from your dreams – ever!" Mitch reached over and pulled his son over to his chest, gave him a hug, then slapped him on the back in that 'dad' kind of way. "Do you know what you want to study?"

"Yeah," Caleb smiled, scuffing his feet back and forth on the floor – nervous to say it out loud. "I want to be a chef. I'm going to enroll in the culinary program in Pennsylvania Culinary Institute, plus take some business classes. I want to open my own restaurant someday."

His answer caught Mitch off-guard, and he was unable to reply at first, shaking his head in disbelief. "Wow. I… I don't know even what to say, Son. I think that's awesome. You're serious about this?"

"I guess all those years of watching and helping you cook – how you taught me about the flavors and spices – it made me want to learn more. I didn't realize it until I took Jenny to that fancy restaurant a few weeks ago. Her cousin works there as a sous chef and gave us a tour of the kitchen."

Mitch's eyes widened. "You never told me about that. Come to think of it, you never told me about Jenny. Who in the blazes is Jenny?" Mitch looked at Caleb and raised his eyebrow, a smirk on his face.

"Oh yeah," Caleb chuckled. "Well, you guys left on your trip and you've been so busy since you got back that I haven't had a chance."

"I know – it's been a bit hectic with Brad gone. I'm sorry we've been out of touch lately."

"It's okay, Dad. I get it."

"So… Jenny is?" Mitch prodded.

"Jenny. Yeah, she works at the coffee shop in town. We graduated high school together, but I never really knew much about her or got to know her until last summer. I spilled coffee all over her one day – the lid popped off as she handed it to me. I helped her clean it up, then she made fun of me for making such a mess and creating more work for her. I don't know… there was just something about her. She had a nice smile, and I kind of liked her laugh." Caleb's cheeks were a soft shade of red and he couldn't stop smiling as he talked about her.

"I see. Sounds like you really like this girl, or has it already grown past the 'like' stage?"

"It's grown a little past that… for me anyway."

"That's what I thought. And for the record, you didn't really have to answer. It shows all over your face," Mitch smiled.

"Whatever." Caleb laughed. "Don't start teasing me, Dad."

"Me? Tease you? Why… I'm hurt that you would think I would be that insensitive, Son. *Caleb's in love… Caleb's in love…"* Mitch sang, poking fun.

"Seriously, Dad. Cut it out – you are not near as funny as you think you are." Caleb smiled, despite his attempt to hold a straight face.

Mitch's phone rang, Brad's name flashing on the screen. "Hey brother – how did your talk go? Did you explain everything to –?"

"Mitch!" Brad abruptly cut him off. "There's been an accident…"

*****

Brad and Clare arrived at the hospital and quickly made their way inside. At the main nurse's desk, Brad asked where they sent Hannah when she arrived, anxious to see her. They wouldn't tell him anything.

"Can you at least tell me if she's awake? Is she going to be okay? Why can't we visit her? What's happened?"

"Sir, I understand your concern, but unless you're a family member or her spouse, I'm afraid I can't disclose that information or give you any details about her condition."

"But she doesn't have anyone else!" he shouted in frustration. "Her grandmother is one floor up – " Brad stopped talking, turned around and took Clare by the hand, then walked away from the desk.

"Sir! Where are you going?" the nurse yelled down the hall at him.

Clare agreed. "I'd like to know that too. Where *are* we going? Shouldn't we go find Jules?"

"That's exactly what we're going to do."

Brad took Clare up to Lois' room and saw the same nurse that was on duty the other night. She nodded her head at him and smiled, seeming to remember him too, so they walked into Lois' room. Her eyes were closed, and her complexion was extremely pale. Seeing her now, Brad knew in his heart that she didn't have much time left. He sat down on the bed next to her, and gently touched her hand. Clare stood at the back of the room.

"Hi Lois. It's Brad. Are you awake?" he asked quietly.

Lois slowly turned her head and looked him in the eye – a smile immediately appeared. "Well, looky here – visitors," she said. Her voice was scratchy and he could barely hear her. "How are you, young man?"

Brad was lost in thought. *She knows it's almost over, and she is smiling. Should I tell her about Hannah? What do I do?* He swallowed, fighting back the tears. "Hi beautiful. How are you feeling?"

"You charmer you." She smiled a toothless smile. "I've been better I suppose, but I expect to be fit as a fiddle pretty soon. You look worse than me though… what's wrong?"

Her words made Brad laugh, somehow giving him a sense of peace. "Lois, I need to tell you something, and I need your help."

Lois' attention wasn't on Brad though. She peeked around his shoulder and saw Clare standing against the wall, crying.

"Clare, Sweetie! Come over here and give your grandma a hug," she demanded in a sweet tone.

Clare hesitated at first, looking to Brad for some sort of sign that it was okay. Brad smiled and nodded his head in approval, encouraging her to come over. She ran to Lois' side and wrapped her arms around her, sobbing.

"Oh Sweetheart, it's so good to see you. Don't cry my darling girl – everything will be okay."

"I know Grandma Lois – I know. I love you." Clare pulled away to wipe her face.

"Grandma loves you, honey – you are a light in my life, you know it?"

Clare smiled and nodded her head up and down in reply, too upset to talk.

"Lois, I need your help," Brad said.

"Anything, doll, but first you need to tell me what's wrong," she said.

"How did you know –,"

"A mother always knows when her kids are hurting. Now what can I do to help?" Lois asked.

"It's… it's Hannah. She was in an accident, Lois. Her horse threw her during a thunder storm. She has a head injury, but that's all I know. They brought her here by ambulance, but they won't let me see her or tell me anything because I'm not family, or her spouse. I need you to talk to the doctor and give him permission to talk to me. She needs my help, Lois. Would you do that?" he pleaded.

Lois tried to sit up on her own, but was unsuccessful. Brad raised the bed to help her, and she pressed the nurse's call button.

Within a few minutes, her nurse appeared. "You okay, Miss Lois? What's wrong honey?" the nurse asked.

Brad explained the situation to the nurse and Lois expressed her full approval of his plan.

The nurse looked at Lois. "There is only one way he can help," she began, "but it requires you to give him a medical power of attorney, Miss Lois. Do you know what that means?"

Lois nodded in agreement. "Give him whatever he needs. Please. She's my granddaughter and he loves her. He's going to marry her!" she smiled, then coughed several times. Unable to catch her breath, the nurse quickly reached around behind her and pulled out Lois' oxygen mask and placed it on her face.

"Alright, if that's your wish." The nurse turned to Brad. "Mr. Young, you'll also have to sign it in the presence of two other witnesses."

Brad's face was morose, lost in thought as he recognized that Lois' time was growing short. His mind had drifted, not hearing the nurse.

"Mr. Young, did you hear me?" the nurse reiterated.

"Huh?" he replied.

"The witnesses. Do you understand what is required?"

"Yes, I'm sorry. Well, Clare can be a witness, and maybe you could be the second? Please?" Brad asked the nurse.

The nurse looked at Lois, and Lois motioned for her to draw closer so she could whisper something in her ear. Lois said a few words, then the nurse stood back up and looked at Brad. "Alright. I'll be your second witness," she agreed.

Brad was a bit puzzled, but didn't question what had just transpired. "Wait. Does it have to be notarized or go through some other long process? I need this to be effective now or it doesn't me any good!" he asked, beginning to panic.

"No. The state of Washington doesn't require it thankfully. It's saved many a life."

Everyone finally in agreement, the nurse left to retrieve the documents and brought them back in for them to sign. "This now allows you to make decisions on Lois' behalf concerning Hannah's care… as well as Lois."

"Wait. What? What do you mean Lois' care? I thought this was just supposed to be for Hannah?" Brad suddenly realized this was the result of the whisper and looked at Lois, then took her hand and squeezed it in approval.

"She wanted herself included too," the nurse explained, handing Brad the form, but stopped just short of giving it to him. "This is a big responsibility, Mr. Young. Are you sure you're up to this?"

"Ma'am… these women are not only my past, they're my future. They mean everything to me. I'll do anything for them," he replied, then signed the form.

Lois removed her mask, then reached out and took Brad's hand and squeezed it tight. "Go find our girl. I need to know that she's okay."

"Clare – are you ready?" Brad asked.

"Um, why don't you go on? I think I'll wait here with Lois and keep her company. Just hurry, okay?" Clare said.

Clare knows too. She needs to say goodbye. He thought.

"I will, Scooter."

Brad hurried back downstairs and over to the main nurse's station, handing the first nurse the signed form and asked once again about Hannah's status. The nurse read the form and looked up at Brad, almost perturbed that he'd found a way around the system.

"Where is she? Can I please see her now or talk to the doctor, please?" Brad pleaded.

"They moved her to ICU, Mr. Young. The doctor is in with her now – I'll page him."

Brad's heart sank, mentally preparing himself for the news he was about to receive. A few minutes later, the doctor walked up to him.

"Hello Mr. Young, I'm Dr. Kinzel. Let's take a walk," he said, matter-of-factly. "Ms. Blake suffered a serious head injury during the fall. There is a great deal of swelling and fluid has built up around her brain. We're keeping an eye on it, and my hope is that it will go down on its own, but if it gets worse, we'll have to put her in a drug-induced coma to keep the swelling down. If that doesn't work, we may have to operate to relieve the pressure. There is a very high risk with that type of surgery though, due to her hypertension. Do you know if she is on medication for high blood pressure?"

Brad closed his eyes, remembering Hannah whining about her meds. "Um, yes. She has medicine, but she told me she can never remember to take it. I don't know how long it's been since she had a dose." He stared at the floor in a daze.

"Well, we'll start her on BP meds and do the best we can. Stay positive."

"Thanks, Doc. Can I see her now?"

"Of course. She's still unconscious, and seems to be stable right now, but that could change at any moment. Please don't stay long, Mr. Young."

Brad nodded in agreement, and the doctor pointed him to her room. He approached the door and paused, staring in at her. He walked inside and sat next to her on the bed. Hard as he tried to prevent them, the tears began to roll down his cheek upon seeing her red curls strewn around the pillow. He leaned in and kissed her scratched-up cheek, then detected a familiar smell permeating the air around him – an unmistakable scent. It was masked by a sterile hospital odor, but he knew it well. He moved in closer, and inhaled slowly.

Cucumber-Melon. She still uses the same shampoo after all these years. I didn't even know they still sold it. He smiled, then picked up a long curl, stretched it out, and then let it spring back into place. Like he used to do. "I finally get you back and this has to happen." He stroked her head softly. "I know you have no reason to give me a second chance, but I hope you do. I was so stupid to let you go all those years ago," he whispered. "Oh, and I have a gift for you. I'm giving the winery back to you – free and clear. You need to wake up so I can tell you in person, okay? I love you, Jules." He kissed her cheek again and sat quietly holding her hand.

Clare pulled a chair up next to Lois' bed.

"Do you want me to read to you, Grams?" Clare asked. Lois turned her head and smiled, her false teeth no longer in her mouth.

"Sure, Sweetie. But first, come sit next me so I can tell you something," Lois said in breathless words. Clare did as she asked.

"Am I in trouble?" Clare asked with a chuckle.

"Far from it my dear. I need you," Lois took a big breath, "… to give Jules a message for me."

"Grams… come on. You can tell her yourself. She's going to be fine – trust me."

"I know, but I might not be here by the time she gets better."

"Where are you…? NO. Don't you dare talk like that, Lois. You are going to get better. You will – you have to!" Clare's anxious voice rose.

"My sweet, Clare," Lois coughed – barely able to whisper. "It's okay honey. I will always be with you, but my time on this earth is coming to an end. I want you and Jules to take care of each other. Promise me that, okay?"

"I promise," Clare said, holding Lois' hand, tear trickling down her pink cheeks.

"I need you to tell Jules that there is always *grace* after the storm." Lois coughed.

Clare's chin quivered as her tears poured down. "I… I promise, Grams. What does it mean though?" Clare asked.

"She'll know, don't worry. You'll both know one day," Lois smiled.

"I love you," Clare said, and wrapped her arms around Lois. "Don't go yet, Grams," Clare whispered in her ear, crying softly.

"I'll be here forever, Clare," Lois said, pressing her hand over Clare's heart. "Now, why don't you read to me while I rest?"

"Yes ma'am." Clare wiped her eyes, then picked up the book from Lois' nightstand and sat down in the chair. She read aloud, starting at the beginning. Lois smiled and closed her eyes.

*****

Brad stood next to her, dashing in his black and white tuxedo. The winery was full of beauty, flowers of every color blooming all around them. Catching rays of sunlight, the pearls and beads sewn on Hannah's gown glistened, twinkling like stars at night. She looked into the crowd of guests seated behind them – her mom and dad were smiling from the front row, looking so proud. Mitch and Laci – holding their new baby boy – Clare, and many other family and friends were gathered around, anxiously waiting for the ceremony to begin. She didn't see her grandmother at first, but as she turned toward the door, she saw her enter. Lois was never more radiant, wearing a lovely lavender dress and hat to match in true 'Lois' fashion. She had a glow about her that Hannah hadn't seen in years. Lois walked up to Brad and Hannah, and took their hands.

"Grandma, the ceremony is about to start. What are you doing?" Hannah asked.

"I came to say goodbye my dear. I will always be with you, but my time here has ended. Before I go though, I need you to promise me that you'll give Brad a second chance. He's a 'keeper' that one – your one true love. I'm so grateful that the two of you found your way back to each other. The timing was all in God's hands from the very start." Lois looked over at Brad. "Thank you for saving my granddaughter, Brad. Without you and your love, she would have been a wandering soul. Love her well for me."

Brad smiled, but Hannah looked lost and confused.

"Grandma, where are you going? Why would you say goodbye before my wedding? I don't understand." Hannah looked around and the seats that were once filled were now empty – only her parents remained. They stood up and walked over to Lois, taking her by the hand.

"Mom? Dad? Aren't you staying?" Hannah questioned them. Her voice cracked, tears flowing from her eyes.

"We love you, Jules. We will always be here my darling," her mother said softly – her voice like an echo ringing in the distance.

"Grandma, Mom, Dad… what's going on? Please don't leave!" Hannah was sad, and suddenly realized what was happening.

"I need to go now my dear, but know that you are the pride and joy of my heart, and I love you so much. Take care of each other, and above all else, remember that there is always grace after the storm." Lois kissed Hannah on the cheek, and walked out the door – Hannah's parents at her side.

Hannah knew that was the last time she would ever see her again, yet managed a smile and turned back around.

"Brad!" Hannah yelled. "Don't go! I can't lose you too!"

Slowly, Brad drifted backwards – moving farther and farther away from her. She reached out, but was unable to touch him. He smiled. "I did it for you, Hannah," Brad whispered.

Hannah could barely hear him, his voice distorted as if under water. Her heart was overcome with a palpable, aching pain and she started to cry, then doubled over and grabbed her chest.

"She's gone," she whispered softly. "She's gone."

*****

"The tall grass hid him from her eyes as he galloped toward the ranch, but as he got closer, her face lit up at the sight—" Clare's reading was interrupted by a long, loud beep coming from one of Lois' machines. She flew out of the chair… the book fell to the floor.

"Grams, wake up! Grandma!" Clare shouted over and over, but there was no response. Her hand shook as she tried to press the call button, but two nurses had already rushed into the room. "What's wrong with her?" Clare asked in a panic, but they didn't answer. Another nurse entered the room pushing a big cart, and Clare immediately recognized the paddles sitting on top. The loud, continuous beep blared from Lois' machine. Clare knew what it meant. Lois' heart had stopped.

"Miss, I need you to step outside please," the nurse said to Clare.

"Is she going to be okay?"

There was no response. The nurses were already working on Lois, hooking her up to the paddles and trying to revive her. Slowly, Clare backed away and walked out of the room. Her chest was heavy and tight as her tears poured down like rain. In the hallway, she waited, pacing back and forth. Waiting.

"Clear!" the nurse shouted. The paddles cracked, sending a shock through Lois' chest and causing her limp body to bounce up off the bed. Clare screamed and covered her ears to drown out the noise - the dismal scene was more than she could bear. *She can't be gone! She has to be okay – she has to open her eyes and breathe! Hannah has to see her…* Clare wanted to run away and hide, but she couldn't leave.

A loud, solid tone emanated from Lois' room and Clare rushed inside, the nurses turning off her machines. Lois' body lay on the bed, lifeless and still – her skin white as snow.

"NO!" Clare screamed.

"She's gone, Sweetheart. I'm so sorry. We did everything we could," the nurse said.

"Grandma!" Clare pushed her way past the nurse and ran to Lois' bedside. "Lois?" she said softly, crying. "Grandma? Please open your eyes… *please!*" Clare pleaded. Lois' eyes were closed - her mouth agape and her lips caved in. Clare threw herself on top of Lois' chest, her cry so loud it echoed down the hall. "No!" she cried.

The nurse walked up behind Clare and patted her on the back. "I'm so sorry for your loss. I hate to do this, Sweetheart, but I'm going to have to ask you to leave the room, okay? I'll give you another minute to say goodbye."

Clare sobbed, then took a deep breath. "Wait! What about Jules, her granddaughter? She's downstairs. Brad went to find her. She needs to know."

"We'll call down and have someone tell her."

"No! I'll tell her. I need to tell Brad too. Please… don't call. Let me tell them," Clare begged.

"Alright Sweetie. I'll get you her room number."

Brad's head was bowed, silently praying for Hannah to wake, when he was startled by her faint whispers. Words. She was talking, but her eyes were still closed. He stood up and started to talk to her.

"Jules! Baby, I'm here! It's Brad. Can you hear me?" he asked.

"She's gone. She's gone," Hannah mumbled . Her head moved side to side slowly as she whispered the same phrase over and over, but her eyes never opened. Seconds later, a loud repetitive beep blared from her vitals monitor, the speed increasing between each one. Brad watched as the blood pressure numbers began to rise on the screen and his eyes grew wide, filled with hope she was waking up.

"Nurse! I need some help in here!" he yelled.

The nurse rushed in to check on her and Brad stepped away to let her work, bumping right into Clare as she came running through the door, out of breath.

"Clare!" Brad was glad to see her, but immediately noticed her fire-red eyes were filled with tears. "Clare? What's wrong?"

Clare gasped for breath. "It's Lois. I'm… I'm so sorry," she sobbed, "but I didn't have time to come get you. She's gone, Brad! She's gone!" Clare threw her arms around Brad's waist, hugging him tight and soaking his shirt with her tears.

"Oh, God no. Clare… I'm so sorry." Brad hugged Clare tight and tried to console her as she mourned, still keeping his eye on Jules. The nurse had turned off the monitor alarms and he could still hear her whispering the same words.

After a few minutes, Clare quieted her crying, and she too heard Jules' murmuring. She pulled away from Brad and looked over at her. "Is she awake? What's going on? What is she saying?" She sniffed and wiped her eyes.

"She's been saying it for the last few minutes now – *'she's gone'*, *'she's gone'* – saying it over and over, then her blood pressure shot up and that's when the nurse ran in. She's not awake though, at least I don't think so. Dreaming maybe. The nurse is checking on her now."

"She knows," Clare whispered, her eyes wide in shock.

"Knows what?" Brad asked.

"Jules knows about her grandma," Clare smiled.

"What? That's impossible. There is no way she could know."

Clare looked up at Brad. "Some things in this life are impossible to explain or understand, but trust me… she knows. I'd bet my life on it."

They walked back over to the end of Hannah's bed, her muttering now barely audible. The nurse had just finished listening to her heart. "What happened to her? Is she okay?" Brad asked the nurse.

The nurse folded the stethoscope around her neck. "She's dreaming, which is actually a good sign. Must have been a doozy of a dream though – her BP spiked pretty high. That's not good. One more episode like that and it could do even more damage," she replied.

"Wait. What kind of damage?" Clare asked, her brow furrowed.

The nurse placed her hand on Clare's arm in comfort. "Her brain is functioning normally for now, but it's in a fragile state. If her blood pressure doesn't stay at a normal rate or lower, her heart could fibrillate and that could cause her to have a heart attack. She's resting now and it's down, so she's out of danger. Let's hope it stays that way." The nurse smiled and walked out.

Another hour passed by, and Hannah eventually stopped her rambling. She remained unconscious, but no worse and no more dreams. Clare called her foster parents to give them the news about Lois, and they gave her permission to stay at the hospital for the night with Brad.

She sat down in the chair next to Hannah's bed with a magazine in hand, and it wasn't long before she nodded off from sheer exhaustion.

Brad watched her and realized how long and hard this day had been for her. A day that started off as a fun outing with her big sister, ended up being the worst day ever. She suffered the loss of Lois, her surrogate grandmother in all respects, and was now worried about the possibility of losing Jules too. *Lois. I can't believe she's gone.* The reality hit him. He had lost a friend too, even though they only knew each other a short time. His face resting in the palms of his hands, he wept softly, careful not to wake Clare. The love of his life lay in front of him, fighting for her life and he couldn't do anything about it. She didn't even know about her grandmother's death. *How will I tell her? Please God, please bring her back to me!* Before he could pray another word, one of Hannah's monitor alarms began to beep again incessantly.

Clare was awoken immediately by the sound and they both rushed to Hannah's bedside to find her eyes wide open, staring at the ceiling.

"Jules! Oh thank you God! You're awake!" Brad's heart overflowed, finally able to talk to her.

Hannah turned her head toward Brad, but her eyes and face showed only anger. Clare was standing on the opposite side of Hannah's bed. She looked up at Brad and shrugged, not sure what to make of Hannah's reaction.

"Hey sis… I'm here too. I'm so glad to see you!" Clare said. Hannah looked over at Clare and smiled. "Hey, Sunshine!" Clare said in a sweet voice.

Hannah's nurse entered the room. "Let's give her some space while I give her a check-up, okay?" the nurse asked, then pointed them away from Hannah's bed. She disarmed the monitor alarms and started her evaluation.

They stepped away, but Brad couldn't take his eyes off of Jules. He couldn't understand why she reacted to him that way, but chalked it up to her being scared, not realizing what was going on. "It's okay Jules – Clare and I are here. You're going to be okay!" he yelled over at her from the other side of the room.

"She sure looked pissed at you," Clare said.

"Really? I hadn't noticed," Brad replied, trying to brush it off.

"Who is going to tell her about her grandma? When do we tell her?" Clare asked.

"Let's worry about that later. I'm sure the doctor will let us know when the time is right."

The nurse walked over to them.

"How is she? Is she going to be alright?" Brad asked anxiously.

"She's stable, and her blood pressure is normal, but the doctor needs to evaluate her and check the swelling in her brain – see if it's gone down."

"Can I talk to her now?"

"Keep it short. She's had a head trauma and is still on shaky ground. One at a time," the nurse replied.

"Clare? Do you want to talk to her first?" Brad asked.

"I think you'd better do it. I'm not sure I can see her yet. I'm afraid I might not be able to hold it in about Lois." Clare stepped into the hall to give them some privacy.

Brad took a deep breath, then walked to Hannah's side. She turned her head toward Brad and blinked several times, then closed her eyes and took a deep breath, seeming frustrated. After a few seconds, she opened her eyes again.

"Get…," she paused, "… out," Hannah said in a cracked voice, her brow furrowed. "Go." Her voice was getting stronger. She turned away from him.

Brad took her hand, but she pulled it away from him hastily. "Jules… I know you're scared, but everything is going to be okay. The B&B is fine and I'm taking care of everything so just relax. Do you remember what happened?" Brad wanted to explain why she was there, thinking it would help her make sense of things and calm down.

"Go now!" Hannah yelled, the beeps from her heart monitor going off more rapidly.

The nurse came running into Hannah's room. "Mr. Young, I'm afraid you'll have to leave. We have to keep her blood pressure down. Please, step outside," she urged.

"I don't understand! What did I do?" Brad left without a fight, but his heart ached at the thought of Jules not wanting him there. *She's obviously scared and confused, probably doesn't even remember what happened. She did hit her head after all.* His mind raced, fearing the worst.

"What happened?" Clare asked as Brad entered the hall.

"She doesn't want me in there. She told me to 'get out'."

"She's just scared, Brad. Don't worry."

"No, it's more than that. I should go – let her get some rest."

Clare's eyes suddenly grew wide. "Brad, wait! I know what's wrong! She still thinks you're selling the winery! That's the last thing we talked about before the accident – she doesn't know the truth! You have to tell her."

"I'm such a fool. Of course! I totally forgot in all the chaos today. But I can't tell her. She won't listen to me – you should tell her."

"Oh no! I can't. You don't want me to tell her, trust me. I'll just screw it up. I think this is something you're going to have to tell her on your own, but maybe now isn't the best time."

"Yeah, you're right. I don't know what I was thinking. She needs her rest. Why don't you go in and see her? I'll talk to the nurse and ask her if we should tell her about Lois or if we should wait."

"I'm scared, Brad. I don't want her to be mad at me. I need her to be okay." Clare's eyes welled with tears.

Brad put his arm around her shoulder in a side-hug as they both stared into Hannah's room through the door. "She could never be mad at you. You're her sister remember? Trust me, I'm the one she likes being mad at. You however… well, you're her hero. Go on," he urged.

"I hope you're right."

Clare walked into Hannah's room, quietly moving toward her bed. The nurse was still in the room keeping an eye on her blood pressure, but nodded to Clare and smiled, approving her presence in the room.

"Hi Jules… it's me, Clare."

Hannah opened her eyes slowly, smiling up at Clare. She tried to speak, but her throat was too dry.

"Here, give her a drink of water." The nurse said, handing Clare a cup of water. Clare put the straw in Hannah's mouth and watched her take a few sips.

"Thank you, Clare," Hannah said in a dry voice. "I… I'm so sorry," she stuttered.

Clare sat down on the edge of Hannah's bed. "What are you sorry for? I was the one who wanted to go horseback riding. If it hadn't been for me wanting to go, we would never have been in that storm. I'm the one that's sorry, Jules." Clare looked down at the bed, tears rolling down her cheeks.

"Clare. I love you. I wanted to give you…," Hannah took a breath, "… to give you your birthday wish. I had so much fun. *He's* the one that ruined everything," she said, pointing to Brad still standing in the hall. No sooner had she said the words, and the monitor began to beep incessantly.

"Calm down, Hannah," the nurse said, then looked up at Clare. "Miss, you're going to have to leave now. She needs her rest."

"I… I know – just one more minute, that's all I promise," Clare pleaded.

"One more," the nurse agreed.

"I love you too, Jules, but there's something you should know. I wasn't going to tell you, but… but I was the one that messed everything up. I overheard Brad talking to that guy and it sounded like he was going to sell the estate, but I didn't hear the whole conversation. That's not what he is doing. I didn't fully understand it, and I jumped to conclusions. He told me everything. Brad's the one I called when you got hurt and if it weren't for him, you might have died out there. He called the stables to send help, and he kept talking to me on the phone the whole time. I was so scared, Jules. I don't know what I would have done without him. He loves you. He loves you so much. He's making everything better at the winery for you – trust me. Just give him a chance okay? I was wrong." Clare talked so fast, she could barely catch her breath between words, then waited for Hannah's reaction after telling her the truth.

Hannah smiled as a tear rolled down her pale face, then suddenly an image flashed through her memory. It was an image of her dream. *Grandma. She said goodbye to me. She's gone! Oh God, no… please no!* She started coughing and the beeps from her monitor sped up, but this time her heart rate kept rising, climbing higher and higher. Within seconds, she was in cardiac arrest. Two more nurses ran inside and pushed Clare away from the bed.

"Jules! I'm sorry!" Clare shouted. "Please, Jules! Don't you leave me too!"

Brad ran in to the room and pulled Clare out, still screaming Jules' name. He held Clare to his chest as she cried, watching the nurses as they worked to keep Hannah's heart beating.

Thud thud…

Thud thud…

Thud thud.

Whatever happened that night, whatever memory Hannah experienced, increased her already high blood pressure to the point that it caused a mild heart attack. Thankfully, they were able to restart her heart. Combined with the swelling in her brain, however, she drifted into a coma.

They waited…

One week passed.

The doctor tried to encourage them. "It's the brain's way of protecting itself – just be patient", he said.

They waited…

A second week, come and gone. Still no change.

Day after day, Brad was slowly losing hope.

I'm tired of being patient, he thought.

13 – Beginning Again

Mitch stared at his phone as he sat with Laci in her doctor's office waiting room, anxious for Brad's call, and nervous for their first sonogram appointment since the miscarriage. He remembered vividly the last time they were there, how they had exited through the back door. A solemn ending to a once hopeful beginning. Today however, they began again.

"Brad will call as soon as Hannah wakes up. She's *going* to wake up. She has to," Laci said, trying to assure him.

"It's been two weeks and she's still not responding. She could be in a coma for months, or years – what if she never wakes up?" Mitch rambled. His heart was keen to Brad's pain, knowing how it felt when he almost lost Laci to cancer last year.

Laci shifted in her seat to face him. "Look at me, Luke Mitchell Young. I know this baby is going to be fine and I know Hannah will wake up. Trust me. I just know it. We have to have faith, okay?" She took his hand and gave it a squeeze.

"Laci Young?" the nurse called out from the side door. Mitch smiled and kissed her on the cheek, then they walked back to the exam room.

After Laci was prepped and ready, the sonographer left and the doctor came in the room to perform the sonogram. "Good morning, Laci, Mitch. How are you both today?" the doctor asked, making conversation to lighten the tension in the room.

"Hi Dr. Greene. We don't usually see you this early in the visit. Is everything okay?" Laci asked.

"I'm sure everything is fine. I wanted to perform the ultrasound myself though, in light of your history. I hope that's alright."

"Of course, that's fine. I'm glad you're here… makes me feel better actually," Laci smiled.

"Well, let's take a look and listen then, shall we? This time, I'm going to use a 3-D Doppler ultrasound. We can listen for the heartbeat, and check to see how the blood is flowing through the baby's umbilical cord at the same time."

The doctor moved the wand over Laci's tummy and within seconds, a loud pulse came echoing through the little speaker. A strong heartbeat.

"Thank God! I hear her!" Laci exclaimed.

Mitch couldn't speak. The joy on his face was enough and no words were needed. Their baby was healthy and everything looked good. The doctor pointed to a blob on the screen, and as they watched, they saw a tiny little arm raise up, then go back down again.

"Oh look! He's waving to mom and dad!" the doctor said, pointing to the screen as they watched the baby's hand go up slowly "Congratulations to you both. You have a healthy baby in there. It's a little early yet to see what the sex is, but we should be able to tell next month."

Laci looked at Mitch. "Mitch? I… I don't want to find out this time. Let's be surprised."

"What? Are you sure?"

"I don't care what we have. I want it to be like Christmas morning when it arrives!"

Mitch laughed. "You would find a way to tie this to Christmas."

"She's actually pretty close, Mr. Young."

"What do you mean?" he asked.

"Based on her measurements, it looks like it just might *be* Christmas when this baby arrives. I'd say your due date is on or around December 23rd."

Laci's eyes grew as big as bottle caps. "Are you kidding me? Oh Mitch… this is going to be the *best* Christmas ever!"

Back home, Laci and Mitch shared the good news with their kids and Mitch's mom, then Laci called her parents to tell them. Everyone was overjoyed to hear the good news about the baby, but Mitch felt somewhat guilty for celebrating, knowing Brad was hurting on the other side of the continent. He picked up his phone and dialed.

"Hey little brother. How are things in the NC?" Brad asked, his voice melancholy.

"Everything's fine here, but I'm calling to see how you are doing. How is Hannah? Any change?"

"Nothing. I visit her every day and still no change. I can't help but think I did this to her somehow. She was so mad at me that night."

"Don't go there. You said yourself that Clare shared the truth with her before she took a turn for the worse. You can't blame yourself," Mitch tried to console him.

"Something happened though. Clare said she was smiling at first, but then it was like she had a terrible thought and it caused her heart rate to shoot up."

"Hang on to her smile and don't give up. She needs you there. Clare needs you too. When Hannah wakes up, she'll have to regain her strength, and then she'll have to cope with the loss of her grandmother. It's still amazes me how everything happened at once."

"Yeah, that little thunderstorm caused a whole different type of storm around here. My head is still spinning."

"I was in the middle of storm once, and I heard Laci's voice. It changed the course of both our lives. Maybe that's the only way God can get our attention sometimes – he wakes us up with a storm so he can pour out his grace. Hang in there, okay? I don't think he's finished yet." Mitch always had a gift for putting Brad at ease, no matter what was going on.

"I'm ready for a little grace I can tell you that. In the meantime, Clare and I are taking care of guests and working on getting things ready for the grand re-opening of the B&B. She's been a huge help. I'm not sure I could keep everything running if she wasn't here. She's a special kid – I can see why Jules is so crazy about her, although she drives me *crazy* sometimes. Teenage girls are a complete mystery to me. One minute she's fine and happy, the next minute she's whining and crying about her hair. Who does that?" Brad laughed.

"I know what you mean. Laci's little Emma is growing up fast. She'll be thirteen soon and I've just learned to leave the house or go hide in the winery when she is in one of her 'moods'. It's the safest place I know."

"Well, I'd better get back to work. Tell Laci and the kids I said 'hey'."

"Um… there's one more thing actually. I wasn't going to tell you, but I don't think I can keep it from you much longer," Mitch was hesitant.

"Spill. What's going on? It's okay – I'm a big boy," Brad joked.

"Well, God willing… you're going to be an Uncle again soon. Laci's pregnant."

The momentary pause felt like forever as Mitch awaited Brad's reply. "Let me guess… she got pregnant on your little road trip up here, didn't she? She had to have. Jeez… she's pretty fertile for a forty-something gal isn't she?"

"Hey buddy, that's my wife you're talking about."

"Well, she is!" Brad laughed. "Look, I'm really happy for you Mitch – for both of you. Honest. I can't wait to have another little niece or nephew."

"Thanks brother. We're pretty excited, especially after today. We saw the baby wave at us during our sonogram appointment – right on the screen! Heartbeat was loud and strong too. That was a huge relief."

"I guess her visit to the rain paid off in more ways than one then. Maybe there really is something to her theory."

"I think there is – it's served her pretty well so far," Mitch replied.

"Thanks for telling me. It's nice to hear some good news for a change."

"Try to stay positive about Hannah. She's going to come out of this and you two are going to be together. I'll let you go, but keep me posted okay?

"You got it. Love ya," Brad said.

"Love you too, man."

Mitch made his way out to the winery and saw Laci sitting in the office, but she didn't notice him approaching. Before walking in, he simply stopped to stare, still in awe that she was his. She was wearing her favorite pink Cannon Beach t-shirt, and that day, wore her glasses instead of contacts. It changed the whole look of her face – somehow making her look even smarter than she already was, if that was even possible. Laci was back to her old self – happy, content, full of life, and beaming her beautiful smile. Her blonde hair fell around her shoulders in loose curls – what she called her 'sexy hair day', and it brought a smile to his face. *How did I ever get so lucky?* He thought. *I know it was you, God, but it's still hard to believe sometimes. Why is it, that even after we both spent over 20 years with another spouse, I feel like she was always meant to be mine? I guess timing really is everything…* Laci looked up and smiled, waving him in.

"Hey Darlin', what are you doing out here?" he asked.

"Needed a little breathing room I guess. The kids were going nuts in there with all the baby news. They're already working on a list of names. Travis thinks we should have a boy and name him Jake, after his favorite cartoon character. Emma started to argue with him and said we were having a girl."

"Did she suggest a name too?" Mitch asked, sitting on the desk beside her.

"A few, but she was mostly messing around with Travis. She said it's too soon to pick a real name."

"Ah. Well, maybe she's still a bit uncertain about things. That's normal."

"I know. Until I'm as big as a house, I guess I'll be a bit uncertain too."

"Do you have a name in mind yet?" Mitch asked.

"No, but whatever name we do choose, I want it to be written on our hearts. The minute we say it, it will be a name that simply feels right to all of us. Does that sound silly?"

"Of course not. I believe this baby will be a new beginning for our family. The tie that binds, so to speak."

Laci stood up and wiggled between his legs, wrapping her arms around his waist. "You never cease to amazing me, Mr. Young. Have I told you how much I love you lately? Because I'm absolutely crazy about you." She smiled and brushed his lips with a gentle kiss.

"Good, because you're stuck with me, Darlin'," he said. He pulled her in tight, resting his chin on her head, and enjoyed the tenderness of the moment.

After a few minutes, Laci looked up at him. "Now, are you going to update me on Brad and Hannah? I know you called him."

"Nothing gets past you does it?" he laughed. "Well, I wish I had good news, but there's no change. She's still in a coma, and he's strung out worrying about her, taking care of Clare, remodeling the B&B, helping guests, and spending every other waking minute at the hospital with Hannah. I feel helpless. He was with me every minute when Karin was sick and never left my side. I can't help but think I've abandoned him when he needs me most."

"Don't you dare think like that, Mitch Young! You are an amazing brother and he knows it. He doesn't expect you to leave your wife and kids. He didn't have any other family *but* you back then remember? It makes a difference. You're supporting him by being here and taking care of your family's business – just like he did when you were with me. He'll get through this, and she is going to wake up. It's all in God's timing – and his timing is not always our own."

"You're right. I'm just worried about him that's all."

"I know, babe. I know."

*****

The patio and fire pit were finally finished and Brad stood back to take in the view, wishing his Jules was there to see it with him. He smiled, and knew in his heart she would see it soon though. After a quick shower, he got dressed, prepped the breakfast for the next morning, and headed off to the hospital. When he arrived, he found Clare sitting by her bed, reading Hannah's favorite Nicholas Sparks book, *The Lucky One*. She visited her every day and read for at least an hour. After finishing the book, she would start reading it again from the beginning. Clare was determined to be at her side when she woke.

"Hey Squirt… care if I sit in a spell?" Brad asked.

Clare tilted her head back and smiled at an upside-down Brad, standing directly behind her chair. "I guess. You're a crappy reader though. You might even wake her up and scare her with your horrible pronunciation and monotone voice. Better stick to talking out loud for her sake, dude," Clare giggled.

"Ouch, that hurts. You really know how to hurt a guy when he's down," Brad joked, walking around in front of her.

He had grown quite fond of the back and forth banter between him and Clare, and was thankful that he had her in his life. "I got some good news today. Want to hear?" he asked.

"Sure! Let me guess… you're a new member of the AARP?"

"Ha ha… very funny. No, I'm actually going to be a new uncle soon! Laci is pregnant."

"Oh that's awesome! Will she bring the baby up here so we can see it after it's born?" Clare's excitement made Brad feel even better.

"I'm sure they will. You'll be the baby's honorary aunt you know, seeing as you're like my little sister now too."

Clare's expression shifted from one of excitement to humbled, shocked by Brad's comment. "Are you serious? You really think of me like your little sister after all I've done? If it weren't for me, Jules wouldn't even be laying there right now."

"Stop. You're not allowed to take on that burden remember? That was our deal. And yes, I am proud to call you my little sister," Brad knelt down next to her, now at eye level. "You saved my life, kid. I don't know what I'd have done these last several weeks without you."

"You're not bad for a 'Putz' either I guess," Clare laughed and punched Brad in the shoulder, nearly knocking him off balance.

"You're too kind," he replied.

"Well, I need to head out. I've got homework to do. Finals are coming up," Clare said. They stood up and she hugged him goodbye.

"Will you be out for dinner tonight?" Brad asked.

"Nah. I need to study. Thanks though. I'll be out tomorrow."

"Okay Squirt. Have a good night."

"You too. And call me if –"

"I know… if anything changes. Don't worry, I will," he smiled.

Hannah's room was mostly quiet – accompanied by a constant beeping melody from her machine. At times, it sounded like a freight train blaring through the silence. Other times, it sounded far, far away, like a distant echo. He was about to sit down when Hannah's doctor stopped by to do his last rounds and check on her.

"Hello, Mr. Young. How are you this evening?" the doctor asked.

"I'd be a lot better if you'd give me some good news, Doc. Anything at all."

The doctor folded his clipboard into his chest and smiled. "Well you're in luck then. I did a scan of her brain today and all of the swelling is gone. She's out of danger, Mr. Young and with any luck, she'll be waking up very soon. I can't say for certain when that will be, but the odds are definitely in her favor. Don't give up on her," he said.

Brad's heart overflowed and he covered his mouth with his hand, unable to reply at first.

"So you're telling me she's going to wake up, and she'll be okay? I mean… will she be the same Hannah she was before?"

"I'm optimistic that she'll wake up at some point, but with any brain injury, we won't know the extent of the damage, if any, until she's awake. Stay positive, Mr. Young. Given that it's only been a little over two weeks so far, I think she's got a great chance of a full recovery. Once she does wake, she may have some trouble speaking at first or getting her balance, but again, it's too early to tell. She may have no trouble at all, so let's not jump to conclusions yet, okay? I have a good feeling about her. She's a fighter that one."

"Oh you have no idea, Doc… that redheaded beauty is as strong as they come," Brad smiled.

After the doctor left, Brad decided to sit on the bed next to Hannah. He scooted her legs over and nestled in beside her. On the nightstand was her favorite cucumber-melon scented lotion, so he reached over and poured some on her hand, then gently massaged it into her soft skin. "Did you hear the doc, Jules? You're getting better! The swelling is down in your brain, so that means you have to wake up now – no more excuses, Red," he said aloud, then paused. "You know, if you were awake right now, this would be a lot more fun. I might even give you a back rub if you were really nice. Alright then, if you're going to keep sleeping, I'll fill you in on the latest. My sister-in-law Laci is going to have a baby. She's due at Christmas. Can you believe it? I'm going to be an uncle again." He looked at her face and brushed the hair from her eyes, gently stroking the side of her soft cheek, then sighed.

"Come back to me, Jules. I need you here with me. Andréa said to tell you that she needs a girl's night out, and we need to have our grand re-opening of the winery soon. I can't do it without you," he paused, holding back the tears.

"You'll be glad to know that I finally finished the wine bar, and remodeled the patio. The fire pit is ready to go too, so I think it's time you stop messing around and wake up, dang it!" his voice was louder than he realized.

Hannah's nurse stepped in the room. "Mr. Young, is everything okay in here?" she asked, having heard him from outside.

"Oh, sorry Annie. I'm just giving Jules the third degree for sleeping in so late," Brad smiled.

"Well, you give her the third degree for me too, Sweetie. Maybe that will do the trick today," she smiled and went on her way. Annie was a good-sized African-American woman, probably in her late sixties, and originally from Louisiana. She would bring in some of her amazing bayou cooking to make sure Brad had a good meal every night.

The nurses had all become quite fond of him and Clare over the last couple of weeks, now considered 'regulars' unfortunately.

"Jules… I need to tell you something. I've told you before, but I need to tell you again. Your grandma passed away the day you had your accident. We laid her to rest in the back of your family's estate next to your parents. There wasn't really a service – I figured you'd want to be there, you know? I'm so sorry, Jules." He squeezed some more lotion in his hands, then started working on the other hand.

"There's something else you need to know. Even though Mitch and I own your estate right now, we won't for long. You see, we are donating it back to you and Clare. It's yours, and you should run it. It's my gift to you. I love you, Jules – I always have. I was a fool to leave you back then, and I knew it the minute I walked away. Please wake up, Darlin'. I'd rather have you awake and mad at me than this. Clare and I both need you."

You are my one and only, you big Putz! Why on earth can't you hear me? I've been screaming at you for days now but nothing I do makes any difference. I can't break free of this place. I should have listened to my heart that day. I knew you couldn't have sold my family's estate like that. You have to help me find my way back, Brad. I need you too! I know my Grandma is gone. She said goodbye to me and I'm okay. I know about Laci too – and I saw their baby. It's a boy. You're going to have a new nephew! He's beautiful, and looks just like Laci - he'll be very special. Thank you for taking care of Clare for me. It sounds like you two have become friends. I always knew you had it in ya. She's right though, you are a terrible reader. Grandma was right too… you are a keeper. I love you, Brad Young! Now if I can just get back and –

Brad was busy massaging Hannah's hand when he felt her wrist twitch. He jerked his head up in excitement, hoping to see her eyes open. He searched her face, anxiously waiting for a sign – for something else to happen. Waiting.

Nothing. Probably just reflexes, he thought.

I did that! You felt it too, didn't you? Hold on… I'll try to do it again, only bigger this time. Don't give up on me, okay? It's my love for you – I know it now. I have to let go of the past and grab hold of my future with you. It's you, Brad – it's always been you!

Without warning, Hannah's other arm twitched and even shook the bed a little. Then she squeezed the hand he was massaging. Brad hopped off her bed and started pacing the floor. It was happening!

"Annie, get in here! I think she's waking up!" he yelled.

Finally! You see me! I'm coming back to you, Brad. Now if I can just open…

Annie came running in the room and checked Hannah's vitals. She pulled back her eyelids and flashed a light in her eyes. "Her pupils are dilating. It looks like our girl is waking up," she said with a big smile on her face. "You must have really told her a thing or two, didn't you?"

Brad smiled. "I think the hand massage did the trick," he jested.

Hannah's monitor started to beep – each one coming faster and faster as if the machine itself were coming to life. Intently watching her face, Brad waited patiently, and then he saw it. A slight movement in her eyelids. Again, they fluttered.

Once. Twice. Three times.

Finally, her eyes were wide open. They bounced around the room, unable to focus on any one thing, until she looked at Annie and her gaze remained fixed on her.

"Good morning, beautiful!" Annie said to her in a loud voice. "My name is Annie. I'm your nurse. You've been asleep for almost three weeks… it's nice to have you back. I need you to follow my finger if you can, okay?" The nurse moved her finger from side to side and Hannah followed it – slow and steady. The second pass however, Hannah didn't follow the nurse's finger back to the other side. Her gaze stopped at Brad.

Brad's eyes lit up as he smiled at her, unable to hold back his tears. "Hey beautiful. I've missed you," he whispered.

Hannah blinked slowly, as if she was answering him in her own way, then smiled a crooked smile.

"Mr. Young, would you mind stepping out for a few minutes. The doctor is on his way, and I need to check some of her reflexes and give her a thorough exam. I promise it won't take long," Annie smiled.

"Sure, of course." Brad took Hannah's hand in his. "I'm not going anywhere okay? I'll be right outside that door. I love you, Jules. I love you with all my heart." Brad lifted her hand and kissed the top, then gently laid it back down on the bed. "Thank you, Annie."

"My pleasure, Mr. Young. Now go get some dinner and don't worry," Annie replied.

Brad left Hannah's room, overwhelmed by what had just transpired. He walked aimlessly down the hall, lost in thought and decided to go outside and get some fresh air. On his way though, he came upon a small chapel and instead, walked inside. The doors closed behind him – alone in a quiet, peaceful place. He walked to the front, sat down in a small pew, and lowered his head into his hands. In that place, he wept more than he had in years and felt the weight of his burdens lift off. The words flowed out of him…

"Lord, I am so grateful for that woman and for you seeing your way to open her eyes again. Thank you. I know I don't deserve her love. I've screwed up more times that I can admit. I guess you already know that though, huh? I'm so sorry I left her all those years ago. I knew then she and I were meant to be together, but I took my own path. And no, that path didn't quite work out the way I had hoped. So, if it's okay with you, I'd like to have a chance to make it right. I need her in my life, Lord. I think she needs me too. I don't do this praying thing all that well, but I'm hoping you can see your way to opening her heart so she'll let me in. I'll do right by her – I promise. All I need is another chance – a chance to begin again. Jules is my new beginning."

He wiped his eyes, and walked out.

Brad grabbed a sandwich from the vending machine, then after a call to Clare to give her the news, and a short call to Mitch and Laci, he made his way back to Hannah's room. The doctor was visiting with Nurse Annie in the hall.

"Hey Doc. Everything okay in there? How is she?"

"Mr. Young, congratulations. We took her back for an MRI and it came back clear – no damage whatsoever." Brad sighed a breath of relief. "It's remarkable actually, and she is already doing better than expected – she's even talking. Some slight stuttering, but otherwise no trouble. Even that will pass soon. I'd say she might even be able to go home next week if she continues to do well," he said with a smile.

"What? Are you… are you serious? She's really okay?"

"Go see for yourself. She's asking for you. But keep it brief – it's late and she needs to rest. She's a lucky young woman, Mr. Young."

"I'm the lucky one, Doc." Brad's face beamed. He looked inside Hannah's room, and saw her looking right at him. *It's now or never, Brad. Don't be a wuss! Just tell her.* He was more nervous than he had been in years, but he walked in using his 'John Wayne' stride, as if it would give him some sort of added courage.

Hannah smiled as he sat down on the side of her bed, and at first, no words were exchanged. Finally, she spoke.

"I…," struggling to speak at first. "I've missed you too," Hannah said. Her sweet freckled-face gleamed.

Brad eyes filled with tears, then he leaned down and kissed her cheek, brushing the hair from her eyes. "God, I love you, Jules. Do you know how scared I was? I thought I had lost you forever. I can't lose you – not ever, do you hear me? I know this probably isn't the time, but you need to know that I was never going to sell the estate. What Clare overheard was me making it into something you would have forever – I'm donating it back to you, Jules. And another thing, I don't care what I have to do to prove it to you, but I'm here to stay – forever. I am, and have always been, madly in love with you Jules McRae, or Hannah Blake, or whatever other names you have. There has never been, or ever will be, any other woman who I want by my side all the days of my life. You're it for me, Red… my one and only. I don't have a ring or anything yet, but I'll get you one bigger and better than the last one, I promise."

"Brad… I –," she tried to interrupt.

"Hold on Darlin', I'm not finished yet. What I'm trying to say is, I should have never left you back then. You were the best thing that ever happened to me and I'm not about to walk away again. I love you, Jules. You don't have to give me an answer now. I know you've been through a lot, but I couldn't wait any longer. Basically I'm asking if you'll marry me. I want to take care of you and love you forever, and run the estate by your side. So, that's it I guess. Now you can talk."

"Gee… thanks," she replied with a quiet giggle. Hannah's arm shook as she lifted it to touch his cheek. "Last I checked, I – already – had – a ring." Her words were broken and slow.

Brad's mouth dropped. "Does that mean what I think it means?"

"I would check the YES box if there had been a note, but I didn't see one." Hannah's smile lit up the room.

Brad was so happy, he lunged forward and tried to kiss her, but in his clumsy excitement, his arm gave out from under him and his forehead smacked against her lips. Her lips were so dry the impact cracked her bottom lip open and caused it to bleed.

"Ouch… that kind of hurt," she giggled. Her speech was improving by the minute.

"Aww geez, Jules. I'm so sorry! Are you okay?" He felt horrible, then grabbed a tissue and gently held it to her lip.

"No, I think I'm crazy," she said in a muffled voice through the tissue, then pulled it away. "I'm crazy in love with you, and as it turns out, I'm even crazy enough to marry you. Now hurry up and kiss me before I change my mind," she smiled.

Brad pushed her red curls out of her face, and tucked them behind her ear. Even in that moment, seeing her laying in that hospital bed wearing an ugly gown, no make-up, and not smelling her best, she was the most beautiful woman in the world. He slid his hand behind her neck and slowly leaned in toward her. Their lips met with a familiar tenderness, and right then, the past melted away.

After a few seconds passed, she pulled away. "By the way, I know."

Brad looked confused. "What do you mean, 'you know'?" he asked.

"I know Grandma is gone – she told me goodbye."

"But how? I don't get it." Brad couldn't fathom her having knowledge of her grandma's passing.

"I heard every word. I was asleep, but my mind was awake," Hannah swallowed, then pointed to her water cup.

"Oh, here. I'm sorry. I bet you are pretty thirsty."

Hannah took several drinks of her water, then continued. "I had a dream, but it wasn't like a normal dream. I don't remember everything, but I saw Grandma there, and she told me 'goodbye'. She also told me to give you a second chance – that we were brought together because of… God's perfect timing." She smiled, and a few tears rolled down her red cheeks. Exhaustion had set in, obvious as she took a deep breath. "I should have been there with her. Did she suffer much?"

"No, not at all. Clare was reading to her and she just went to sleep. She was in no pain and Clare said she was even smiling."

Hannah smiled. "That's exactly the way she would have wanted it. She adored Clare. I'll miss her so much, but I know she's in a good place. She's at peace."

"Lois was quite a lady. I knew I liked her the minute we met. I'm sorry, Jules. I hate that you had to lose her during all of this, but I'm so glad you were able to say goodbye in a way that was special to you," he paused and stared at her. "I don't want to leave, but I need to go and let you rest – doctor's orders. You've had an eventful evening."

Hannah squeezed Brad's hand, then motioned for him to come closer. "Brad?"

"Yeah, Jules?"

"I… I love you," she whispered.

Before Brad could reply, they heard loud, clunky footsteps echoing down the hall outside Hannah's room, and within minutes Clare appeared. Brad laughed.

"Hi Clare," he said, without turning around.

"Hey Putz," she replied. Hannah's eyes grew wide at her reference to Brad. "Hi, Jules! God, it's good to see you! Oh, and don't worry… that was just a joke between us. We're cool, don't worry," Clare explained. Hannah smiled in relief.

"Well, on that note, I'll take off and let you two have a minute to catch up," Brad said, kissing Hannah goodbye.

"Oooh! Someone made up with his girlfriend," Clare teased, giggling.

"Goodbye, Clare. See you tomorrow. Don't stay too long, she needs to rest and you need to study," Brad said as he walked out, waving his hand in the air.

"Yeah, yeah….I'm good," Clare replied. "He's so over-protective now," she smiled.

Hannah reached up to Clare, wanting a hug. Clare hesitated at first, but wrapped her arms around Hannah and broke down crying.

"I've missed you, Jules. I was so…" Clare cried. "I was so scared I'd lost you too."

"I know, sis. I'm back now, and I'll be home soon," Hannah replied.

14 – Timing is Everything

Summer was in full swing. The pink roses Hannah's dad planted years ago were blooming, along with the wildflowers that surrounded the estate. Bugs and birds filled the air with their chirping and buzzing, making the season complete. Hannah was recovering nicely since she came home from the hospital, and as she settled back into the routine at the B&B, she felt happier and more confident as each day passed.

Between Brad's carpentry skills and Laci's behind-the-scenes website updates and marketing savvy, the winery was receiving more attention than ever. Guests were calling in from all over to book their stay, and the winery business had almost doubled since they started changing things, adding the Young Vines label to their inventory and pulling in more grapes from around the local region. It was Brad's love for Hannah however, that moved him to make the estate into something more than just a business. He wanted it to be her future, where her passions could be lived out and she would have a legacy to leave her family in years to come. He put his whole heart into fixing it up for her, despite all the obstacles. The results were breathtaking and guests were raving about it – calling it the perfect sanctuary – a place to escape and relax.

The grand re-opening event was that weekend and everyone's emotions were running high – especially Hannah's – wanting everything to be perfect. Before the accident, she had one speed… fast. Since then, she wasn't quite back to her regular pace, which frustrated her beyond belief. Brad, however, was taking matters into his own hands and called for reinforcements, unbeknownst to her.

*****

"So, you're all set for tomorrow right? Everyone is packed and ready?" Brad asked Mitch, stressing out about the weekend ahead.

"We fly out at seven a.m. our time, and by the time we land, rent a car and drive there, we should arrive by early afternoon. You're cooking lunch, right?" Mitch asked.

"You know it, brother. Just get here! Jules is stressing out and she needs all the support she can get right now. Are you certain Laci is up for the trip?"

"Laci is fine. She's five months along and everything is going great. I promise. I wouldn't bring her out there if I wasn't sure. Besides, *my* life would be the one in danger if we didn't come, trust me."

"Alright, I trust you."

"Do you think Hannah has any idea about the surprise you have in store for her?" Mitch asked.

Brad laughed. "I don't think so. I'd be shocked if she did. She's been so distracted with her recovery that she's not been able to do much else, which is how I wanted it. She feels better though, she's even starting to meddle in the event planning and freaking out about all the little details. I need Laci here like *yesterday*, brother." Brad heard Hannah call out to him from the kitchen. "Hey Mitch, Jules just yelled for me so I'd better go check on things. One quick favor though?"

"Anything, what is it?"

"I need you to go to my house and look for a small box sitting in that big chair in my bedroom. It says 'Jules' right on top. I need you to bring the letters that are inside. They are rubber banded together, and the one on top is dated this past March. Can you please bring them? And *please* don't open any of them," Brad pleaded.

"I'll find them, and I won't open even one....promise," Mitch replied. "But I am curious. Who are the letters from?"

"They're from me. I will explain when you get here. Thanks, Mitch. This means a lot. I'll see you soon!"

Brad hung up the phone and ran into the kitchen to find Hannah drying dishes. Her hair was pulled up in a clippie, and a few red ringlets hung down the sides of her face, softly brushing against her cheeks. She looked at him and smiled, blowing a strand from her face. *God if you only knew how beautiful you truly are, Jules. You don't though, and that makes you even more beautiful.* He thought to himself. "Everything okay? Is it that darn garbage disposal again? I swear I fixed it, Jules!"

Hannah laughed. "No silly, I just need *you.*" She tossed her dish towel on the counter and reached out, pulling him into her arms. "Kiss me, you big Putz," she giggled.

"Well, well, well… now *that* would be my sincere pleasure, Red." He took her sweet face in his hands and stroked her soft cheeks, lightly brushing her lips with his.

Hannah felt all of his love in that kiss, and it sent her to a place that she wanted to stay forever. *He's mine again…* she thought.

Brad pulled away slowly. "So, are you sure everything is okay?" he asked, sensing an underlying story to her spontaneous kiss.

"I'm good, honest. I'll admit to being a little stressed about the event, but that's only because I want it to be perfect."

"Look, I told you to leave all the details to me, or most of them anyway. The chef has everything planned, we have wine for every course, the guests are all confirmed, the patio is beautiful and it's going to be amazing. Trust me, will ya?"

"You sound pretty confident. I guess I'll have to," she winked.

"Exactly," he smiled, then kissed her again, drinking in the sweetness of her lips. "Look, I'd love to stay here and kiss you all day, but I have *got* to run into town. Can you handle things while I'm gone? Clare is outside stocking wine and her walkie-talkie is on if you need her."

"Will you ever stop worrying about me? I'm fine! It's been over a month since I came home and I haven't had one problem. Now go, do what you need to do. I've got this. What are you doing anyway?" she asked.

"Oh, just picking up a couple of things for the patio. Nothing big. I'll be back in a couple of hours. I love you." He kissed her on the cheek. "Do you have any idea how happy you make me feel, Jules? It's the only word that fits. I know that probably sounds dumb, but it's true," he added, gushing with a smile the size of Texas.

"You're crazy, but I love you, too. And I feel the same… trust me." She slapped him playfully on the tush.

"Wooh! Hey now, don't get me all excited, Red. I won't be able to keep my focus."

"Oh, get out of here. No excitement until the wedding day, buddy," she laughed.

"That's mean… you know that right? Just flat mean."

"What can I say? I have pretty high standards. Let's hope you can live up to them once the ring is on your finger."

"Ouch… you're tough. I like that in a woman," he said softly, then pulled her close and kissed her again, lingering on her lips as long as he could. Each kiss held more fire than the last, and he longed for the day when she would be his in every way.

Breathless, she pulled away. "Yeah, you'd better go run your errands. I… I need some air." Hannah felt dizzy and off-balance, but in a delightful way.

That day's guests hadn't arrived yet, and after Brad left, the B&B was quiet and peaceful. Hannah went to her room and pulled out the wooden box from her closet. The little blue velvet bag was still inside and drawn tight. She pried it open and emptied the contents into her hand. Her ring – as bright and shiny as the day he'd given it to her. She'd dreamt about it, but never really believed it would be on her finger again someday. After everything she'd been through in her life, it seemed like things were finally coming together – her dreams coming true.

Holding the ring tight in her hand, Hannah decided it was time to walk down the hill and pay a visit to her parents' and grandmother's grave stones. She hadn't visited since coming home from the hospital, and even though she had somewhat said goodbye, it wasn't on her own terms. In a sense, it hadn't become real yet. It was easy to put it off at first during her recovery, but she needed to close the door and make her peace. They had been buried at the base of the estate, on the downward slope of the hill that overlooked the town. She could see everything from there, surrounded by rolling hills, cherry blossom trees, wildflowers, and a few late blooming pink phlox. She sat down, leaning against her grandmother's headstone, and took in the view.

"Hey Grams, Mom, Dad. I miss you," Hannah let out a big sigh, and the tears followed as she continued to talk to the head stones. "It really sucks that you're not here to watch me marry my soul mate, but hopefully you're watching from somewhere above. The winery is doing great and I managed to save the estate – with Brad's help of course. He kind of swooped in and saved the day, which ticked me off at first. I was perfectly happy keeping him in that little box, but *nooooo*, he just *had* to ride in on his white horse all sexy-like, and totally stole my heart in the process. You nailed it Grams. You knew from the beginning that he was still the love of my life, and you weren't going to be happy until we were together again. Nice job!"

She played with the ring, spinning it around her finger, and the tears continued to fall as her heart gave way to the finality of her words. Her grief and love unfolded, mourning the loss of her grandmother at last. Being physically separated from Lois during her final days on earth was the worst part – let alone experiencing what could have been her *own* last days at the same exact moment. Thinking back, she recalled her last moment with Lois and the words she shared, how life was all about timing, and timing is everything. Hannah doubted her words then, but after everything that had happened… those words never rang more true. She closed her eyes and let the memory movies of her grandma play through her mind, everything from their shopping sprees to her make-up tutorials. Each one brought a smile to Hannah's face, and slowly, her tears ran dry.

"Thanks for stopping in to say goodbye while I was 'out'… literally," she giggled at her own pun. "It was good to see all of you again. Weird, but good. I still think I'm a little nuts. It felt so real though, like you were right there with me. Oh, and you'll be happy to know that Brad has finally grown up, Mom. You always said that he would figure it out some day, but I didn't believe you," she stood up and kissed the top of the stones. "Goodbye, Grandma, Mom, Daddy. I'd better get back to work. We have guests coming in and wine to pour. I love you all so much… thanks for watching over me." Hannah stood up, wiping the last tear from her eye, and ran her hand across the top of the stones as she walked away.

On her way back to the estate, she poked her head in the winery to check on Clare.

"Hey girl! You alright in here?" Hannah asked.

"Me? Oh sure," she replied, laced with a hint of sarcasm.

"Hmm. O-k-a-y… what's up? I know better than that."

"It's just… well, with all the excitement around here and all of us so busy getting things ready, I'm starting to worry about where I'll fit in after you two love birds get your 'happily-ever-after'. Are you really going to want an 18 year old hanging around?"

"How many times are we going to have to have this conversation before you get it through your thick skull? You might be 18 in number, but you act like a toddler sometimes, Clare. Did I ever tell you that I wanted to adopt you a few years ago?"

"No. Why didn't you?"

"Because I was single, and had never been anyone's mother before. I had no idea how to take care of a teenager on my own, and was struggling to take care of myself frankly. I was scared, and once the estate started going downhill, I couldn't take on the added responsibility of a kid – even one as great as you. I didn't want to let you down – that's the last thing you needed."

"You could never let me down, Jules. I love you," Clare said.

"I love you too, and that's why I want you to live here with us at the estate. You're a legal adult now – you can choose where you want to live, and you are welcome here for as long as you want. I don't want you to be my 'little sister' anymore though. I want you to be my daughter. Brad does too. We've already talked about it, and I've already contacted your foster parents to talk it over with them. So, take some time and think about it, and…,"

Clare cut her off – overwhelmed with joy, and grabbed Hannah in a tight hug, nearly knocking her to the ground. "Yes, yes, yes! I want you to be my mom! You already are, don't you know that? I love you, Jules. Can I… I mean… is it okay if I call you Mom?"

Hannah's eyes welled with tears. "Well, that's a silly question. Of course you can! I guess that settles that, then."

"Sweet! Which room do I get?" Clare asked.

Hannah burst out laughing, "Something tells me you already have one picked out."

"Yep! I want the one in the attic – and I want to hang lights and fill it with bookshelves and tons of books."

"Books, really? I can't *imagine.* It's only your first love," Hannah replied.

"Ha, ha. You're so funny. I can't help it. I love them," Clare looked down and noticed a glare coming from Hannah's hand. "What's in your hand?"

"Oh this?" she smiled. "This… is the engagement ring Brad gave me when he proposed years ago. I wanted to hold it while I visited Gram's grave." Hannah's cheeks turned pink, remembering the day he gave it to her.

"I can't believe you kept it all this time. I would have hurled it down a tall elevator shaft or threw it off a cliff or something. Why *did* you keep it?"

"I guess part of me always hoped it would bring him back to me. I'm not sure I ever really believed it would work, but I couldn't bring myself to let it go. It was the only piece of him I had left. I've kept it in a wooden box that he made for me, along with his 'Dear John' letter. When he showed up here, I pulled the box out of the closet and tucked it under my bed, hoping it would give me the courage to tell him off or something. Obviously you can see how well *that* turned out. Sounds silly, huh?"

Clare took the ring from Hannah's hands and admired it. "It's not silly at all. It's beautiful, Jules. He loved you. He never stopped loving you, and you know that now. Did you two set a date yet?"

Hannah didn't respond. She simply turned and looked out over the hills behind her, replaying her Grandmother's words about 'timing' in her head. "Not yet, but we will. It's been a little nuts around here. We'll figure it out."

"Well, life is too short to wait around for the perfect day or time. If he doesn't set a date soon, he's really going to earn his nickname of 'Putz' in a big way as far as I'm concerned!"

They laughed together and walked back to the house. Clare put her arm around Hannah, thankful that their journey, although long and sometimes painful, had given her a 'forever family' in Hannah, and now Brad.

*****

"Hurry up, Laci! Our flight leaves in three hours," Mitch shouted, coming down the hall at the crack of dawn.

"I know when our flight leaves, *Darlin'*," she mumbled to herself sarcastically, but Mitch entered the bedroom just in time to hear her reply.

"Hey now, no need to get all sassy on me," he smiled.

"Really? I thought you liked it when I got sassy?"

"That depends… is it 'fun' sassy, or 'I'm-in-trouble' sassy?"

"Yeah… probably not the fun sassy this early of a morning," Laci giggled, then heard her cell phone ring.

"Who's calling at this hour?" She looked at her phone and saw it was Evan. "Oh, it's Evan! Uh, oh. I hope everything is okay."

"Well why don't you answer the phone and find out?" Mitch shook his head at her. Laci stuck her tongue out at him.

"Hey Buddy. What's up?" she said as she answered the phone.

"Hi, Mom. Do you have a sec?" Evan asked.

"Sure, Sweetie. I have more than a few for you. Everything okay?"

"Well, I wanted to catch you before you all left. I… I'd like to move back home, if that's okay."

Laci's mouth fell open and she sat down on the edge of the bed. Mitch looked at her with worry in his face, mouthing the words 'what's wrong' to her. She waved him off.

"Okay. Did something happen? I thought you were going to stay and work there this summer?"

"I was, but I've decided to drop out of school too," he stated.

Laci was silent, not even sure how to reply at first. "I'm sorry. Did I hear you right? Did you just say you're dropping out of school? What about your degree, Evan? You only have one more year to go!"

"Don't freak out, Mom. I'll finish online, I'm not stupid. I just can't be here anymore. I want to be there with you and help run the winery… if Mitch will let me that is."

Laci looked up at Mitch with a little smile on her face.

"What is going on?" Mitch whispered – hands in the air.

Laci shushed him, and he rolled his eyes. "*Why do I even bother?*" he added, talking to himself.

"Did something happen to prompt this? You're not coming home because of me and the baby are you? I don't want you to worry – I'm fine."

"No, that's not it. I mean, I want to be there, but it's more than that. After I almost lost you to cancer, and then you marrying Mitch and moving, nothing has felt right. I feel so disconnected from everything – and I hate school, Mom. Believe it or not, the short time I was able to help Mitch at the winery last year was the happiest I have been in a long time. I loved it – everything about it!" The excitement in Evan's voice was evident.

"Wow. I'm just surprised, that's all. Happy, of course, but surprised. Honey, you can always come home. We have plenty of room!"

After hearing that little tidbit, Mitch stopped in his tracks and stared at Laci, his arms crossed and the '*I need an update*' look on his face. Laci laughed.

"Hold on a sec, Ev," Laci said, then pressed mute and held the phone down on her lap.

"He wants to come home – for good. He wants to run the winery with you! Isn't that great? Especially with Caleb going off to school in the fall!" Laci's eyes widened with her big, cheesy smile.

Mitch nodded with a smile, seeming agreeable to the news. Mostly, he enjoyed how the news made Laci's face light up. The love of his life was happy, and seeing her happy meant everything to him. He gave her a thumbs up. "Sounds good to me! Fill me in later."

She unmuted the phone. "Okay Sweetie, I'm back. Mitch gave me the thumbs up, so if you want to move home, then we're good with that. It's your life, honey. You have to choose what's right for you."

"Thanks, Mom. Tell Mitch thanks too. I'll let you go – I know you are leaving soon."

"Wait a minute though. What about Sarah? Aren't you two getting pretty serious?"

"Umm… yeah we were, but she doesn't want to move. We're just on different paths, so we broke up a few days ago. It's been coming for a while now. That's not why I'm doing this."

"I'm sorry, Ev. At least you figured things out now rather than later."

"I know. I will always care about her, but it's better this way. I may be there before you get back home, so I'll just bunk with Travis if that's okay until I find something of my own."

"Heavens, no! We have plenty of room sweetie. I know Travis will want you to sleep in his room at least one night or two, but I'll make up the guest room so you will have some privacy okay? Be careful coming home. We'll see you so soon!"

They hung up and Laci set the phone down on the bed. She wasn't sure what to make of his decision to move home yet, but selfishly she was anxious to have him back home.

"Okay… are you happy, sad, or surprised? Please just tell me so I know how to respond. I *hate* trying to figure it out on my own," Mitch grinned, trying to lighten the moment.

"I think I'm all those things," she replied.

"That figures. Don't make it easy on me, heaven forbid!" He sat down beside her and turned her face toward his. "Look… whatever Evan has going on is his business. He has to figure things out on his own okay? If moving home helps him do that, then I'm all for it." He leaned forward to give her a kiss, and Laci's heart sped up, as it always did when he kissed her. Their kiss deepened, and she clung to him, as if he might vanish if she let go.

She pulled away slowly. "I thought we had a flight to catch?"

"We'll make it. Besides, this is way more fun," he smiled.

*****

Grand opening day had arrived, and by early afternoon, all but one guest had arrived for the B&B. The dinner event wasn't set to start for several more hours, but Hannah was already overly anxious. She decided to bake some cookies to take her mind off of things.

Clare stormed into the kitchen. “Hey Jules, where is Brad?” Clare asked.

“He’s on the patio. Why?” Hannah’s eyes widened as she took a double-take at Clare, already in her fancy outfit for the evening’s festivities. “My my… look at you! Swanky!”

Clare had fixed herself up nice for the party. Her dark hair was held up in a rhinestone clip, and she wore a sleeveless blue dress covered in sparkly material, bringing out the blue in her eyes. She was also wearing make-up, which was a first. If it weren’t for the high-top Converse shoes on her feet, she would have looked much older than she was.

“Oh cut it out – it’s just a dress. It’s not my thing, but I wanted to look nice for your big night,” Clare replied.

“Clare, you are beautiful in anything. If you don’t want to wear a dress, then don’t wear one. Be yourself, Sweetheart. That’s all I care about.”

“I’m fine. It’s not that bad actually. Makes me feel kind of… nice,” she smiled, looking down at her attire.

“What did you need with Brad?” Hannah asked.

“Oh, I just need to borrow him for a minute. Some guests arrived that need help with their luggage. I’ll go get him.”

“Okay. I can help too.”

“No you can’t. No lifting for another month, remember? Be good, Jul… I mean… Mom.”

Hannah rolled her eyes. “Not you too! I’m fine. When are you two going to let up?”

“When you’re back to one hundred percent, that’s when.” Clare kissed her on the cheek and ran to the patio.

Hannah laughed, then went to her room to get ready.

Brad had already hung the patio lights, and was starting to prep the fire pit when Clare came out through the door.

"Hey Squirt! You're just the person I needed to see. Did you find the item we discussed?" he asked.

Clare pulled the little blue velvet bag out of her pocket and handed it to Brad. "I snuck it out of her room earlier today – she took it with her when she visited the graves yesterday. Lucky for you she told me where she kept it. Why do you need it anyway?"

"I have something else to go with it, but I need the original to make it work," Brad's curiosity got the best of him. "So… where *was* she keeping it?"

"It was under her bed in a little wooden box. It had the words 'My Jules' carved on top." Clare looked in Brad's eyes and smiled. "You made the box for her didn't you?" she asked.

His cheeks turned a pale shade of pink. "Yep. I wanted her to have something I made with my bare hands, besides a ring. I had big plans back then. I was going to write her a letter every year for our wedding anniversary, hoping she would keep them in the box… to remember. Would you believe I still wrote those letters? I have them all in a box at home. I wrote them as if we had gotten married, talking about our kids and all sorts of stuff. Crazy, huh?"

"You two are SO made for each other… seriously, dude. Two peas in a pod," Clare laughed.

"Well, enough of that. I could use your help out here setting tables if you're looking for something to do," Brad asked.

"I'll set the tables, but first you might want to go out front and greet your guests that just arrived… one of them is *with child*…," she said.

"What? They're here and you're just now telling me? Why didn't you say so when you got out here?"

Clare rolled her eyes and shook her head. "I just did, dude. Chill!"

"Okay, okay! Let's go!" They walked around to the front entrance and saw Laci and Mitch – Laci's tummy already showing a small bulge. Brad walked up to Mitch and was overtaken with emotions.

"Hey little brother!" he said to Mitch, embracing him in one of his manly brother hugs, smacking each other on the back a couple of times. His brother was his rock, and now that he was there, the weight of the world seemed to lift off of Brad as he wept on Mitch's shoulder.

"It's good to see you, man. I know it's been a long, rough road. I'm so sorry I wasn't here to help you through it, but really happy things turned around for both of you."

"It's okay. Like you said… it all turned out pretty good. She's handled everything with such grace, it's unbelievable. Even losing Lois in the midst of everything. She's amazing. It sure is nice to see you, though. I've missed you too." Brad wiped his face with the sleeve of his t-shirt, then turned towards Clare. "Mitch, Laci…this is Clare, Hannah's 'little sister' with Big Brothers Big Sisters."

"It's so nice to meet you, Clare!" Laci reached out and hugged Clare's neck without warning, as was her usual custom when meeting friends of the family. "Brad told us so much about you and how brave you were for Hannah."

"Thank you. It's nice to meet you too. I've heard you really like the rain. I'm not a big fan of it myself." Clare replied with a little smile.

Laci giggled. "Yeah, I do. Rain is my thing I guess. It's not for everyone. Speaking of Hannah though, where is she?"

Brad cleared his throat. "Um, she's inside. She doesn't exactly know that I invited you here. She *may* flip out."

"What? You mean our coming here is a complete surprise to her? That's a lot of surprises in one weekend,

Brad Young!" Laci stressed, now concerned about their arrival being kept secret.

"I didn't want to take any chance of her refusing your offer to come up and help, so I didn't give her the option. Figured it was better that way," Brad said.

"Man, you have a lot to learn, dude," Mitch added, shaking his head and smiling.

"Trust me! She won't be mad. I know her."

"Well, let's go surprise her, then!" Laci said.

Brad walked over to Laci and stopped in front of her. "Thanks for being here, Laci. I am so happy for you, and I'm sorry for being such a jerk in the beginning. You are the best thing that ever happened to Mitch, and in all my years, I've never seen him this happy. Until you came along, I would have never believed there was one person that was the perfect mate to another person's soul, but you're most *definitely* his. And now, I've found mine too." Brad reached out and pulled Laci into a hug, squeezing her as tight as he could.

Laci's eyes filled with tears, seeing the beauty in Brad's big heart for the very first time. "I always knew you had it in you… a heart that is," she laughed.

"Touché," he replied. "I guess it softened up with all this rain up here."

"Told ya," she said, and they laughed together as they walked inside.

Brad sat their bags down on the floor. "Hey, Jules – can you come in to the foyer?" he yelled out.

Hannah walked out of the kitchen, drying her hands on a dish towel. When she entered the foyer, Mitch and Laci were standing there to greet her. The look on Hannah's face was priceless, resembling both shock and excitement. She even dropped her towel on the floor.

"Holy, cow! What… what on earth is going on? What are you doing here?" she exclaimed, and rushed over to greet them with a hug.

"We heard there was a big party here tonight. I never miss a good party!" Laci said.

"Laci! Look at your cute little tummy! I'm so happy for you," Hannah began to cry.

"Oh, Sweetie… thank you." Laci tightened her embrace around Hannah and hugged her tight. "We wouldn't have missed celebrating this day with you, not for the world. You're family, my dear!"

Hannah wiped her tears, then looked at Brad. "Why didn't you tell me they were coming?"

"I didn't want you to make a fuss, and I knew you would have if I had told you. I just wanted to surprise you, that's all. Laci said she could pitch in and help us fluff things up for tonight too," Brad added.

"Well, I don't like being kept in the dark, but in this case… I am grateful. Thank you for doing all of this for me," she whispered in his ear, then reached up and pulled him into her embrace, kissing him softly.

Laci coughed a few times, trying to interrupt their kiss. "Not to break up your little moment, you two… but we have a party to start as I recall."

Brad reluctantly pulled away. "Yeah, yeah, whatever. I had to suffer watching the two of you lovebirds for months… this is payback," he replied.

They all laughed, and walked inside. The preparations began.

15 – One Soul

A thick layer of smoke drifted from the fire, filling the air with a sweet, hickory scent as the wood crackled in the fire pit. Happy faces gathered all around, clinking wine glasses with each other, laughing, talking, and the extra happy guy was singing to his lady friend. The salmon was cooking on the grill, almost ready to serve, and the clear patio lights that hung all around began to glow softly, adding a touch of elegance to the evening ahead.

Brad finished getting ready and joined Mitch in the dining room. Clare was there too, hopping around like a nervous kitten. Laci was in event planning mode, making tables look beautiful and already schmoozing with the guests. Hannah was MIA, still closed up in her room and taking an unusually long time to appear.

"Hey, Clare? Would you mind going up to check on her… make sure she's doing ok?" Brad asked, worried something wasn't right.

"Sure. Be right back." Clare ran upstairs and knocked on Hannah's door. "Hey Jules, you about ready? All the guests are here and I'm starving!" There was no reply. "Jules… can you hear me? Can I come in?" Still no reply. Clare became anxious, and opened the door anyway. Jules was laying on the bed sobbing, her headphones plugged in her ears to drown out any noise.

Clare walked over to her side, careful not to scare her, and gently tapped her on the leg to announce her presence. Jules jerked her head up, and ripped the headphones out of her ears.

"Clare, I'm so sorry! I was just trying to relax before dinner." She sniffed, wiping the tears away.

"Yeah… so how's that working out for ya? Because from where I stand, you don't look all that relaxed, Jules. Just being honest." Clare's understated humor always made Hannah laugh.

"Ah, well that's where you're wrong. You see crying can actually release a lot of anxiety and stress, thus making a person more relaxed and stress free."

Clare laughed. "You don't really believe that bologna do you?"

"It sounded good though, right?" Hannah asked, a smile on her face.

"Jules… what's wrong? Are you worried about tonight? Everyone is already having a great time out there, except for us. You're not even dressed – what's up with you?"

"I'm just missing my Grandma, I guess. Seems wrong to do this without her. And… I think this is all wrong. I got a sign and I'm not sure Brad and I are going to work out."

Clare's jaw dropped. "Shut the front door! What do you mean 'you-got-a-sign'? What kind of sign?"

"I lost his ring. I can't find it anywhere, Clare. I know I set it back in the box after I visited the graves the other day, and now I can't find it anywhere. I've looked everywhere!" Hannah broke down again.

Clare sat down on the bed. "Look here, Sister… ha! I guess its Mom now… but whatever. Listen to me. You get up and get dressed. It's probably rolling around here somewhere. Trust me… I know it's in this house, and it's ridiculous to think that losing it is some sort of *sign*. How do you think Brad would feel if he knew your love for him hinged on some old ring? Doesn't seem fair if you ask me." Clare crossed her arms and stared at Hannah, like a mother scolding a child.

"Look at you, Miss Sassy Pants, telling me what to do," Hannah giggled. "You're probably right. It will turn up. I'll keep looking, and I won't say anything. If he asks where it is, then I'll tell him I took it to get it cleaned or something. Thanks, Clare. I had a moment of panic I guess. It's been such a long road getting here, but at the same time, it feels like it happened in the blink of an eye. Part of me just wanted to have the ring for good luck, but you're right. I have Brad back in my life, and he's all that matters."

"Hey, what am I, chopped liver?"

"Oh don't be silly! You know what I mean. I've always had you… and you've always had me. That will never change. I love you girl."

"I love you too, Mom. Tonight is about putting the past behind you, and grabbing hold of everything in front of you, and never letting it go. Now, go get dressed already! Guests are waiting," Clare added.

Hannah reached over and hugged Clare tight, then hopped up to get ready.

Clare came back and gave the others a fictional version of what was keeping Hannah, figuring it was none of their business. They all moved into the foyer to wait. After a few minutes passed, Brad looked up and saw Hannah walking downstairs to join them – his jaw dropped. She wore a slimming black and white dress that clung to every curve, sleek black heels, and her long, red hair was flowed freely all around her face, curls bouncing as she walked.

Mitch bumped Brad's side. "Dude… close your mouth."

Brad cleared his throat and walked over to help her down the last few steps. "May I?" he asked.

"I thought you'd never ask," she replied, and hooked her arm through his.

"You look beautiful, Jules…. absolutely stunning."

"Thank you. Umm…," she lowered her head and paused, then stopped walking as the others went on out.

"Before we go outside, I need to say something," She turned toward him. "Look, there's really no excuse, but I can't seem to find…"

Clare popped her head back inside the door. "Jules! Let's go! You can talk later, okay?" she yelled, knowing exactly what she was about to tell him.

Hannah smiled and shook her head. "I'll tell you later. I love you, Brad. Thank you for tonight… for all of this." She kissed him on the cheek. *How am I going to tell him I lost his ring? Please don't let it be a sign… I can't lose anything else. I need this, Lord. I need him, more than he'll ever know.* Hannah thought.

"I love you too, Jules," He pulled her into his arms and leaned in to kiss her gently, a soft sweet reminder of what was yet to come.

Brad and Hannah walked outside behind the winery, and immediately began greeting guests, hugging necks and reconnecting with friends. Her face lit up as she worked the room, like it was breathing new life into her.

"She looks happy," Laci said, leaning into Mitch's shoulder.

"That's no small part thanks to you, Darlin'."

In the distance, a crack of thunder announced itself and Laci immediately turned around to see the dark clouds rolling toward the estate from over the mountain. "Yes!" she squealed quietly. "And only good things ahead!" she added.

"You know I love you, right? You and your crazy love of rain… I'll never grow tired of it" Mitch leaned down and kissed her softly.

"Hey you two, get a room," Brad joked as he walked up to them. "It's almost time to start, but before we do I need you two on board with something."

"What's up, brother?" Mitch asked.

"I'm not going to wait around for months on end to marry that woman. Life is too short. So, I already called and booked a minister, and I want to take a drive out to Cannon Beach tomorrow and get married on the beach. I checked the weather, and it's supposed to be a beautiful day. Are you up for that? She doesn't know yet, of course… but I'll tell her later tonight."

"You are full of surprises these days!" Laci jested. "You can count us in!"

"I love how you answer for both of us… do I get a vote?" Mitch asked, smiling.

"No. Your vote is now by proxy only after marrying me. My vote always wins."

"I hope you're ready for this, big brother… your life will *never* be the same again," Mitch laughed and Laci playfully jabbed him in the shoulder.

"And you wouldn't have it any other way," she smiled.

They laughed together, and went to their tables.

Brad tapped the side of his wine glass to get everyone's attention and asked them to find their seats. "Hello everyone! Can I get everyone's attention for a few minutes?" The crowd quieted and he continued. "First off, thank you for coming tonight. My name is Brad Young. Not all of you know me yet, but I'm a friend of Hannah's and I started helping run the B&B back in March. I want you to know how much we appreciate you all being here to help us celebrate the grand reopening of Hannah's family estate, Foxhead Bed & Breakfast and Winery." Everyone clapped, and Brad motioned for Hannah to stand. The thunder clattered again. "I'd also like to thank my sister-in-law for bringing us this rainstorm. I think she orders them in advance with the big man upstairs." The guests laughed in reply.

Cheeks now flushed and red, Hannah waved and found the nerve to speak. "Thank you everyone. It's been a long road getting here, but I'm so grateful to all of you for your support and friendship. I see many of you here tonight that have been with me on this entire journey and I am forever grateful. Especially to you, Andréa!" Hannah lifted her glass toward her dear friend who sat at the table next to theirs.

"I'm always here for you sweet girl!" Andréa shouted, and everyone laughed together.

Hannah sat back down, and Brad continued his toast. "Hannah is the heart and soul of this place. Without her, it just doesn't work. It's her family's legacy, and part of my job was to save that legacy. You see, I'm actually from North Carolina, and I run a winery there with my brother, Mitch and his wife Laci, who are both here with us tonight." Mitch and Laci gave a little wave to be gracious. "Those two stumbled across this estate one weekend during a romantic getaway, not realizing that Hannah was about to lose it in foreclosure. After Hannah's parents died, she kept running this place and also had to take care of her ailing grandmother, who has since gone on to be with the Lord. Hannah offered Mitch and Laci a place to sleep for the night and after a good heavy rain, Mitch and I were buying this estate. That's an entirely different story of its own, but suffice it to say, the rain played a big part," Brad laughed and shook his head. "It was my job to come up and finalize the sale, and get things up and running. What we didn't realize, was that the owner, Miss Hannah here… was also a love from my past… the love of my life to be exact." The crowd 'oohed and aahed', but Hannah's gaze remained fixed on Brad as he spoke, tears spilling down her cheeks.

"Back then, I knew Hannah as Jules McRae… not Hannah Blake. Apparently that was her nickname, but it's the only one I knew. I fell in love with her the first time I set eyes on her. I even asked her to marry me, but I screwed it up and lost her. I remember my daddy always telling us boys that God worked in mysterious ways… we just had to pay attention so we don't miss the moments of grace He gives us. After I got up here and saw her again after all these years, I realized that was God giving me a little grace even though I didn't deserve it. She didn't make it easy on me though. After the accident, I was worried I would lose her again… forever, and I couldn't bear living one more day without her," Brad stared in Jules' eyes as he continued. "She's a tough cookie though, this girl… and after everything we've been through these last several months, I was given a second chance. She agreed to marry me again!" he smiled, pulling Hannah up out of the chair and to his side while everyone whistled and clapped.

"Hannah already knows this, but part of the agreement in our purchase of this estate was to donate it back to her after ninety days, so as of last month, Hannah Blake is once again the sole owner and proprietor of Foxhead Estates, and rightfully so." Guests clapped and hollered in support of her new status, a few shedding tears.

"Okay… I won't drag this out much longer, I'm sure you're all starving and ready for some of that amazing salmon over there, so I just have one more thing to add," Brad reached inside his jacket pocket and pulled out a little box. "Jules… I know you already said you would marry me, but I didn't have a ring to give you. So, I had a little elf do some work for me, and I decided to take the ring I gave you years ago, and make it new again. Like us. We found each other once, then parted ways. Our souls remained connected though, gently drawing us together again after all these years. Even your grandmother knew it."

Hannah's mouth dropped open. "What? You… you told my grandmother about this?"

"Yeah. I went to the hospital one night, when she first went into the hospital, and asked her permission to marry you. It's funny, but Lois knew we would be together again from the moment I arrived."

"You're right. She *did* know. She... she told me there would be grace after the storm, in my dream." Hannah's head was spinning, almost in a daze.

Clare shot up out of her seat. "Wait a minute!" she shouted, "Grams said that to you in your dream?" The crowd was silent.

"Yes," Hannah looked directly at Brad. "In my dream, you and I were getting married. Laci and Mitch were there too – holding their baby boy."

Laci looked at Mitch, shaken to the core by Hannah's statement. A chill fell over her, apparent by the goosebumps on her arms. Mitch pulled her close and held her hand tight.

Hannah continued, "... then Grams and my parents walked up and said that very same statement to both of us. Why is it important, Clare?"

"Jules... your grandmother told me the same thing that night in the hospital. Right before she died. She... she wanted me to tell you that there is always 'grace after the storm' – that you would know what it meant. With everything that happened though, I was so upset and worried about you, that I forgot to tell you until now. Lois is here, Jules. *That* is your sign," Clare added, then walked over and gave Hannah a big hug. They cried together. "See? You're exactly where you're meant to be," Clare whispered in her ear.

"Thank you, Clare. I love you!" Hannah squeezed her tight, overwhelmed by the timing of the moment.

Clare turned to Brad. "Sorry to interrupt... please continue." The crowd laughed quietly.

"Thanks Clare."

Without another word, Brad picked up a small black box, then dropped down on one knee, taking Hannah's hand in his. "Hannah Jule McRae, my Jules, the love of my life and the mate of my soul… will you please be my bride once and for all?" he asked.

Hannah couldn't catch her breath. She looked down and saw the ring – the same ring he had given her years ago, but it was now set inside a circle of diamonds that shone as bright as the sun – complete. Tears flowed from her eyes as she held out her hand, quivering like a newborn foal. "I have been and forever will be yours, Brad Young."

Brad slipped the ring on her finger, then stood up and pulled her into a kiss, breathing her in as he lingered in the moment. Just for fun, he dipped her backwards and quickly brought her back up, their guests clapping and crying, enjoying the moment along with them.

"Let's eat!" a guest called out – it was the happy guy who was singing to his lady earlier.

Brad and Hannah laughed, pulling away from each other reluctantly. "Okay, okay. Everyone raise your glasses to my future wife! To Hannah, to Foxhead Estates, to new beginnings, and to grabbing hold of happiness wherever you can, whatever that looks like."

"Cheers!" everyone shouted in unison.

The evening was filled with laughter, tears, joyous reunions with friends and family, good food, and great wine. As the guests mingled and enjoyed themselves, Brad took Hannah aside for a walk down the hill to get some air and steal a few minutes alone with her. They stopped at the bench overlooking the hillside and sat down.

"How are you feeling? This hasn't been too much has it?"

She looked at him, scooting close to him as he wrapped his arm around her. "I haven't felt this good in years. It's all because of you. You make me so happy, Brad, and somehow you've managed to fill all the empty places inside of me that were longing to be whole again. I sometimes wonder how I ever made it this far without you. I love you so much." She leaned over and kissed him softly.

"I love you too, Darlin'. It still amazes me how all this happened, but I know it was God who brought us together again. Speaking of which… I don't think we should wait around to make it official Jules, so I need to ask you something…" Brad took a deep breath, nervous about disclosing his plan. *You have nothing to lose and everything to gain here dude… just buck up and ask her already! She already said yes, remember?* Giving himself a pep talk.

"What is it? What more could you do to surprise me? The ring was pretty incredible."

"I brought Laci and Mitch up here for the grand opening, but I also want them here for our wedding day…." He waited for her reply.

Hannah raised a brow. "What are you talking about? How is that supposed to happen? It takes months to plan and prepare for a wedding. I'm sure they're not staying that long."

"I don't want to wait, Jules. We've been through too much and I want to marry you as soon as humanly possible. Tomorrow to be exact," he exhaled.

She leaned away and her eyes blew up like balloons. "Wait a minute… did you say tomorrow?"

"I did. I want us all to drive up to Cannon Beach tomorrow. I want to marry you, Jules. I don't want to wait any longer. We've waited far too long as it is. What do you say? Everyone else is on board, and I've already talked with a local minister who can meet us there. You can invite whoever you want… but it's time for you to be my wife. I can't wait another day."

Brad's big brown puppy dog eyes were irresistible to her, and as the wind tossed his dark brown hair back and forth, she melted. She sucked in her breath at the thought of finally becoming his bride, and it moved her to tears. "It sounds perfect, Brad. Better than perfect… let's do it!" she squealed, and threw her arms around him and held him tight.

He pulled away just slightly, then took her face in his hands and slowly pressed his lips to hers and sinking into her tender lips. Hannah's body was riddled with chills, and since he was wearing her favorite cologne, the smell made her head spin all the more. She felt his warm hands glide up and down her back, shivering at his touch and longing to feel his bare skin on hers, but the kiss would have to be enough for now. She would happily wait for him – for the moment when their two hearts and bodies would become one soul. Brad was everything she had ever hoped for in a soul mate. The one who knew her heart better than any other… even after so much time had passed. She was amazed at how one word from him during her day could send her heart aflutter, and the way he could see through to her very core, knowing exactly when she was having an off day. They were connected in ways that even she couldn't understand – a connection that would last a lifetime.

Out of breath, she pulled away. "I'm glad the storm has passed."

"Me too, Jules… me too."

They walked back to the patio to wrap up the evening and say goodbye to their guests. The event was a success, and several were asking about prices and already making reservations for parties. Brad was busy doing his 'smooth salesman' act, so Hannah walked over to Laci and took her by the arm, guiding her across the patio.

"Hey girl! Where did you two slip off to, and where are we going?" Laci asked.

"Well, apparently I need a wedding dress..." Hannah's eyes beamed with delight.

Laci squealed after hearing her news. "SWEET! I knew you'd say yes! But wait, where are we going?"

"To visit the queen of fashion – sitting right over there." Hannah pointed to her friend.

"Andréa?"

"Yep – she's the master, and the only one who can pull this off in less than 24 hours. You *sure* didn't give me much time to plan!" Hannah laughed.

Andréa was talking with friends when they walked up next to her. "Ahhh! Jules, Laci! You two are a hoot!" Her passionate enthusiasm overflowed, "I *knew* you'd fall for him again, Jules!" she boasted, then looked at Laci. "And *you* Miss Laci... I had a feeling about you the minute you walked into my store. You have the magic touch, missy."

"Andréa... pipe down! We need to talk dresses. I'm getting married tomorrow."

"What? Wait... that's ridiculous! Tomorrow? Are you serious?"

"Yes, tomorrow, and yes I'm serious," Hannah affirmed.

"Oh my, you're not kidding! Oh my goodness! We have to get to my store. Right now. Let's go!" she demanded.

"I still have guests, Andréa. I can't just walk out," Hannah replied.

"Brad! Get over here!" Andréa shouted.

Brad heard her little chirp over the clamor and walked over. "What's up?"

"We're leaving big boy. Can you wrap things up here? We have to get to my shop and find this woman a dress apparently... you sure don't have much patience do ya?"

"I've been patient for nine years, Andréa. This is long overdue," he replied, laughing.

*****

Laci walked down the hall to Hannah's room and knocked on the door.

"Hannah? Do you need help getting ready, sweet girl?" Laci asked.

Thank God! What took her so long? I can't go out there looking like this. "Uh… yes. Please come in!" Hannah replied, a desperate tone in her voice.

Laci walked inside her room and saw Hannah trying to fiddle with her hair and flower piece. Luckily, she arrived just in time. Hannah's red hair was shooting out in all directions and the flower hair piece was sitting crooked on her head… it was a disaster.

"Don't touch it… just stop. Let me have the brush," Laci said politely.

"I know it's bad, trust me. I'm not 'girlie' like you. Most days I just throw my hair up and go, or wear a hat. I miss Grandma… she would know how to fix it for me," Hannah's head dropped.

"She's here, Sweetie, trust me," she paused. "Do you remember when we first met and you told me how much you hated the rain?" Laci asked.

"Yes. I didn't know you then, or your belief in all the good that rain brings. Gotta say – I thought it was a little weird," Hannah laughed.

"That's okay. Mitch did too at first. You've had to deal with so many storms lately-literally–and you've done it with incredible grace. But you've forgotten one important piece. You have to look for the beauty that only comes after the storm has passed. The storms have passed, Hannah, at least for now. It's time to embrace all the good things you have around you now." Laci reached around Hannah's shoulders and gave her a tight squeeze.

"I wouldn't have found him again if it weren't for you and your rain. I'm a believer now, don't worry. Thank you, Laci… for having faith in us… in me. I love you, sis," Hannah smiled.

"You and Brad were always meant to be together, and were already being drawn together long before you ever realized. Mitch and I just happen to be in the right place at the right time to help connect the pieces. You did all the rest, sweet girl," Laci wiped her tears. "Ugh! Enough sap – my makeup is already a mess. Now let's see what we can do about your hair. I'll do the best I can, and hopefully Grams will approve," she smiled.

*****

It was a glorious July day, and the sun was shining low on the horizon, not quite sunset yet. Perfect weather for a wedding on the beach. The wind was surprisingly calm, and the whooshing sound from the waves crashing into the shore – one at a time – was the only music required.

Hannah stood barefoot in the sand, staring into Brad's eyes and waited for the words to be spoken. In her arms, she held a little bouquet of yellow and white flowers tied together with a thin pink satin ribbon. She looked stunning in her short, white chiffon, spaghetti-strapped dress. A ring of tiny white flowers sat atop her head and a little pearl necklace laid gently on her neck. Clare stood next to Hannah, wearing a similar band of yellow flowers on her head and a long, pale yellow skirt with a white blouse, the sleeves dropped down off the shoulders.

Hannah turned to Clare and pulled up her sleeves. "Will you stop fussing? I'm eighteen now Jules. It's okay if my shoulders show a little," Clare laughed.

"I know, I know… I can't help it. I just want you to stay young as long as you can okay? Don't be in a hurry to grow up," Hannah began to cry.

"Don't you *dare* cry before the ceremony even begins! I can't handle it," Clare said.

"I'm doing my best. I'm still new at this remember? I'm just so proud of you, Clare, and I am so glad you are here to share this with me today. I love you, girl."

"I love you too… Mom," Clare smiled, then kicked her foot around in the sand, uncomfortable with touchy-feely moments. "Alright… let's get this show on the road okay?"

Brad didn't disappoint in his tan Dockers, the bottoms rolled up exposing his bare feet. His white button-down shirt showed off his tan skin and dark brown chest hair. He and Mitch looked more alike that day than ever with their matching outfits and goatees.

Laci stood by Hannah's side wearing a long white skirt, and a lovely yellow blouse that fell loosely around her shoulders and tummy, her little baby bump already growing larger by the day. She couldn't help but stare across at Mitch as the minister spoke, admiring her handsome husband and still reveling in their love for one another. Mitch caught her gaze and he winked at her. 'I love you', he mouthed silently, and she smiled in reply.

The ceremony was simple – an intimate gathering with just Mitch and Laci, Clare, Andréa and a guest, the chef from Romuls, and a few other close friends from town. The vows were mostly traditional, with some added words from the bride and groom.

"Hannah, do you have any words to share?" the minister asked.

Squeezing Brad's hands, she began. "I lost you once, and I kept the ring you gave me in hopes that it would bring you back to me… somehow, someway. I wasn't always a true believer though. I wavered. I had given up, thinking I would never be with the one true mate to my soul. God never played a big part in my life until recently, but I will always be grateful that He didn't give up on His plan to reunite us again. Grams was right – 'God's timing' is not always our own. It could have been a *little* sooner," the others giggled quietly, "… but I understand now why it wasn't. I wasn't able to love you the right way back then. Today, I love you more than I ever thought I could love another person. You are everything to me, and I now give you every part of me. My heart has been, and always will be, yours. Forever."

Laci sniffed, wiping her tears. Mitch shook his head and smiled, loving that his wife was always the first one to cry at weddings.

"Brad, it's your turn if you'd like to say something," the minister added.

Brad took a deep breath, still finding it hard to believe they were together, on the beach, about to become man and wife. He let go of Hannah's hand for a second, then turned around to Mitch. "Hey… I need the letter," he whispered.

"I've got it – don't panic, big brother." Mitch reached into his pocket and pulled out a piece of paper, then handed it to Brad and smiled.

Hannah's eyebrow raised a little. *He WROTE his vows? What the…. I didn't write anything down! I thought this was supposed to be off the cuff? Oh boy. He's going to make me cry now. I can't cry!* "What did you do?" Hannah asked, smiling.

Brad cleared his throat. "After I left you, it didn't take me long to figure out that I had just lost the best thing that had ever come into my life. It took me months to function normally again. I lost my job, my friends, and ended up moving back home to start over. That's when I wrote my first letter to you – on what would have been our one year wedding anniversary. I figured the only way I could move forward was to talk to you… to ask for your forgiveness. The letter however, was written to you as if you were already my wife – telling you things that I would have said on our anniversary if we had been together." He took a quick breath, then continued. "I wrote you a letter every year on that day. Eight letters now in all." He held up the paper in his hand. "This one is the most recent, and oddly enough, written while Laci and Mitch were here with you just weeks before we would meet again." He unfolded the letter, and read…

My Jules, my bride...

My beautiful wife. The love of my life. My arm candy, who looks so good in that little black dress you always wear on special occasions. If I could do it all over again, if I had my way... I would give you everything you desired – for you to live out your passions, help others in need, and enjoy life to the fullest.

I would start in January, kissing you at midnight on New Year's Eve, and every day after.

In February, I would make you my one and only Valentine as we shared our favorite chocolate.

In March, I would thank my 'lucky' shamrocks that I was blessed with your love.

In April, I would dance with you in the rain.

> In May, I would love you in a bed filled with petals from the flowers grown in our garden.
>
> In June, I would toss sleepless in your arms on hot summer nights, longing for your touch.
>
> In July, I would hold you close while we watch fireworks in the sky, admiring you from the glow of their light.
>
> In August, I would learn new ways to love you more with each passing day.
>
> In September, I would labor by your side, taking time to enjoy the fruits of what we accomplished together.
>
> In October, I would sneak up on you and give you a thousand treats and kisses on a full moon.
>
> In November, I would be thankful for our life and that you came back to me after all these years apart.
>
> In December, I would ask Santa to give me this list of wishes all over again, forever.
>
> And if I do get a chance to do it all over, I would wish for ten thousand nights and mornings waking up next to you... and then ask for more.

When Brad looked up, he saw alligator tears sliding down Hannah's face. He folded the letter and tucked it inside his pocket. "Jules… I love you and I want to spend the rest of my days with you if you'll have me. I wrote that letter never expecting to see you again. It was my prayer, but I never expected to receive an answer. It was my dream, but I never expected it to come true. Yet, here you are standing before me about to become my wife, proving that God's perfect timing is not always our own. I also remember your grandmother telling you that your name meant 'Daughter of Grace'…"

Jules' eyes grew wide and her mouth dropped open, finding it difficult to breathe. "I never told you that," she said softly, now tasting her salty tears on her lips.

"I was standing in the foyer, eavesdropping. Sorry. I didn't want to interrupt," He smiled, then shrugged his shoulders as the wedding guests snickered quietly. "Anyway, she was right. You are God's gift of grace to me, even after all the stupid things I've done, and all the storms we've both endured… He saw fit to give us a second chance. That is the very definition of grace. I love you with all my heart, and no matter what happens to us, no matter where we are or where this life takes us, this love for you will forever live on in my heart."

Hannah looked at the minister, "Can I please kiss the groom now?" she asked, then broke into laughter as tears poured from her eyes and rolled down her bright pink cheeks.

"Oh, of course," the minister chuckled. "I now pronounce you Mr. and Mrs. Young. By all means… kiss your groom!"

There wasn't a dry eye among them. Clare was especially emotional, opening her second pack of travel tissues. She had never felt happier than she did at that moment, watching her once 'big sister', then best friend, and now adopted mother, find true happiness with the man she was always meant to love.

Hannah tossed her petite bouquet behind her head and threw her arms around Brad's neck, nearly knocking him down on the sand. He smiled his rugged smile, and pulled her into his arms, her feet dangling above the sand. The increasing rhythm of his heartbeat was music to her ears as she enjoyed the warmth of his lips, still sweet from the lip balm he'd applied earlier. Their first kiss as husband and wife was like air to Hannah's lungs, finally with the love of her life. As their kissed lingered on, the guests became a bit restless.

"Alright you two… save some for the honeymoon!" Clare shouted.

The newlyweds pulled away from each other as the group broke into laughter, then Brad pulled his brother off to the side.

"You're gonna tend house for us tonight right?" he asked Mitch.

"I'm all over it, brother. All I need are the keys and you are free to go off the beaten path for a while. Don't get too crazy though old man… I have a flight to catch in a couple of days," Mitch winked.

"Thanks, Mitch. Thanks for everything – for always being there for me. I don't know what I would have done without you all these years." Brad hugged his brother, then handed him the keys.

"That's what brothers are for, right? I'll always be here for you, man. Now go enjoy your new wife. You two deserve this more than any two people I know." The wedding party walked around the beach for a tad longer, taking in the view, then said their goodbyes and headed back to the estate. Andréa had given the newlyweds the perfect gift – spending a couple of nights at her condo right on the beach – their honeymoon suite was only a few feet away from the ocean.

Brad and Hannah walked hand in hand along the shore, watching the sun set over the water. The waves were picking up speed as the tide rolled in, splashing the bottom of Hannah's tea length wedding dress.

"We'd better get back to the room – you're going to be soaking wet soon," Brad said.

"Not yet. Just a few more minutes… please? I want to see the sun go down – it becomes a beautiful watercolor painting when the orange and pink mingle together. That's my favorite part!" She leaned against his chest and he wrapped his arms around her, holding her close.

The ocean had always captivated Hannah – a beautiful and dangerous wonder at the same time. She marveled as the golden rays reflected off the water's surface, like a piece of twisted, stained glass, standing in the arms of her beloved.

"Okay… we can go now," she said softly. She turned and kissed him gently before they returned to their room.

It wasn't just any wedding night. It was a passionate reunion of first love – a culmination of emotions that had flowed through them since the day they met, and every day since over the last nine years. It was finally their turn – sharing all the love they had for one another and breathing in their new life as one. Hannah's body quivered as Brad took her in his arms, laying her in the bed. She sensed they were both a bit nervous, and excited, and anxious… and happy all at the same time – beyond anything words could describe.

Brad pulled Hannah on top of him, wanting her to face him. She wore an elegant, sheer pink robe with satin trim, slightly agape and revealing a glimpse of her full breasts peeking out from under her long hair. Her hands ran gently over his chest and she smiled down at him, seeming to enjoy the feel of his thick hair between her fingers. He closed his eyes, excited by her touch. Slowly, he pulled the tie from her robe and slid it off one sleeve at a time, letting it fall to the floor. Beholding her exquisite beauty, he caressed every part of her, and loved her gently – his one true love. They gave in to their intense desires, and fulfilled every request of the other.

Hannah's heart overflowed with a fire that had burned for Brad since the first day they met, nearly consuming her when she lost him. Now, that same fire grew even stronger as she took him in, wrapping him inside the warmth of her love – a love that would last a lifetime. His soft hands caressed her body, bringing immense pleasure and delight, and she longed for more – not wanting the night to end. His lips were sweeter than her best wine, and like the finest whiskey, he loved her smooth and strong. Never were two people more in sync or connected, and as the intense rhythm of their bodies steadily increased, Hannah's love erupted and spilled out in moans of sheer ecstasy.

The candles burned low, and they rested in each other's arms. Brad turned on his side, and pulled Hannah in toward his chest. He cradled her head in the nook of one arm, and wrapped his other arm on top of her, cupping her breast in his hand. Every curve of her warm body was curled tight inside his. He draped his leg over her thigh, and she stroked it, tickling him lightly with her fingernails. There, in the arms of the man she loved, she drifted off to sleep.

They began as two wandering hearts… now bound as one soul.

Epilogue

Mitch and Laci waited in the doctor's office lobby, her first checkup since returning from their trip to Washington. Laci's foot tapped incessantly against the wood floor, as her anxiety before these visits were always nerve wracking. She stewed and worried, awaiting the doctor's news – that the baby was still healthy and growing strong, but always fearing the worst until she heart the words.

Mitch put his arm around her and pulled her close. "Stop fidgeting, Darlin'. Everything is fine – just believe it. Besides, Hannah dreamt we had a little boy remember? We just have to believe it will come true. Think about something that makes you happy – like Evan coming home today." Mitch's sweet southern voice always comforted her like some magic spell.

"You're right. I'm just a worry-wart – I'll be fine after I hear his heartbeat," she paused. "I can't believe he is moving back home to stay. It will be nice having him around again. I've missed him. Maybe he'll even meet a nice girl here. Caleb could always introduce him to someone he knows!"

"Oh no. Don't start. I think Caleb has enough to worry about right now without trying to play matchmaker. Evan will be a nice addition to the winery though, especially since Caleb will be leaving soon. We're trading one son for the other I guess," Mitch's voice dropped. "It will all work out. Caleb needs this – he's on the right path for his life and going away to school will help him grow."

"Yeah, I only hope he can stay focused. This 'Jenny' girl seems to have turned his world upside down. I'm worried he's getting too serious too soon."

"He's an adult, Mitch. You have to let him find his own way. You raised him right and he'll make the right choices for his life. He's a good young man."

"Thanks. We both have some pretty special kids.

"We do, don't we?" she kissed his cheek.

Mitch looked up and saw their regular nurse enter the lobby. "I think we're up next, Darlin'." The nurse called Laci's name. They walked back to the exam room, and Laci prepped for the usual routine, her anxiety working overtime as she waited.

Dr. Greene entered the exam room and smiled, hearing Laci's fingernails click against the edge of the table. "Hi Laci. You seem more nervous than usual today. Anything going on?"

"Huh? Oh, no. It's just been a long couple of months with traveling and family stuff. Being away from home is getting hard on me. I get tired so easily around this time."

"Mitch, would you mind giving us a couple of minutes alone? I'd like to ask Laci a few questions – doctor to patient. We'll only be a minute."

"Sure, Doc. You good, Lace?" he asked.

"Yeah, I'm good. It's okay," Laci smiled, but on the inside, she was an emotional train wreck. Mitch walked out of the office and closed the door behind.

Dr. Greene took Laci's hand to offer some comfort. "Now. Do you want to tell me what's *really* going on? Something isn't right with you."

"It's not the baby. At least, I don't think it is. I just don't feel right. I can't explain it. Last time, I knew something was wrong with the baby even though I didn't want to believe it. This time, I think it's me. I can't put my finger on it. I'm worried that my cancer is returning. I'm scared, Dr. Greene."

"Well, let's not jump to conclusions yet. I'll take a few blood samples today. I had planned on checking your enzyme levels anyway. What are you feeling? Is it something you can articulate or is it simply a *feeling* right now?"

"I guess it's a 'not-quite-right' feeling. Physically, I feel fine, outside of being tired," Laci replied.

"Is there anything else going on at home? Marriage okay? Kids?"

"Marriage is amazing. He's the love of my life and I couldn't be happier. My oldest son is moving back home, and Mitch's son is leaving for college soon. My dad had a heart attack, and my mom isn't in the best health either. I can't stand not being at home to help them."

The doctor sighed, and then a smile spread across her face.

"What? What is it?" Laci asked, even more worried.

"Did you hear yourself rattle off all of those huge worries in your life? You are extremely stressed, Laci – *way* too much on your plate right now and that has to change, my dear."

"Yeah, I guess there is a lot going on. I haven't thought about it much. I was so involved with Brad's happy reunion and helping with buying the new winery, plus running events here, that I haven't had much time to myself."

"What do you love to do, to calm yourself and relax?"

"I love to write, play the piano, and run. I haven't been able to run lately, for obvious reasons, but I do miss walking in the woods," Laci smiled as she remembered walking with Mitch to their special bridge over the river.

"Then do more of those things – doctor's orders. You have to make time for yourself, Laci. You're carrying the weight of the world on your shoulders and it's not your job. Your job is you, and taking care of this little life in your tummy," The doctor placed the heart monitor wand on Laci's tummy, immediately picking up a strong heartbeat, "and this little life sounds like he's doing quite well," she added.

Laci let out a huge sigh of relief and smiled, shedding a few tears. "Can we let Mitch in now?"

"Of course" The doctor opened the door and motioned for Mitch to join them.

"All good in here, Doc?" he asked.

"Well, listen for yourself, dad." She found the baby's heartbeat again, announcing himself with a loud screech through the monitor. They laughed.

"Sounds good to me. You okay, Darlin'?" Mitch took Laci's hand and leaned down to kiss her on the cheek, wiping away what was left of her tears.

"I'm better than good. We're going to have a baby…."

"By the way, are you still certain you don't want to know the sex of the baby? We can look today if you want," the doctor stated.

Laci looked at Mitch and smiled. "Nah… I think we might have a pretty good idea. We'll wait and see."

"Then I'll see you both next month. You're in the home stretch, Laci. Only four months to go. Get plenty of rest, and whatever you do… enjoy being pregnant. Stop worrying."

"I will. I promise."

During their drive back home, Mitch took Laci's hand and lifted it up to his lips, kissing it lightly, in his loving way. "Can you believe he'll be here in four more months?" he asked.

"I… I'd rather not think that far ahead yet. Let's take it one day at a time, okay? It's easier that way."

"Stay positive, Lace, and have faith. Lean on the one who brought us together – who gives us the rain, and storms, and even the snow."

Laci gazed out the window as they drove. "Snow. What a beautiful way to end the year… meeting our baby, and the hope of frozen, delicate rain drops floating down to earth as snowflakes, covering everything in a soft white blanket."

"It will be the best Christmas yet – receiving the gift of our child. Maybe if we have enough faith, it will be a white Christmas," Mitch replied.

"Well, I have hope in the rain. Lois said there was always grace after the storm. So surely there must be a little faith from falling snow, right?"

Mitch smiled. "Absolutely, Darlin'," he let out a little laugh.

"What?"

"Aw, just thinking, that's all. If someone had told me four years ago that I would be here right now, madly in love with a woman who loves the rain, about to be a dad again… I would have said they were crazier than a crawdad in heat."

"Well, that's an image now burned into my brain. Thanks for *that*," Laci laughed.

"It's true! I'm the most blessed man on this earth, and it's all because God had a plan for us. He even had a plan for Brad and Hannah. We both got our second chance at love. That doesn't happen to just anyone, Lace."

"Timing is everything."

Laci's heart was filled with joy, thinking about everything that had transpired over the last several months. Everything from losing their child and feeling the loss of that life – how it caused her heart to wither and become hard – to finding her way back to the rain, remembering God's promise of His grace. She was also privileged to be a part of Brad and Hannah's journey back to one another, and her heart was once again, full of hope.

The winding road that lay ahead of them, albeit lined with joy and love, would also be paved with unexpected challenges; learning how to be parents together, making room in their hearts for a new child… and learning to let go of another.

LETTER FROM THE AUTHOR

Through both my non-profit work in my local community, and seeing the results first-hand from the impact my best friend has made in the lives of not one, but two of her 'little sisters'; I know that the Big Brothers Big Sisters organization is making a BIG difference in the lives of our young people.

"For more than 100 years, Big Brothers Big Sisters has operated under the belief that inherent in every child is the ability to succeed and thrive in life. As the nation's largest donor and volunteer supported mentoring network, Big Brothers Big Sisters makes meaningful, monitored matches between adult volunteers ("Bigs") and children ("Littles"), ages 6 through 18, in communities across the country. We develop positive relationships that have a direct and lasting effect on the lives of young people. Big Brothers Big Sisters provides children facing adversity with strong and enduring, professionally supported one-to-one mentoring relationships that change their lives for the better, forever. This mission has been the cornerstone of the organization's 110-year history. With 325 agencies across the country, Big Brothers Big Sisters serves approximately 200,000 children, their families and 200,000 volunteer mentors".[1]

To learn more about how to become a Big Brother or Big Sister, contact your local BBBS organization and help a young person today at www.BigBrothersBigSisters.org.

Sometimes all it takes is for someone to care about them, and show them they matter!

About the Author

Sandy recently moved back to her hometown of Mt. Vernon, IL and lives there with her two youngest kids. She currently works in Marketing for a local Children's Home and is busy working on another book.

Books from 5 Prince Publishing

www.5princebooks.com

Abandoned Soul *Doug Simpson*
Copper Lake *Ann Swann*
Throne of Jelzicar/Warriors of Gravenlea *S.D. Galloway*
Fatal Desire *Christina OW*
Unwrap the Romance *Anthology*
An Ill Wind *James P. Hanley*
Stargazing *Bernadette Marie*
The Grand Dissolute *Joel Van Valin*
Old Amarillo *Sara Barnard*
Nobody's Business *M.J. Kane*
Walker Pride *Bernadette Marie*
Reasons Box Set *Lisa J. Hobman*
A Secret to Keep *Railyn Stone*
The Three Wives of Adam Monroe *Bernadette Marie*
How to find Happiness *Lindsay Harper*
The Dacque Chronicles *Doug Simpson*
Redemption Series *Melynda Price*
An Everlasting Heart Series *Sara Barnard*
Fatal Obsession *Christina OW*
The Doom of Undal *Katrina Sisowath*
The Escape Clause *Bernadette Marie*
Permanent Spring Showers *Scott Southard*
Reasons to Stay *Lisa Hobman*
Wings *Pete Abela*
Reasons to Leave *Lisa Hobman*
Love Finds its Way *Wilhelmina Stolen*
The Paper Masque *Jessica Dall*
The Silver Unicorn *Wayne Orr*
The Merger *Bernadette Marie*
Lessons from a Two Year Old *Pete Abela*
Christmas Presence *Lisa J Hobman*
The Copper Rebellion *Jessica Dall*
The Christmas Tree Guy *Railyn Stone*
The Calling *Jim Hanley*
Braving the Darkness *Melynda Price*
The Three Mrs. Monroes- Vivian *Bernadette Marie*
How to Have a Happy Marriage *Lindsay Harper*

CPSIA information can be obtained
at www.ICGtesting.com
Printed in the USA
FFHW021801041219
56476150-62284FF

9 781631 121463